AT FIRST MEOW

THE BAYOU RESCUE SERIES #2

LEIGH LANDRY

---

*T*aylor Bourque was never listening to her best friend ever again.

The gutted house on pillars loomed before her. While it seemed out of place in the tiny pocket of suburban homes, its Acadian architecture appeared right at home with the bayou as a backdrop.

Maybe Ellie had sent her to the wrong place. This couldn't possibly be the location for Taylor's job interview. Could it?

The building was undergoing major renovations. Paint had been stripped, the roof re-shingled, and the boxing completely replaced. There was no railing on the porch, just an open deck, and there were holes where windows would eventually sit. The buzz of power tools and banging of hammers blasted from those openings.

Taylor stared at the bright blue poster board tacked to the side of the building that read, "St. Martin Animal Sanctuary," in thick black marker. Pink glitter and rainbow stickers were splattered around the words as if an eight-year-old had made the thing.

Ellie had told her this was a new animal shelter, but Taylor's so-called friend had neglected to say *how* new.

This place wasn't even operational. From the look of things, it wouldn't be for a while. How could they have animals, much less need a vet tech?

She did a mental time calculation. It was Wednesday afternoon. She'd taken the entire week off for some soul searching and job hunting. She could walk away now and still have time to hunt for more work prospects.

A woman stepped out onto the porch. She had a wavy auburn bob with bangs pinned back from her face, and she wore a blue plaid flannel shirt opened over a gray thermal undershirt, sawdust-coated faded jeans, and high-top hiking shoes.

The woman smiled down at Taylor. "Can I help you?"

"I'm not sure." Taylor said, regretting her decision to show up for this interview along with every decision that had led her to this moment. "There might be a misunderstanding. I was here to apply for a job, but it doesn't look like—"

"The tech. Yes, right place." The woman hopped down the steps and held out her hand. "I'm Sierra. You must be Taylor?"

"Yes." Taylor shook the woman's hand, noting her firm grip as she took another look at the building. "You guys are... operational?"

"Eh, sort of." Sierra glanced over her shoulder, then turned back to Taylor and shrugged. "It looks worse than it is."

Taylor couldn't help being drawn in by this stranger's enthusiasm and confidence. She was a sucker for positivity. That had bitten her in the butt more than once. Seemed like it might again.

"You have animals?"

Please don't let there be animals with that racket inside.

"Oh gosh, no." Sierra's bob shook with her head. "Not yet. We've got some cats at the house down the road." She pointed at a brick house nestled in the cul-de-sac. "My business partner has a black cat rescue we're incorporating into this operation. But we also have a few animals from other rescues lined up and ready to move in as soon as it's safe here."

"Just cats and dogs?" The word "sanctuary" was so vague that it left Taylor with a sense of dread.

Sierra winked. "Still working out the details."

Taylor's brain screamed at her to run at the sight of that mischievous wink, but Taylor couldn't help being sucked in by its siren call charm. She'd worked on small mammals and even some birds at her other jobs, but she'd been able to avoid reptiles until now.

She should get back in her car before this misunderstanding turned into a huge mistake. Well, another huge mistake.

"This is a part-time position?"

Why was she asking that?

Why wasn't she in her car and heading back down that gravel driveway past the rows of pecan trees?

"For now," Sierra answered. "As you can probably guess, hours might be a little erratic while we work around contractors."

"That makes sense." At least they seemed to be taking into account the safety of any incoming animals. She couldn't work anywhere that wouldn't. And just because it was an animal rescue, she couldn't automatically assume that they would. Lots of people start rescues with the best intentions, without the know-how or skills to properly care for the animals.

"Once we're up and running, we'll need someone full

time. But we could run with two part-timers if that works better for whoever takes the job."

Taylor definitely needed full-time work. Fast. She had rent and bills and student loans, and she needed to get out of her current job as soon as possible. Yesterday would be ideal. If her present situation hadn't been so pressing, she'd have turned right around before walking up those porch steps. No matter how much working in animal rescue appealed to her.

Sierra nodded toward the building. "Come on, I'll give you a tour of what we've got so far."

Ignoring her brain's blaring warning alarms, Taylor followed Sierra up the unfinished steps and through the open front door. The inside looked exactly as she'd imagined. Like a house, not an animal shelter.

"We're going to screen-in the porch as a sort of airlock for any potential escapees," Sierra said. "We'll be using this front room for a meet-and-greet area with comfy furniture and a dinette table for meeting with adopters and filling out paperwork. But it'll also serve as a comfortable space for staff to relax and take meal breaks."

Taylor took it all in. The main room was structurally complete. Drywall up. Air vents installed. And the kitchen cabinets, counters, and plumbing were installed in the adjoining space. But it was still far from operational. The entire area needed flooring, paint, molding, and closet doors.

Sierra continued her tour, walking backward and gesturing toward the small kitchen area.

"The kitchen has a sink and counter space to prepare meals and clean dishes." She pointed to the back. "There's also a room through here for laundry, with a second door opening to what will be our vet clinic."

Taylor nodded while Sierra waited for her to take it all in. Everything sounded good. Maybe too good.

They walked down the hallway with Sierra pointing into

rooms as they passed. Each room contained a small unfinished closet and was in the same condition as the main greeting area, but Taylor imagined they could finish these much faster. Once they had paint, they could move in kennels or leave them open for larger dogs and begin housing animals pretty quickly. Especially since the place already had electricity and water.

They passed each of the rooms, including the last one where all the noise was coming from. A man was cutting what looked like a piece of closet door framing.

"We're planning to do all the finishing details working from back to front, so we can begin basic operations," Sierra confirmed.

"Is there a/c yet?" Air conditioning was an absolute must for South Louisiana summers, but heating was the bigger concern for now. They didn't have a long winter, but they still got below-freezing temperatures, and there was at least a cold month or two left on the calendar.

"They're installing the unit next week," Sierra said. "There was no point until they were done with the walls, doors, and windows. But we'll have that set up before we bring any animals in."

The plans were sound. Well-thought-out. Taylor had no reason to be suspicious, but something still held her back.

She'd never heard of these people. What made them think they could run an animal rescue facility?

"Sorry, this is a lot to take in," Taylor said, realizing she was gawking wordlessly. As usual for her, but she'd learned over the years that people who didn't know her sometimes took offense at the visual representation of her thought process.

"Oh, for sure. This last room will be the office, and across the hall is what I hope you're here for."

Taylor shook her head and dug in her tote bag for a

folder. She opened it and handed a sheet of paper to Sierra. "My resume."

Sierra took the paper with an odd grin on her face. "Thanks, but I've already checked you out."

Well, that wasn't creepy at all.

"You did?"

"I've got a couple friends at the newspaper who know their way around a background check," Sierra clarified. "Or at least how to get someone else to run one for them."

"That's good, I guess," Taylor said. "For you, I mean."

"Honestly, I'm more concerned with initial impressions and how you are with animals. So if you're interested, there will be a trial period. We can see how we all mesh and if you want to stick around. I know you've got experience, but not everyone's cut out for animal rescue. No matter how much you think you love animals." Sierra frowned. "Sometimes the more you care, the harder it is."

Taylor followed every word of Sierra's logic until that last bit. How could caring possibly be a detriment? Don't they *want* employees who care about animals?

She was moving away from private veterinary work for a lack of caring. Well, that was part of the reason. But not a lack of caring from her or her coworkers. From the owners. Some pet owners just didn't give a crap about their pets. At least, not until it was too late. It was an exhausting battle, and in private practice, she usually couldn't intervene.

But with animal rescue, she wouldn't have to plead with owners to do the right thing. She could do what needed to be done. She could make a difference. All *because* she cared.

"Are you scaring off potential employees already?"

Taylor faced the owner of that booming voice: a fierce-looking woman carrying a tray of coffees. She was a good six inches taller than Taylor, with curves Taylor could only dream of on her own scrawny frame. She wore a Fleetwood

Mac T-shirt, dark stretch jeans, comfy-looking rainbow loafers, and killer red lipstick with thick mascara and black hair in a messy ponytail.

"I'm not scaring anyone," Sierra said defiantly as she took a coffee. "Am I scaring you?"

"Just a little." Taylor laughed. "I'm honestly trying to figure out how you guys pulled this together and paid for it all."

She probably shouldn't have said anything. It was never professional to bring up money right away. Or at least that's what she'd heard. But if she planned to sign on to something brand new, she needed to make sure she wasn't jumping into anything shady.

And these women had enough mischief in their eyes to contain some serious shady potential. Taylor could only hope it was a use-your-powers-for-good situation here.

"Scrimping, hubris, and a whole lot of begging." The other woman held out another coffee for Taylor. "For now, let's just say it's complicated. But all above board, I promise. I'm Liz, by the way."

Liz had been the one who'd reached out to Ellie for staff recommendations. Besides being Taylor's best friend, Ellie worked at the vet clinic, where Liz took her rescued cats. Since Elie usually had good instincts about people, Taylor had felt inclined to trust this Liz person as well and didn't think twice about showing up for this interview.

Trusting Ellie and Liz might prove to be her second big mistake of the year, and they weren't even through January yet.

"Thanks." Taylor took the coffee and tasted it. Dark, rich roast. No sugar. She nearly spit it out, but swallowed politely. Not, apparently, without notice.

Liz laughed. "Come on, we've got creamer and sugar in here along with plans for you to look at."

Liz led the way with her remaining coffee, while Sierra held out a hand in the doorway for Taylor to follow next. After a fleeting moment of hesitation and with a soundtrack of hammering in the background to guide her along, she entered the clinic-to-be.

2

---

 iz gestured for Taylor to sit in one of two folding chairs at the card table centered in the room. Sierra grabbed cream and sugar from a mostly empty bookshelf and placed them on the table.

Taylor sat and tore open three packets of sugar, even though she really would have preferred six in this diesel. But she didn't want to reveal her intense sugar habit so soon after meeting new people. So she poured just three packets into her cup, along with a creamer container, while Sierra leaned against the wall and sipped her own coffee.

Liz slid a sheet of paper toward Taylor and twisted it around for her to examine. It was a shoddy, blueprint-type map. Plans for what would be a mini vet clinic.

"Long term, we'd love to do all of it on-site. Hire a vet. Do surgeries and everything in a room in this building," Liz said. "This room will be our home base for care. We'll outsource major issues or maybe bring in a vet once a week. Not sure exactly yet. For now, you would be it, along with one of us to assist until we can pull in more staff or volunteers."

She would be it?

All of her alarm bells and whistles rang out loudly in her head. Her instincts had been right. She should have hauled ass back into her car and hightailed it out of here.

So why hadn't she?

More importantly, *why was she still here?*

The simple answer was that she needed a new job. She needed to get out of the current situation she'd gotten herself into, and this seemed like the universe plopping a speedy alternative in her lap.

The more complicated answer was that something in her *wanted* this job. She liked the idea of working in animal rescue, and as bizarre as it sounded in her head, Taylor liked the thought of working with these women. They made her feel like the three of them could somehow save the world together. Or at least a few animals.

"I would be... it?" She tried to sound confident, but her voice trembled slightly.

"We mostly need someone to do intake evaluations, scan cats for ringworm, give vaccines and meds, and help us assess when an animal needs more care than we can handle here," Sierra said. "Does that sound like something you'd be interested in?"

Yes.

Absolutely.

This was exactly what she'd come for. To give animals who'd gotten a shitty deal a second chance. To patch them up when life had failed them. Here, she wouldn't be at the mercy of an owner's decision. She could give the animals that came in the care they needed.

But, like always, she couldn't jump on the decision. She needed time. Time to let the details sink in. Time to come up with questions. Time to make sure her answer was a definitive yes.

"You don't have to decide right now," Liz said. "Ignore

Sierra. She's never taken over five minutes to consider a thing in her entire life."

"Hey, that's not true." When Liz shot her a look that seemed to be a familiar form of communication between the two business partners who were obviously long-time friends, Sierra replied, "Fine. That part's true. But you don't have to say it like it's a bad thing. My quick thinking and acting got us this far, didn't it?"

"Take all the time you need," Liz said, ignoring Sierra's question. "We can discuss pay and hours later. Decide if you want on board first. Because that's the most important part for us. Trust me. No one lasts long in animal rescue if they don't have a passion for it."

That was more reassuring than Sierra's earlier comment about caring too much.

Passion she wasn't worried about. It was the newness of this place that held her back.

The business didn't have a track record. No other staff to talk to. It would be a complete leap of faith. Not something she usually did, and when she did… well, that kind of impulsiveness had landed her here looking for a new job.

But she *did* have passion. And that passion made her want to leap in with these two.

"I can let you know in a couple days," she said. "Probably by tomorrow. I just want to sleep on it."

Sierra took a sip of coffee instead of responding. Taylor took it as a sign that the woman was trying to hold her tongue.

"Of course." Liz tapped the paper in front of Taylor. "What do you think of the plans? We'd love your input, whether you decide to take the job or not."

Taylor studied the paper. Liz and Sierra had marked off space for an exam table, a sink cabinet, and lots of shelving. "You'll want to have a fridge for meds. At least a small one, even under the exam table. I know you have the kitchen, but you won't want to leave an animal in here to walk over to the kitchen every time you need dewormer."

Sierra narrowed her appraising eyes at Taylor, while Liz nodded and said, "Good call."

"Everything else looks good," Taylor said. "Although, honestly, I might not be the best judge of this since I don't have any experience outside of private practice."

"That's okay," Liz said. "I know enough about the rest of the rescue stuff and have friends who do, too. We all have to outsource in our home rescues though, so we don't know what should go in an exam room. I appreciate your input. Thanks."

"You're welcome," Taylor said. "I really do like the idea of this place."

Liz smiled and opened her mouth, but Sierra jumped in first. "But you don't know if you want to jump on a zooming train that just left the station."

Taylor stifled a laugh. She couldn't help liking this woman despite being so obviously different from her. Sierra and Liz seemed to balance each other out. She got the impression this would be a fun place to work, but she wasn't in the habit of deciding things only based on impressions.

Well, not *good* decisions.

"We can't all be Sierras," Liz said with a shudder. "That would be terrifying."

"A world full of me?" Sierra said. "Are you kidding me? That would be awesome!"

As amused as she was by their banter, Taylor wasn't sure what to do. She didn't feel like she had enough information yet to make that decision, but she didn't know what information was missing.

The sound of car tires crunching over gravel caught her attention from the small, window-shaped hole in the wall.

Sierra raised an eyebrow at Liz and asked, "Expecting anyone else?"

Liz shook her head. "Contractors were on their way out when I got here. Said they wouldn't be back to install the windows until late afternoon tomorrow. Maybe they forgot something?"

Sierra leaned out of the open hole. "Not unless they drive an electric blue Prius."

"I'll go check it out," Liz said.

"No, I'll go," Sierra said. "I'm scarier."

"That's exactly why you *shouldn't* go."

"What if it's someone who needs scaring?"

Liz sighed. "Let's both go."

Taylor stood along with them. "I should probably head out, anyway. Get out of your hair and all. I'm sure you both have lots to do."

"Nah," Sierra said. "I mean, yes. But you stick around. Wander and get a feel for the place. See if you have questions. We'll be back in a few minutes."

Taylor watched them both leave, then did a slow, full rotation in the center of the room.

She stopped and closed her eyes, imagining the space filled with the items in the design draft. Imagining a cat on the exam table. Imagining *herself* on the other side of that table, with Sierra or Liz keeping the cat calm while she prepared a vaccine.

The ease with which she could imagine herself here was shocking.

Also? It felt right. Like she belonged here.

But Taylor didn't make decisions based on feelings. Especially not after the one and only disastrous time she tried that. She needed to make sure there weren't any reasons to say no before she said yes.

She hoped like hell she didn't find any reasons to say no.

For the first time in as long as she could remember, Taylor wanted something with all her heart. She wanted *this*.

―――――

THE MOMENT AUSTIN cut off the engine, a howl erupted from the back seat. The dang cat had done that at every red light and during every silent break between playlist songs the entire way to Breaux Bridge.

And every single time it happened, Austin had jumped behind the wheel. Once, his foot slipped off the brake with the howling jolt, but thankfully at a slow intersection.

The cat must have a built-in amplifier in his throat. One that made him sound like a Sasquatch. Or how Austin imagined a Sasquatch would sound. He'd never be caught dead watching any of those paranormal hunting docu-things. Just not his kick watching people skulking through the woods with night vision and conspiracy theories. Even if he did think there had to be *something* out there.

The cat behind him howled. Again.

"Dude, this sucks. I know. I really do." He turned to face the gigantic carrier crammed behind his passenger seat. "But I don't have a choice here."

Howl

"You're killing me, cat."

Howl

It pressed its nose against the bars and stared at Austin with that smushed face and those huge owl eyes. The same face and eyes Austin had seen twice a year for the last eight years, and at least once a month for four years before that. Ever since this beast had wandered into his uncle's house when it had been just a tiny kitten.

Austin had been sixteen and was helping his uncle remove an old couch when this guy strolled inside between

Austin's legs, hopped onto his uncle's new purple sofa, and never left.

He took one more look at those big, desperate, confused eyes and exited the car. It was the only thing he *could* do. He couldn't take the cat back to his apartment on the Northshore. The landlord had a strict no pets policy. And he'd tried every other relative and friend of his uncle's. No luck. They either couldn't or made up excuses.

This was the big guy's best option. Or so he'd been told.

He'd called a few rescues in the area, but none of them had room. Or if they did, they advised against putting a senior cat in their facilities. The stress alone would kill the poor guy.

Austin had already lost his uncle. He couldn't bear to have a part in killing his uncle's cat on top of everything.

"Howdy," a bright voice called out from the steps of the house.

"Hi." Austin tugged at the purple carrier until it broke free from the car. He closed the door and carried his ward toward the two women standing on the porch steps. Both wore jeans and T-shirts but couldn't be more different. The one on the left had a vampy pin-up aesthetic, while the other woman looked like she'd be perfectly at home wandering off into the woods for an extended stay. "Is this... um... St. Martin Animal Sanctuary?"

It couldn't be.

This place wasn't even a fully formed building, much less a fully functioning business. This was bad. Even for a non-profit.

Both women had soft stances, but something in their eyes told him that either woman could—and most definitely *would*—break him in pieces if he stepped one foot out of line in their presence.

Whoever they were, he liked them already.

The woman with the red lipstick pointed at a bright blue poster board with glitter vomited all over it. "That's what the sign says."

The sign looked like a homecoming week spirit poster. But if that's how they wanted to run their business, who was he to judge?

"Can we help you with something?" The other woman in flannel eyed the carrier as he walked toward them. "You got a bear in there?"

As if he heard his stage cue, the cat let out another earth-rumbling howl.

"Not quite. It's a cat. Tink."

The woman with the lipstick blinked twice fast. "Did you say Tank?"

Austin sighed. "Tink."

The woodsy flannel woman fought back a laugh, while the cat howled once again at the mention of his name.

Her friend relaxed her stance, and a look of concern replaced her steely glare. "Is it hurt?"

"No ma'am," Austin said. "Just voicing his opinion."

Tink did a lot of voicing his opinion lately. He'd always been a talker, but over the last few days, he'd had a *lot* to say. Not that Austin could blame him. The situation was shitty all around. If he could get away with howling at strangers, Austin might do the same.

"We aren't open yet, as you can see," the woman in flannel said. She wasn't swayed by Tink's howling, and she was even less impressed with Austin.

Of course, she was judging him. He was dropping off a cat like it was a bag of used clothes. Whatever she thought of him, he thought worse of himself.

"I can kind of see that. But I had a couple of other places that suggested I try you all." He stood a few feet in front of the bottom step and looked up at the women. "Please, if you could just help me out. Or help me find someplace else to go. My uncle died last week, and I can't find anyone to take his cat."

"Have you tried your own place?" The woman's red lipstick curled into a snarl.

Her friend elbowed her. "Stop it. I thought you said I was the scary one?"

As far as Austin was concerned, they were both pretty scary. But scary in a way that told him they'd probably take a bullet for a cat they didn't know. He was counting on that, actually.

"I tried. Begged my landlord. He won't budge on his policy." Tink howled again, as if to plead his case. "Please? They said if I take him to the shelter, the stress might kill him."

The snarling woman sighed and looked at the sky. Her flannel-wearing friend asked, "How old is he?"

"Twelve," Austin answered.

The women exchanged A Look.

"Yeah, I know," he said. "That's why I'm here. I can't drop him just anywhere. I need to know he's going to be okay."

He looked at the construction mess behind them again and reconsidered his assumption that Tink would be okay here.

But he was out of options. He needed someone to take this cat so he could finish settling his uncle's estate and get back home before practices began.

He was already missing tryouts. The assistant coach was handling that and sending him the stats and video clips so they could consult on who'd make the team this year. Most of the lineup was set since they didn't lose a bunch of seniors. But there were a few open spots in question, and Austin hated not being there for tryouts.

If anyone else in the family had stepped up to help with his uncle's affairs, he could have been back already.

"I have an idea," the woman in flannel said.

"Uh-oh." Her friend's face tightened like she'd been on this ride before.

The woman with the idea winked at her friend and stuck a hand out. "I'm Sierra. This is Liz. We've got an exam room inside. Let's see what you've got here."

---

3

*A*ustin followed the two women into the building and down an unfinished hallway. They turned at the end into a small room with nothing but a folding table, a couple of metal chairs, a mostly empty low bookshelf, and a woman standing in the center with her eyes closed.

She was a head shorter than him, with a thin frame. Probably not an athlete. Although maybe a casual runner. She looked built for marathons. Straight blonde hair trailed over her shoulders, and she wore a fitted, navy button-down shirt with the sleeves rolled up, black jeans, and yellow Converse shoes.

The woman opened her eyes and startled when she saw the three of them in the doorway. Her eyes immediately drifted downward to the carrier in Austin's hand. Tink howled to confirm his presence as well.

"Sorry, didn't mean to scare you," Liz said. "We've got someone we'd like you to take a look at."

The blonde woman's gaze raised from the carrier to lock with his. Austin forgot to breathe while he stared into those big brown eyes.

"Austin, this is Taylor, our potential vet tech," Sierra said. "Taylor, this is Austin. Austin and…"

Austin found his breath and realized she was waiting for his answer. "Tink."

Taylor's gaze drifted back to Tink with his face smushed against the bars again. She took a step toward Austin and squatted to peer inside the carrier. "Is he okay?"

Not even a throwaway comment or giggle at the ridiculous name for such a beast. Like she'd seen worse.

"He's angry and old and confused, but in good health as far as I know," Austin said. "My uncle was very good about taking care of him."

"Your uncle's cat?"

"He passed away a few weeks ago."

What a way to start a new year. He'd kicked off January by losing his favorite relative, becoming the sole adult responsible enough to take care of everything, and gaining temporary custody of a twenty-pound, hairball-hacking beast of a cat.

Taylor stood and made eye contact. Her expression was soft and sincere around that sharp little nose. Those brown eyes of hers drew him in once again. "I'm sorry."

"Thanks," he said. "This is… uh, the exam room?"

"It will be," Liz said. "Taylor, would you mind taking a look at the cat for us? We'll step outside."

She tugged at Sierra's shirt sleeve, and the two women squeezed past Austin out the door.

"Wait," Taylor called after them, a hint of fear in her voice.

Sierra leaned her head around the door frame with a mischievous grin. "Consider this an audition."

"An audition?" A horrified Taylor stood frozen as the two other women disappeared.

Austin looked over his shoulder, then back at the woman remaining in the room with him. "Those two seem… fun."

"If you say so." Taylor looked around. "There's no door and no window. How is it even safe to let a cat out in here? Never mind the fact that there's absolutely no exam equipment."

Austin placed the carrier on the ground beside the folding table. "I'll hold him on the table. He knows me. And he isn't much of a runner, as you'll see. I'll make sure he's safe while you look at him."

She pulled her attention from the open hole in the wall and looked at Austin. Deciding if she could trust him.

A wave of relief washed over him while a rising tide of hope filled his chest. Yes, this was the place for Tink. With this woman watching over him, Tink would be safe and cared for. He just had to convince her and the others to take the cat.

And maybe convince this woman to work here? They'd said "potential" vet tech and "audition." Whatever that meant.

Taylor stared at the carrier, considering his offer and the situation. Her lips parted slightly as if she knew her answer, but wasn't ready to release the words just yet. Hands down, she had the cutest risk-assessing face he'd ever seen.

Not that he was interested in a cute vet tech from Breaux Bridge. Not when he lived two hours away and had his hands full with his uncle's estate and baseball season kicking up.

He didn't need a date. He certainly didn't need a girl-friend. Not now, at least. He'd love to settle down with someone eventually, but his life and priorities just didn't match up with that at the moment. What he needed right now was someone to take his uncle's cat. That was all.

That's what he kept telling himself.

But the more he watched her consider options with those big brown eyes of hers, the more he reconsidered what he needed. Or, at least, what he wanted right now.

She finally decided and nodded. "Hold him on the table."

Austin exhaled and somehow tore his eyes away from her. He opened the carrier door and stuck his hand inside. "Okay, buddy. Let's do this."

TAYLOR STOOD PATIENTLY while Austin pulled the cat from the bright purple carrier and placed it on the table.

"Cat" was a loose term for this beast.

Tink.

The beast's name was Tink.

The table groaned beneath the gray tabby's bulk. Taylor didn't have a scale, but the thing had to weigh close to twenty pounds. Not the biggest cat she'd ever seen, but definitely near the top of the list. And it wasn't just over-weight like she typically saw with spoiled older animals. This cat was simply huge. Long-limbed and big-boned, with enormous eyes and a head that seemed far too small for its body.

"Wow."

It was all she could say. Mostly because she didn't want to say anything offensive about this guy's dead uncle's cat, but also because she suddenly couldn't think straight with this man standing mere inches from her.

At first, it was his eyes. Crisp, blue-gray irises beneath thick eyebrows and a mess of short, light brown hair. He was tall enough that she had to crane her neck to look into those eyes.

Then it was the short beard, which he rubbed every time he mentioned the cat. Nerves. He clearly cared about this animal, despite being here to dump it on strangers.

He wore a dark gray T-shirt that clung to his lean muscles and a pair of worn-in jeans. Both looked so soft that she had to fight the urge to reach out and touch them. She silently thanked the universe for this rare warm January day that prompted those bare arms.

But it was his *smell* that really did her in. Taylor was used to smelling unpleasant things all day. Urine. Poop. Anesthetic. Professional grade cleaners. Sometimes she couldn't get the smell of blood out of her nose when she tried to sleep at night. Those were the nights she wished she'd become an accountant like her sister, Geena.

No one wore perfume or cologne at the clinic. There was no point. You can't out-scent ammonia. Plus, strong perfumy scents irritate some animals. So no one around her, not even the head vet… well, not during work hours… wore cologne.

This guy, though.

This guy smelled like a cedar grove. Woodsy and cool, with a hint of spice. Was it possible to fall in love with someone simply because they smelled like a *tree*?

Taylor wanted desperately to take a few steps away. Away from this man and his trees and the heat emanating from his muscled arm nearly brushing against hers. But he was holding and petting a cat that needed her attention.

"I'm honestly not sure what I'm supposed to do here," she said. "I'm kind of limited in what I *can* do, and I don't even work here, so I don't know what they need to know."

"Trial by fire job interview? Those are always fun."

His smile curled up a little higher on one side than the other, turning Taylor's insides to mush.

The cat.

Keep talking about the cat, she reminded herself. Or anything else that would make him stop smiling and stop smelling so damn intoxicating.

Bonus: the cat might relax more if it heard Austin's voice while she examined it. With the open window and doorway both nearby, she wanted this cat as chill as possible.

"What do you do for work?"

"High school coach," he said. "And I teach history."

She slowly placed a hand on the cat's head and gave it a couple of small pets before scratching its ears and around to the side of its face. Then she held up its smushed face to look into those big round eyes. They were clear. Really clear for his age. That was good.

She scratched the side of his face again. "Can you use one hand to scruff him while I look in his mouth?"

"Scruff him?"

Not a cat owner himself, obviously.

She talked him through how to get a firm grip on the massive scruff, explaining that it wouldn't hurt Tink and that it was for the cat's safety.

"What school?" she asked.

"Not here," he said. "Northshore High."

"What sports?" She hoped he'd start giving more than two-word answers as she gently pried open the cat's mouth and examined its teeth.

"Baseball," he said. "I'm supposed to be there for tryouts this week, but my uncle had other plans for me."

She kept her eyes focused on the cat's mouth despite the annoyance building inside her. The cat's teeth looked good. Looked like the owner had them cleaned recently. Huge canines, so she quickly released her hold, even though the cat wasn't protesting much at all. Unlike its guardian here. "I'm sure your uncle is terribly sorry to have inconvenienced you with his death."

Austin released his hold on the cat and began stroking it again. A horrified look came over his face.

"I didn't mean it like that," he said. "I know it looks bad because I'm dropping off his cat, but I swear I would keep him if I could. And I tried to get people to take him. Bunch of selfish jerks, my whole family."

He sounded genuinely upset about having to hand over

this cat, but she couldn't let the "other plans" comment slide. It sounded like typical sports guy stuff. They always think the world revolves around them.

"Well, he looks really healthy. I'm sure Sierra and Liz will help if they can, and you'll be able to get on with your life." She hadn't meant that to sound so nasty.

Okay, maybe she did.

"I told you, it isn't like that," he insisted again. "I've got a responsibility to those kids. Some of them have scholarships and college at stake. Not to mention those afternoons on the field... I get to talk to them nearly every day. Find out what's going on in their lives. Help give advice and an ear to listen when I can and when they let me. I take all of that seriously."

Taylor blinked back at him. Had she misjudged this guy after all? Had the fact that her current boss played in a local baseball league clouded her assessment of this person because of... all of *that* mess?

"Sorry."

"It's fine," he said. "I know this all looks bad. But I swear, I don't want to leave this cat here. I just don't have any other options. And I'd have another home for him and be back coaching those kids if the rest of my family weren't a bunch of selfish vultures."

"Families suck sometimes."

Hers didn't sound nearly as bad as his, and she wasn't super close to her extended family, but she wanted to strangle her own sister often enough to feel this was a fair assessment.

"Yeah, mine especially. They're not making any of this easier." His muscular shoulders rose and fell with a heavy sigh. "Sorry. I'm just under a lot of stress right now, since I'm the only one handling the whole estate."

She ran her hands over the full length of Tink while he made the softest purrs she'd ever heard from a cat that large.

Her fingers caught on a textured collar hidden beneath the massive folds of thick skin and muscle around the cat's neck. When she moved the fur aside to look at the collar, she nearly gasped out loud.

"Did your uncle live near Oak Shadows Apartments?"

He cocked his head to the side. "Yeah. How'd you know?"

She pointed at the collar and looked up at Austin with her mouth hanging open. "I think I know this cat."

4

———————

*A*ustin stared at Taylor in confusion. "Did you know my uncle?"

"Not exactly," she said, examining that collar.

Austin hadn't even realized Tink had a collar until she'd excavated it from all that fur. Just another thing for him to feel guilty about. Sheesh, he was a mess.

"So you didn't exactly know my uncle, but you know his cat?" That didn't make sense at all, since the cat never left his uncle's side and was strictly an indoor pet, as far as he knew. His uncle would never take the risk of Tink getting lost or hit by a car.

"The collar." She ran her fingers along the gaudy, fake, heart-shaped gemstones along the purple collar with red trim. "He has a matching harness, just like this. I would pass your uncle walking with his cat on that harness when I'd run along the river on the weekends. I just didn't put together that this was the same huge cat. And I never got close enough to realize *how* huge his cat was."

A runner. He'd been right.

Focus, Austin. Not the point at all here.

Then he realized she had to be wrong. Aside from it sounding both ridiculous and completely plausible that his uncle took this cat out for regular strolls on a leash, there was one key detail that showed her connection was misguided.

"That can't be right," he said. "I have a box of Tink's things in my car. You can dig through it but there was no matching harness."

"So you're telling me there's another man in my neighborhood who walks along the same river with an identical cat and matching harness?"

When she put it all together that way, it did sound pretty convincing. "I'm not telling you anything except I didn't find it."

"There had to be one," she said. "You must have missed it or put it in a different box."

"I think I would have noticed a bedazzled cat accessory. I'm telling you, there's no harness."

Although the more her story settled into his brain, the more it sounded precisely like something his uncle would have bought for his cat. He could *see* them walking together with it. The man wasn't exactly conventional. Part of what Austin had always loved about him.

But if Taylor was right, what had happened to the dang thing?

"Well, that's weird." She shook off the mini-mystery and pet the cat's head. "Anyway, it's nice to officially meet you, Tink."

"How does he look?" A booming female voice called out from the doorway. Liz and Sierra both waited anxiously for the answer.

"Really good," Taylor said. "I can't do a full exam here, but no signs of any health issues. He seems to be in perfect shape for a senior cat."

"Great," Sierra said.

Austin turned to the two women. "So does that mean you can help me out?"

The two owners looked at each other, clearly used to years of communicating wordlessly. Sierra turned back to him and said, "I'm sure one of us can hang on to him until we find a permanent home or a foster."

Every muscle in Austin's body unclenched as the realization settled in that Tink would be safe. "Thank you. I can't tell you how much this means to me."

Liz nodded. "We'll need you to fill out owner surrender paperwork. Unfortunately, we don't have any here at the moment, so you'll need to come back sometime this week to fill that out."

"I can come back tomorrow."

"Works for me," Liz said. "I'll leave some papers out front for whenever you stop by."

"Great."

Guilt stabbed at his belly once again. Guilt that he was relieved and almost elated by these people's help. Guilt because it meant he'd be leaving alone today. Without Tink.

That had been the whole purpose of this trip, but now that the moment was here, he struggled to leave. But he couldn't exactly live here in the half-finished shelter. Even if the place had any windows, he couldn't move in and plop a mattress on the floor to live here with the cat.

He'd considered a similar plan, though. A few days after his uncle's funeral, while he'd been going through stuff and making lists of all the things he needed to take care of, he'd sat on the floor at the bottom of the steps, exactly where they'd found his uncle.

Tink had crawled into his lap and slept. While they sat on the floor together, Austin contemplated whether he should stay there. Buy out whoever they discovered his uncle had left the house to and move in with Tink.

But he eventually remembered the kids back at Northshore. He couldn't just abandon them for a cat. Right?

He held out his arm to shake Liz's and Sierra's hands. "Seriously, thank you."

Then he turned to Taylor, who was silently petting and scratching Tink while the others worked out the details. He wasn't sure what to say to her. She wasn't the one in charge here. Didn't even work here. But she'd been so gentle with Tink, and gentle with him once she'd heard the whole story. Even though he didn't feel like he deserved any kindness for what he was about to have to do.

"Thanks."

With one hand still on Tink, Taylor shook Austin's hand. Her palm and fingers were warm from spending so much time in the cat's fur, but a zing of energy sizzled his skin along with that warmth the second their hands connected. Her big, soulful eyes widened, and he knew she felt it too.

"You're welcome."

Her voice was sweet and soft, and he was now equally regretting having to leave her as well.

Get it together, Austin. You don't even know this woman.

Before he'd gotten the news about his uncle, Austin had made a resolution for the year. No more starting things he couldn't finish. He always meant well, but so many great ideas went flat because he couldn't follow through on everything. This year, he swore to himself that his job and those kids were his only priority. At least through baseball season. That meant everything else, including his personal life and especially any dating prospects were on hold until the end of the school year.

His uncle's death might have thrown a bit of a wrench into that plan, but it was a temporary one. Asking out a woman who lived two hours away from him at the beginning of baseball season would be a much bigger wrench.

Austin stood in front of Tink and took the cat's face in both hands, giving him a good last stare. "You be good. Okay, buddy?" He swallowed a lump forming in his throat. "These people are gonna take good care of you. I know this is all a lot, but you're in good hands." He blinked back a surprising well of tears and kissed the cat on his smushy little face. "I'll miss you, big guy."

As he turned away, he saw Taylor quickly wipe her face as she took his position again to hold the cat.

Austin headed for the door and gave everyone a quick wave. "Thanks again. I'll be back to sign the papers."

"Take care," Sierra shouted as he hurried down the hallway and out of the house.

He made it all the way inside his Prius before he couldn't hold back the tears any longer. That was also the exact moment he realized he forgot to give them the box with Tink's things.

There was no way he was going back in there. Not now. Not like this.

Tomorrow.

He could drop off the box tomorrow when he returned to sign the paperwork.

He wiped his face and turned on the engine. Then he backed up and headed down the gravel driveway, notably missing the loud howls that had accompanied him on the way in.

HOWL.

The cat looked up at Taylor with its enormous eyes and squishy little face. Taylor couldn't help feeling bad for the cat. He'd been through a lot. Losing his person, his home, and the guy he probably thought would be his new person. Now he was in a weird new place with a bunch of strangers. Poor guy.

"So are we rock-paper-scissoring for who's taking him home?" Sierra stared at the cat on the table.

"The hot guy already left," Liz as she walked back into the room. "And I think Marc would definitely object to you taking Austin home."

"Probably," Sierra said. "But I was talking about the cat. Besides, I think Taylor's already marked her territory."

Taylor's back straightened, and her cheeks flushed hot with embarrassment.

Her potential employers thought she was flirting with their first potential client. Or whatever they called people who dropped off animals at a shelter. No matter what they were called, it was a bad look for Taylor in a freaking job interview.

Even worse was the idea that she might have been giving off a flirting vibe. As if she wasn't in enough trouble after the dating disaster she'd stepped into at her last job.

Shit.

No, her current job.

The job she technically still had and would have to keep even longer if she screwed up this interview.

Heck, this place might not even get off the ground, and Taylor could be looking for another job in a few weeks or months, anyway. But vet techs were always in demand. Her entire future didn't depend on this one interview, right? No matter how much she liked the idea of working here.

"I didn't—"

"Ignore Sierra," Liz said. "Although I'm pretty sure the hot guy was into you, so maybe you want to stick around for when he shows up tomorrow." She said the last bit in a sing-song voice.

"Ooh, I can see it now," said Sierra. "You'll raise the guy's dead person's cat together and everyone can live happily ever after."

Taylor was speechless. Utterly speechless. These women were *a lot*.

And yet she couldn't help wanting to be part of this inner circle they had.

"Tink would be better at your place," Liz said, circling the conversation back without missing a beat. "With all the other cats at mine, he'd have to stay in a bathroom. Will Marc be okay with you taking him?"

Sierra shrugged. "We'll find out, I guess. I'll tell him the other option was bringing the guy home. That'll soften the news."

"I'll take him."

The room went silent as Sierra and Liz both turned to Taylor. Liz looked mildly surprised, but Sierra had a knowing smirk.

"The cat, I mean." Taylor's cheeks burned even more. "If that's okay with you both. I'd be glad to foster him until you find a permanent home. Or at least until this place is fixed up."

Taylor wasn't sure where those words came from.

She felt a weird connection to this cat. It was like he was her extended neighbor. Like… her neighbor, twice removed. Or something. She didn't understand relationship mathematics.

Then, it hit her. She wouldn't pass them walking together on the weekends anymore. Seeing that beast and his person happily strolling down the sidewalk always brought a smile to her face, no matter how crappy her week had been. She always looked forward to waving as she jogged past them.

Now she was grieving for someone she didn't even know. His nephew had seemed pretty upset about the loss, so he must have been a good guy. The uncle. Not the nephew. Although the nephew too…

Nope, not the point.

No matter how hot he was or how much his blinking back tears over this cat made her insides ache, Austin was none of her concern. Taylor was here for a job, not matchmaking.

And whether she took the job or not, she could at least take this big guy for a while.

Surely Ellie wouldn't mind.

And if she did, too bad. That's what she got for not warning Taylor about the state of this place.

"Does that mean you want the job too?" Liz asked.

"I'd still like to sleep on it, if that's okay."

"Sure thing," Sierra said. "He's all yours."

"Tell you what," Liz said. "You take him home tonight. Sleep on that job offer—which we are officially offering—and you come back here tomorrow to either fill out new employee paperwork or to fill out foster paperwork if you decide not to work for us. Deal?"

Taylor looked at the cat again, wondering if she'd lost her mind. But she nodded anyway. "Deal."

5

Somehow, Taylor had hauled the gigantic carrier up the steps to her second-floor apartment. After placing it in a corner of the living room, she'd left him alone to go out for food for herself and food and litter for her new roommate. An hour later, the cat still hadn't given up the safety of that carrier.

Taylor set up bowls of food and water within his line of sight and placed a huge litter box in the bathroom where debris would be easier to clean off of the linoleum than the carpet.

"Your move, big guy."

No response. Not that she expected one. He'd stopped howling once she brought him inside, after he finally realized Austin was gone.

I'd probably howl too if Austin dumped me.

Nope. Not thinking those thoughts. Get it together.

Taylor was done with men. And anyone else, for that matter. Romantically. Sexually. And anything along those lines.

Halfway through her burrito, Taylor heard the familiar

sound of keys in the front door. Burrito in hand, she turned to greet her roommate.

Ellie had put her nose ring back in—her daily routine once she was out of claw range. Her dark skin glowed in contrast against her dulled aqua scrubs, and her perfectly contoured makeup and thick mascara still looked as flawless as they had when she'd left that morning. Her short natural curls were pulled off her forehead by a bright purple, pink, and aqua scarf folded and tied neatly at the base of her head.

Taylor held up her hands. "Don't freak out."

"As if you—" Ellie stopped short and closed the door behind her. A second later she caught sight of the huge crate. "What the hell is in that?"

"I told you not to freak out. His name is Tink, and he's scared, so lower your voice."

Ellie dropped her purse on the couch. "You know we can't have a dog, right? I mean, you're the one that pointed that out to *me* in the lease when I wanted to bring home that tripod we treated a few months back."

"It's not a dog."

Ellie put a hand to her heart and gasped. "You were at that shelter place today. What did they send you home with? Also, is it going to eat me?"

"They didn't send me with anything. I volunteered to keep him. Just until they find a permanent home."

Ellie snort-laughed. "So he lives here now. Half a day in animal rescue and you've already been suckered into bringing shit home." She closed her eyes and shook her head. "Wait a minute. What are we talking about here if that isn't a dog? Is it a raccoon? What?"

"It's just a cat. Calm down."

"A *cat*?" Ellie shrieked again. "In *that* crate?"

"Yes, a cat. He's sweet but scared. His owner died. Apparently, the rest of the family is garbage, and Austin couldn't keep him."

"What the hell is an Austin?"

"The owner's nephew."

A sly grin grew on Ellie's face. "He's hot, isn't he? I can see it in your face."

"Stop. It doesn't matter."

"He *is* hot." Her sly grin grew smug. "I knew it."

Taylor rolled her eyes. "By the way, if you're such a fortune teller, you could have warned me the place isn't even a real business yet."

Ellie shrugged. "Would you have shown up if I had?"

"Probably not, but you could have given me a heads up."

"Aren't you glad I didn't?"

Truthfully, she was. As terrifying as that place had looked initially, Taylor felt more and more like this was a place she wanted to be a part of. She still planned to sleep on the final decision, but she was pretty certain. She just wasn't about to admit all of that to Ellie.

"Maybe." Taylor took another bite of her burrito.

Ellie sat on the couch and peered into the carrier holes from a respectful distance. "Aren't Liz and Sierra great?"

"I can see why you like them. For many obvious reasons."

"I mean, yeah. Speaking of hot, right? But they're pretty amazing otherwise too."

"They're… infectious," Taylor said. "In the best way."

"That's an excellent way to put it." Ellie gave up trying to get a good look at the gray tabby cat inside the dark carrier without freaking him out. "Has he come out at all?"

Taylor finished the burrito and shook her head. "Not unless he came out while I ran out for supplies."

"We can put him in the bathroom for the night. Or maybe in your bedroom. A smaller room might help him feel more secure at first."

"Good idea. Want to help me move him now?"

Taylor closed the door, and they each grabbed an end of the carrier. Twenty pounds wasn't heavy by itself, but the size of the carrier made it awkward to move him around. She was going to have bruises from where the thing kept bumping against her leg with every step.

They placed him in a quiet corner of Taylor's bedroom and opened the carrier door again. A few moments later, they'd put his food, water, and litter in Taylor's room and closed the bedroom door to give him some peace and privacy.

Taylor threw away her takeout trash. "Sorry. I'd have grabbed one for you if I'd realized what time it was."

"It's fine. I'm not hungry."

"Rough day?"

Ellie was a vet tech at a different clinic from Taylor, but the job was the same everywhere. You left work either starving or too upset to eat until the next morning.

"Not the worst." Ellie collapsed onto the couch. "I'll probably have some popcorn later. After a shower."

"I can make some," Taylor said. "A big batch with real butter. We can watch whatever you want. I'm too tired to make any more decisions tonight."

"Sounds like a plan." That grin returned. "After you tell me all about this Austin person."

"There's nothing to say. He dropped off his cat and left."

"Bullshit. Tell me everything," Ellie said. "I need the distraction."

Taylor couldn't deny her friend a distraction. Not on a tough workday. "Okay, but don't read anything into this."

"No promises if I smell something juicy."

"You know that man I told you about that I would see every weekend when I'm out jogging? The one who walks his cat?"

Ellie laughed. "Oh yeah. Wait… oh my gosh, is that who came in today?"

"No, Austin is his nephew. Or was." Taylor gestured at her bedroom. "Tink was his uncle's cat."

"No way!"

"Yes way," Taylor confirmed. "The nephew seemed not at all surprised that his uncle had been regularly walking his cat by the river. The nephew, Austin, is from out of town and was just in to settle affairs."

"So if the uncle lived around this neighborhood, and the nephew is from out of town, why was he dropping off a cat at a non-operational shelter out in Breaux Bridge?"

Taylor shrugged. "No one else would take the cat. It's twelve years old."

"That sucks. No wonder he's scared."

"The nephew seemed pretty upset about having to leave him."

Ellie scoffed. "But not upset enough to keep him."

"He said he begged his landlord and his family, but no luck."

"So you had time to talk about his family?"

"Stooooop," Taylor said.

"Why? He's hot. He loves animals. You're clearly into him, don't deny it. This seems like a no-brainer to me."

"Have you forgotten?" Taylor asked. "No-braining is why I was over there looking for another job."

"Is this guy your boss?" Ellie asked.

"No."

"Is he married?"

"I have no idea. And I'm not asking, because it doesn't matter. I'm dating myself. Or some brand of self-help. I'm taking a break from making horrible mistakes."

Ellie shrugged. "Not all of them will be mistakes. That

boss of yours owns all the blame for the current situation. Ugh, I hate him."

"Me too."

She hadn't wanted to sleep with him. Not at first. Sure, she'd been attracted to him, but she'd also known he was married. That was a line she hadn't wanted to cross. But he'd kept pursuing her. Kept flirting. Kept inviting the entire office out for Friday night drinks. Then, he'd offered to give her a ride home on one of those Fridays.

She'd felt so guilty about the whole thing. About her lapse in judgment. About his wife. About all of it.

Then she'd found out it was his *thing*.

He'd also slept with his last vet tech. Probably more. And no one in the clinic had thought to warn her.

Not that she'd needed a warning. She knew better.

She'd made an awful mistake. One she didn't plan on making again.

But she still needed out of that job. And she needed to train her brain to not fall for jerks anymore.

"It doesn't matter anyway," Taylor said. "Austin lives two hours away."

Mischief danced in Ellie's eyes. "But how long is he in town for?"

"Don't you have to take a shower?"

Ellie stood and stretched. "You're taking the job though, right?"

Taylor glanced at her closed door, thinking about the scared cat on the other side. Visualizing her afternoon at the shelter site. Replaying her conversations with Sierra and Liz. Thinking about all the animals like Tink that she could help.

"Yeah," she said. "I think I am."

Austin dug through the box he forgot to bring with him earlier that day while the phone rang on speaker. "Hey, Mom. Do you know what happened to Tink's harness?"

"Didn't you drop that beast off today?"

Austin ignored the question, along with his mother's continued refusal to call the cat by its name. "A neighbor said Uncle Kenny used to walk the cat on a leash, and I can't find the leash or the harness. I don't remember seeing them anywhere, and I've been through this whole house."

"Kenny used to *what?*" His mother's tone dripped with judgmental disbelief. "Never mind. I don't want to know anymore. Your father's family always was... well, it doesn't matter. I don't know what you're talking about, anyway. What do you need this thing for? Please tell me you don't still have that animal."

"That *animal* was my uncle's beloved pet," he said. "And I already found a place for him, but I'm dropping off a box with the rest of Tink's things tomorrow, and I can't find the leash and harness."

"I'm sure they'll survive without it. Or they'll buy a replacement."

Austin loved his mother, but everything was replaceable in her mind.

"Do you know if anyone came by the house before I got here? Maybe Tink was wearing it, like they'd been about to go on a walk before..." He still wasn't used to saying his uncle *died*. Austin wondered if that would ever get easier. "Maybe someone took it off Tink and still has it?"

"The police found the cat with your uncle after that woman called them to check on him. That's all I know."

He couldn't help notice she used *that woman* the same way she'd used *that animal*. Everything was *that something*. Whatever she didn't approve of at the moment.

In this case, *that woman* referred to Uncle Kenny's best

friend, Patricia. The person who'd called the police when Uncle Kenny hadn't shown up at the bookstore where they'd planned to meet that Saturday afternoon. The police had brushed her off at first, but by that evening they'd agreed to do a welfare check and found him at the bottom of the stairs with Tink lying beside him as if they'd been napping together.

"Honestly, Austin," his mother continued. "I don't know why this is such a big deal."

It wasn't. At least, it shouldn't be.

But Austin couldn't let it go.

He had no reason to believe Taylor would make up a story about his uncle walking the cat, but that would mean the leash and harness should be here somewhere. Unless the police had taken it with them.

His mother was right. It wasn't a big deal. But it just didn't make sense that the items were missing. And he hated when things didn't make sense.

"I guess it isn't."

"Austin, honey. You've been doing too much. Why don't you come over for dinner tomorrow night?"

"I can't," he lied.

"Well, this weekend, then." Her tone told him this was not up for debate. She'd keep listing days and calling until he agreed to her terms. "Take a break. Have dinner with us. I'll make something you love. Any requests? I know you aren't cooking for yourself in that house."

His uncle's house was only fifteen minutes down the road from his mother's here in the city of Lafayette, so it wasn't like he couldn't accept the invitation. As opposed to most weekends, when it would take a two-hour drive each way to visit. And with baseball season kicking up, he wouldn't be able to accept any dinner invitations for at least the next few months.

The *us* in the invitation held him back. He'd already seen enough of his mother over the last couple of weeks, but he'd avoided the *us* part so far.

"For the record, I do cook."

Boxed pasta and rice with ground meat counted as cooking.

He was actually an excellent cook and enjoyed cooking for other people because it made them happy. But he didn't care much about food. Food was fuel. Sometimes it was tasty fuel, but most days he ate because he had to, not because he considered every meal an event like his mother and the rest of his family.

"Then it's settled. Friday evening," his mother said, pretending he'd agreed to the invitation. But they both knew he would eventually, so there was no point in carrying on the charade. She paused a moment, whether contemplating or for dramatic effect, he couldn't tell. "Feel free to bring a date."

At the mention of the word *date,* his mind immediately flashed an image of that vet tech.

Traitorous brain.

He'd met Taylor briefly to do a difficult thing. His brain had simply crossed the wires with the emotional stuff. That's all.

He had no plans to ask Taylor out. Certainly not to throw her to the sharks at his mother's dinner. That would be cruel.

No. Out of the question. No matter how strong a pull he felt to date again and find something serious. Someone he could come home to and cuddle on the couch with every night. Someone he might settle down with and make forever plans with.

It just wasn't the right time for that.

Aside from being swamped with his uncle's estate in the short term, he also didn't see his schedule easing up any time soon. His number one priority beyond this week was those kids back home. He had meetings, practices, games… commitments he didn't plan to bail on for a new relationship. And no one would want to go into something new, knowing they wouldn't be a priority for him.

He was trying not to start anything he didn't intend to finish. Anything he wouldn't have the time, energy, or flexibility to finish. Anything like a romantic relationship.

"Mom, I told you, I'm not seeing anyone. And if I was seeing someone, it would be a person who lives two hours from here. You know, where *I* live."

One perk of the Northshore coaching job had been the distance from his family and this city. A fresh start, yes, but also room to breathe.

"Well, there's always an extra seat at the table," his mother said.

He dropped the conversation rather than get into all the reasons she shouldn't get her hopes up. But the main reason was he needed to stop giving his brain reasons to flash images of a certain blonde.

"Lots to do here," he said.

"If any of your father's godforsaken relatives had the decency to help you out, you'd have more time to enjoy your visit here."

"Mom, this isn't a visit. I'm…" He stopped himself and sighed. She wasn't completely wrong, and most of his own frustration was aimed directly at the same place as hers: his father's side of the family. The adults who should have been helping him with all of this, not waiting to see what remains were left to pick through. "I'm handling it."

"I wish I could help you. We could get through everything much faster. I could make a few calls, and—"

"Nope." He almost laughed at that. They both knew if she stepped within fifty feet of his uncle's house the vultures would magically appear to defend their territory. He wasn't about to use his mother as bait, but the thought had crossed his mind when she'd offered last week. Ultimately, he'd decided it was easier to handle everything alone. "It's less messy if you stay away. But I appreciate the offer."

"I can handle mess, son. I've been handling mess all my life. Those people don't scare me." Her pitch rose along with the pride and defiance in her voice. "But I'll do whatever is easier for you. Just know that I'm here and the offer stands."

"Thanks, Mom. I'll see you Friday."

He ended the call and glanced at his uncle's clock on the living room wall. The clock face was a psychedelic mashup of flowers with Jeff Goldblum in the center. He couldn't see the numbers or the hands from across the room.

Why was he even trying to figure out what time it was? For the first time in years, he wasn't on a schedule. Even his appointment to fill out Tink's paperwork was a vague "sometime tomorrow."

He couldn't get rid of anything until after he knew what was in the will, so he could only box everything up for now. But that meant he had time to drive out to Breaux Bridge again tomorrow to drop off Tink's things *and* have dinner later this week with his mother and whoever else she invited.

He squinted at the clock again, then tried the Galaxy Quest clock in the study that he could see through the open doorway. But that one was just a picture of the cast with purple clock hands and no numbers, so it was impossible to read from here. Checking the time on his phone would be easier from now on.

Austin decided to order delivery again. He'd been through everything edible in the kitchen and was resisting the idea of buying groceries, even though he would be here long enough to need a few more things.

After placing his order, he grabbed the notepad where he was keeping a running list of things he needed to do. It was filled with phone calls he needed to make, paperwork he needed to fill out, and places he needed to go. He contemplated adding one more item to the list. One more thing to do, because he couldn't let go of the question still gnawing at the back of his mind.

Where were that leash and harness?

With a heavy sigh, he grabbed the pen and wrote another item at the bottom of the list: *call Lafayette PD*.

---

6

*T*aylor stepped out of her car and immediately covered her nose with the back of her hand.

Skunk. Had to be. Probably under the house, if she had to guess.

But even skunk smell couldn't dampen her mood that Thursday morning.

She felt a little better now that she'd been away from her current job for several days. After realizing how badly she'd screwed up and how much she didn't want to see her boss anymore, Taylor had put in a vacation request. She hadn't known what she would do this week. Hadn't planned on looking for another job. She just knew she had to get away from that place for a while.

Over the weekend, she'd decided that she needed to leave for good. That realization had boosted her mood, and after a few more days away, she'd felt so much lighter.

By Thursday morning, as Taylor stood in front of the future St. Martin Animal Sanctuary, she felt confident she was exactly where she was supposed to be.

Taylor saw the bright blue glitter-bombed poster board

with fresh eyes. It now represented everything about this shining, scrappy, hope-filled place.

There was no sound of power tools buzzing this morning. Instead, Taylor heard heavy banging from the back of the building.

When she walked through the open front doorway and into the main room, Liz greeted her with a big smile.

"Hey there. How was the first night with your new roommate?"

After Taylor had gone to bed, Tink had finally felt safe enough to explore the bedroom and try some wet food. The smell of that food, however, had kept her up way past her normal bedtime. The food smell *and* the massive dump he took an hour after she'd fallen asleep. Plus, he'd spent a solid five minutes making a racket to cover it in the box.

"Good. He's eating and using the litter box," Taylor said. "He spent most of the night sleeping in his carrier though."

"The best kind of roommate," Liz said. "Pretty much expected with all the change he's had. Thanks for taking him in."

"Anything to keep him out of the parish shelter."

Liz nodded, then raised her brow. "Am I handing you a foster app or an employee packet?"

Taylor had tried to talk herself out of this last night. She'd even made a list of pros and cons. The pro side was filled with things like paying bills and leaving her current toxic work situation and all the feel-good vibes she'd get from animal rescue. The con side, however, was mostly empty. It was just a big question mark. She knew there had to be a downside, but she couldn't think of what it might be.

Basically, the unknown downside *was* the unknown.

Ater fear-spiraling for half the night, she'd come to a decision. A decision that made her giddy with the thrill of ditching her current job and taking a leap of hope with these two women.

With complete confidence, Taylor said, "Employee packet."

Liz gave a thunderous clap of her hands. "Hot damn, I knew it." Her red lips stretched into a wide smile as she nodded toward the table beside them. "Glad to have you on board."

"Thanks for having me here," Taylor said. "I'm really excited to be part of—"

Her sentence was interrupted by a series of loud bangs that shook the entire house.

"Don't worry about that," Liz said once the banging subsided. "It's windows day! Should have had them a while ago, but stuff happens. I'm just glad we got them in before the rain tomorrow."

Liz gestured at a chair with a stack of papers and a pen on the table in front of it. "Here. Have a seat, and I'll leave you to fill it all out."

"Thanks." Taylor sat and looked through the stack. All employee forms. Not a foster application in sight. "You knew I would take the job, huh?"

Liz winked. "Had a feeling."

———

WHEN SHE'D FILLED out the last paper in her stack, Taylor walked down the hall to find Liz in the exam room, looking out the new window.

"All finished?" When Taylor nodded, Liz pointed at the window and asked, "What do you think?"

"Looks good."

"They should all be in by the end of today, and the exterior doors are going in tomorrow. So the building will be completely secure for the weekend." Liz ticked off tasks on her fingers as she spoke. "Flooring, paint, and molding next week. Then interior doors. Should be able to move stuff in the week after next."

"Do you think all of that will be ready by then?"

It sounded fast, but Taylor had limited knowledge of construction schedules. She'd only heard sad tales of delays and complications, and she wouldn't know the difference between a solid schedule and wishful thinking. But Liz gave the impression that she was the realistic one of this business partnership. If Liz thought they'd be ready to move things in within a week or two, then that was probably a reasonable estimate.

"Give or take a few days," Liz said. "But yeah, I think so. We're going to start with this room and one kennel room, then we'll work our way toward the front. We'll worry about the outside details once everything inside is up and running. Our plan is to get this place operational before getting it pretty for the public. We're here for work, not for show."

Taylor nodded. Definitely the realistic partner. Although Sierra didn't strike Taylor as one to be concerned about prettying things up for strangers either.

"When do you need me to start?"

"As soon as you can. Today would be great if you want to jump right in."

For a second Taylor thought she might be joking, but Liz's expression was dead serious as usual.

Taylor looked around the nearly empty room in confusion. What the heck did they need a vet tech for if they didn't have any animals yet? Was she supposed to... paint? Install doors?

"I'm sorry, I don't understand. What do you need me to do here?"

What she wanted to do was run back and double-check

those papers to see what job she'd actually signed up for. Was this some kind of bait and switch scam?

Liz gestured around her. "This exam room is your domain now. You're going to help us make a list of what you need and order it. You'll submit it for approval, of course, but we're going to hand the space over to you."

Taylor's heart rate kicked up twenty notches, and her breath caught in her throat.

They were putting her in charge of this? She couldn't decide what cereal to eat in the morning. She once researched colors and brands for a week just to order a T-shirt.

How was she supposed to decide what they needed and what equipment to order? She couldn't possibly get an examination space up and running on her own. She'd be researching products for weeks! Months, probably.

"I'll need a couple weeks' notice for my current job." Not that she *wanted* to work there another minute, much less two more weeks. Or that her asshole boss deserved any kind of notice at all. But she didn't want to burn professional bridges or give that jerk any reason to bad mouth her around the professional community. Just in case *this* job didn't work out.

"Of course," Liz said. "Once you do some brainstorming here today, I'll just need you a few hours a week until the construction's done and orders come in to set up this room. In the meantime, we can do most stuff by phone or email, and you can work on lists and orders from home whenever you have time."

"That sounds... perfect."

It really did. As long as she could ask questions and run things by them, this felt like maybe a thing she could do.

With every passing moment, Taylor felt more and more confident in her decision to work here.

"Great!" Liz rubbed her hands together. "Well, I've got to

head out. Sierra's set up a meeting with someone about a fundraising idea. Lord help us all with that woman and her schemes."

"What kind of fundraiser?"

"I guess I'll find out in an hour," Liz said. "Sierra would have left out the important details anyway, so it's better to just show up and find out for myself what she's gotten us into this time."

Taylor smiled. She couldn't help it. And she had a feeling she was going to be smiling like that a lot around here.

"Hello?"

Taylor's eyes widened at the sound of the male voice calling out from the front entrance. Her heart rate ratcheted up without her approval as she recognized the voice.

What the heck was her body reacting like this for? It was just a guy. A guy here to complete some paperwork.

Except she'd completely forgotten he was coming back to do that, and of course it was just her luck that they'd come here at the same time. Again.

Good thing she wouldn't be alone with him in this room. The last thing she needed was to drool over this tree-scented guy who made her heart race against her will. At least Liz was still here to do all the talking.

Liz gave a wink and nodded toward the front of the building. "I'll grab his surrender paperwork and leave you to give that handsome man an update on his cat."

Austin's fingertips clawed at the cardboard box in his hands when he saw Taylor walking down the hall toward him. It hadn't occurred to him she'd be here again. Since she'd been there for an interview yesterday and was back today, she must have taken the job.

Not that it made any difference at all to him. For one, he didn't even live here, so he wouldn't have any interaction with this place after today. For another, she was none of his business.

But good for the animals. Despite her obvious self-doubt yesterday—which he could easily chalk up to being thrown off by the state of this building and the brashness of the two women running it—Taylor had seemed like a genuinely kind and competent person. She'd been patient but thorough with Tink. Exactly what you'd want in a vet tech.

"Hi again." Her voice was delicate as she waved awkwardly at him before stuffing her hands in her back pockets. She was less formal-looking today in lighter jeans and a flowy, cream-colored blouse. But her long, straight blonde hair was still meticulously brushed over her shoulders.

"Hi."

"Here you go!" Liz swooped into the room, waving a paper above her head. She placed it on the little round table near where he stood and breezed past them both. "Just fill that out for me and leave it on the table. Gotta run. I'll be in touch, Taylor."

And just like that, she disappeared outside, leaving the two of them to stare awkwardly at one another again.

Austin shook his head and pushed the box forward, remembering the other reason he was there. "I brought Tink's things. For whoever has him."

He assumed Tink wasn't in this building. He *hoped* not. Hopefully, Tink was happy in a foster home somewhere.

"That's kind of you." Taylor took the box and placed it on the table beside his paperwork. "He's staying with me in my apartment for now."

Austin couldn't help feeling excited about that. At least he knew Tink was in excellent hands. "That's great. How's he doing?"

"Good."

He didn't miss the slight hesitation in her response, but she didn't seem to be lying, so he left it at that. No details needed. No matter how much he wanted to know every step Tink took last night.

Or how much he wanted to keep Taylor talking.

"I'm sorry." He pointed at the box. "I couldn't find the leash or the harness anywhere."

She laughed, a musical little sound that he hoped to hear again as soon as possible.

"I don't think he'll be up for walking with me," she said. "But I will let whoever adopts him know about the walks. Maybe they'll want to try."

His phone rang. When he looked at the screen, his heart stopped for a beat. "I have to take this. Excuse me for a second."

He stepped out onto the porch and answered the phone. It was the police department returning his call from earlier that morning.

"Mr. Champagne?"

"Yes, that's me," he said.

"I'm returning your call regarding the death of Mr. Kenneth Champagne. Our records show no items were taken from that residence since there were no signs of foul play."

"Are you sure?"

"I looked into it myself," the woman on the other end of the call said. "I even checked the evidence log for that day just to be certain someone didn't forget to mark the file. It was an accidental death, so no evidence was collected by the officers on the scene, and the forensics team wasn't called out to the home either."

He'd been hoping there was a simple explanation, so he

could tell his brain to stand down. But now there were even more questions. And the addition of a few alarm bells.

He thanked the woman for checking into it and for going the extra step to make sure the items weren't hiding there somewhere. She told him she hoped he found whatever he was looking for, and he ended the call and went back inside.

Reading the look on his face, Taylor asked, "Is something wrong?"

He sat at the table and slid the pen and owner's surrender form in front of him. "It was about Tink's missing leash and harness."

"I'm sure they'll turn up." Warmth and compassion radiated from her voice.

"It's just weird. The police were the ones who found him, and no one but me has been to the house since then."

"Maybe he got rid of them before he died," she said.

He realized he had a piece of this puzzle standing right in front of him. "You said he walked Tink every weekend."

She nodded. "Right."

"He died during the day on a Saturday. Do you remember seeing him and Tink out for a walk two Saturdays ago?"

"I run every weekend, but not if it's raining." She shut her eyes tight. Her eyes flashed open again. "I remember. I definitely saw him that morning."

Austin's stomach sank. "And do you know if he had that same leash and harness? The one that matches his red and purple collar with the rhinestones?"

If she did remember, then she was the last person to see Uncle Kenny alive. And the last person to see Tink with the missing items.

He held his breath for what felt like much longer than was physically possible. Taylor closed her eyes again and took her time to think and recall accurately, which he appreciated but which also made him want to jump out of his skin while he waited.

Finally, she opened her eyes again and nodded. "Yes. I remember seeing your uncle that morning, *and* I remember seeing Tink with that leash and collar."

7

*A*n icy wave flowed through Austin's body as he sat there with the pen in his hand. He stared at Taylor, processing her confirmation that she'd been the last one to see his uncle on his walk.

Austin had been struggling to find a reasonable explanation for the missing leash and harness. The police must have taken them. Nope. His uncle must have gotten rid of them. Nope.

Unless he got rid of them after the walk.

But why? That didn't make sense at all. It seemed like he loved those tacky items as much as he loved every other tacky thing in his house. Even if he'd upgraded to something even tackier, wouldn't he still have had those new ones somewhere in the house? He wouldn't throw them away, and it didn't make sense that he'd rush out to drop them off at a charity or animal shelter.

"Are you okay?" Taylor looked around the kitchen. "Can I get you some water or something? I don't know what's in this place as far as cups or bottles, but I'm sure there's something. And the tap water is at least drinkable." She looked back at him with a cringe. "Probably?"

Austin shook his head. "I'm fine."

"Well, that's a lie," she said. "At least, you don't look fine. Am I missing something about that leash? It's just missing, right? Stuff goes missing all the time, and I'm sure even more when someone..."

She let the sentence trail off, for which Austin was grateful.

Stuff rarely went missing in his world, but he supposed that was a thing. It just wasn't a thing he could let go of without it bugging him. "You're right. It's probably just missing."

She narrowed her eyes. "What else would it be?"

Austin tapped the paper with the pen in his hand. "I honestly don't know. It's just weird."

"Weird like a cat on a leash weird?" She bit her lip in an adorable display of hesitance. "I'm sorry, but is there something I'm not understanding here?" More lip biting. "How did he die? Sorry if that's too nosy."

Austin was rarely bothered by questions, even nosy ones. But while he usually disliked talking about his uncle's death, he was comfortable answering her. "He fell down the stairs."

"Oh, how awful," she gasped. "I'm so sorry."

Every death was awful, but his uncle's had been particularly shocking. Accidents always are, but part of Austin had expected Uncle Kenny to live forever. Weren't magical beings immortal?

"Thanks," he said. "We don't really know the details. He lived alone."

"Were you close?" She shook her head quickly. "I'm sorry. That's none of my business, and of course, you were. I know you care about Tink."

Austin's heart broke all over again when she mentioned that name. "He was the only relative I liked."

Including the woman Austin was having dinner with tomorrow night. The woman who gave birth to him. The woman who would inevitably grill him about his nonexistent love life and subject him to that insufferable jackass boyfriend-of-the-month. Unfortunately, this jackass seemed to stick.

Taylor sat with a heavy plop on the other chair across the table. "Ugh. I know that feeling. Except I don't think I ever had a favorite in the bunch. Or one I liked at all. My sister and I... tolerate each other."

"Sorry," he said, not liking the fact that he'd completely eradicated her smile with mentions of his dead uncle and horrible family, which apparently brought up her own family trauma. "We should compare notes sometime."

It was a joke, so he was glad when the corner of her mouth rose slightly.

"That sounds like the worst homework ever."

He wasn't sure if it was that he wanted to make her laugh more... like, *really* laugh... or if he'd lost his mind from grief and stress, but he had a thought that went straight from his brain to his mouth. As they often did.

"Would you like to find out whose is worse?"

"Whose what?"

"Whose family," he said.

Taylor looked a little taken back, which he took as a challenge to convince her that this bananas idea—the one he hadn't thought through at all—might actually be fun.

"You want to... what?" She processed a second more. "Compare crappy families?"

He shrugged. "Why not? Do you have plans tomorrow night? Have dinner with me at my mother's house."

She blinked at him. "You want me to go to dinner. At your mom's house. The family you just said was awful."

"She's an awful person, yes," he confirmed. "But she'll be polite to you, and she's an excellent cook. She's been to cooking classes all over the world."

"Is this... a date? Or am I some kind of weird parent-buffer because you know she'll be polite with me there?"

"Can it be both?" Her brow furrowed and raised, and he knew he was losing her. "Okay, full disclosure. She's constantly bugging me about not bringing anyone over, even though she knows how busy I am with coaching *and* that I live two hours away. But also... you seem nice, and I'd love to hang out with you." Her expression softened. He just had to finish the deal. "Plus, I really owe you for taking in Tink."

He flashed his most charming smile her way, only to have it met with a deadpan stare.

"You could have just bought me a gift card."

"I could have," he said. "But this seems more fun."

"Fun for who?"

"For both of us? I hope?" He leaned across the table and smiled at her. The more he tried to convince her, the more he wanted this to happen. He needed to keep talking before his brain caught up and started analyzing *why*. "What do you say? Have dinner with me and experience your own personal episode of *Real Housewives* of Lafayette."

More blinking. "That's not selling it."

He laughed. "*Schitt's Creek*? Like if they didn't end up in a motel?"

She crossed her arms and made a little duck face while she considered. It was the cutest thing he'd ever seen.

Yup. This was a great idea, and he wouldn't let his brain ruin it.

"What do you say? Date? Tomorrow?" He paused, then

added, "If it's horrible, I'll buy you *two* gift cards. One for Tink and one for the terrible date."

And there was the smile he'd been waiting for.

Taylor laughed softly. "Deal."

———

TAYLOR WATCHED Austin drive away from behind the new front room window that had been installed after she'd left the day before. As Liz had promised, the two exterior doors were lined up on the porch, and the crew was grabbing things from trucks and a trailer to put those in that morning.

Just in time. A strong breeze swayed the nearby water oak branches, announcing the approach of that storm front. Winter storms in South Louisiana were a mixed bag. This one wouldn't drop the temperature enough to bring any troublesome precipitation besides rain, but it promised near-freezing temperatures overnight, and tomorrow would be even colder. Right before whatever "date" nonsense she'd gotten herself into.

Had she lost her mind? She wasn't supposed to be dating anyone right now, not after her last disaster, and somehow she'd landed herself in a first date of family drama.

Still, she couldn't deny that thrill she felt at the idea of spending more time with Austin. He was easy to talk to. Even when he wasn't making sense. The thing with his uncle's missing stuff *was* odd, but he seemed a little obsessive about it. Then again, grief did weird things to people.

Even in grief, the guy was downright charming. She was a sucker for charm. Not the smarmy, trying-to-get-something-out-of-you, salesperson-type charm. The genuine kind. Austin seemed to be naturally overflowing with it.

She seriously needed to realign something. Maybe she

should book that chiropractor Ellie kept bugging her to see. Maybe he could realign her spine *and* her judgment.

After catching Austin's paper sliding off in the wind for a second time, Taylor found a cup in the kitchen to place on top of it so it wouldn't blow away before they installed the door. Then she spun to survey the room and wondered what she was supposed to do now.

Liz hadn't given her any instructions beyond Austin and that form. Should she stick around? Liz had left in such a rush, and Taylor had been distracted by that smile.

She was definitely calling a chiropractor. Or finding a therapist. Whoever could get her on the path to better decisions and install some resistance to charm.

Taylor walked down the hall and returned to the exam room. Her domain now, they'd said. Might as well get a jump on brainstorming.

She found a legal pad and pen sitting on the little folding table, so she took it as her sign that this was what Liz wanted her to do next. Hopefully, she wouldn't have to spend all her time here interpreting clues and mind reading.

An hour and a half later, Taylor had three long pages filled with lists and notes and sketches, and she was overflowing with excitement. Sure, a tiny part of her brain was still worried she was making yet another huge mistake, but that voice was getting drowned by the rest of her brain shouting about all the possibilities ahead. All the good she would do.

"I was hoping you'd still be here."

Taylor shook herself from her daydreams to find Liz entering the room. She hadn't even heard her walk down the hall, much less enter the building. Come to think of it, she'd been so engrossed in her brainstorming that she hadn't even noticed if the contractors finished putting up that front door or not. Good thing no serial killers had wandered in while she was lost in deep thoughts.

"I figured I'd get some more lists and notes down while I was here."

"Thanks for handling that form." A smirk peeked out from Liz's stony expression. "I'm sure it wasn't too much torture to sit across from that handsome guy for a few minutes."

"It was fine."

"It was fine? Or was it *fine?*" Liz's voice dropped a whole silky octave with the last word.

"He asked me out," Taylor said, too excited to not tell someone. And to have someone warn her if she was bonkers for agreeing to it. "A thanks. For taking his cat."

"Holy hell, please tell me you jumped on that offer. And that you'll jump on *him* for the rest of us?"

Taylor ignored the crass suggestion and cringed. "We're going to his mother's for dinner."

Liz matched her cringe. "Ew."

"Yeah," she said. "Ew. But I couldn't say no, right?"

"To that man?" Liz shook her head. "I'd be more worried about you if you had. But that is… something."

"If it's awful, he's agreed to buy me gift cards to make up for it."

Liz laughed, a loud, full belly laugh, and pointed a finger at Taylor. "I like your style. Didn't think you had that kind of hard-nosed negotiation in you."

"It was more a joke that stuck."

Taylor looked out the window and recalled the rest of their conversation. Something still felt weird about it all. Something that was none of her business, except the fact that it bothered Austin and made her want to relieve that worry in his eyes.

"How would you know the difference between if someone fell down the stairs or if they were pushed?"

"How in the hell would I know that?"

"Not you in particular," Taylor stammered. "I mean, how would someone know the difference? Do you watch cop shows? CSI stuff? I don't watch much TV, and when I do it's pretty fluffy stuff."

"Well, I imagine the stuff on TV isn't super accurate anyway, so you aren't missing out on much." Liz narrowed her eyes. "Why on earth are you asking about that?"

"Austin's uncle. He was supposedly alone when he died, but there's some weird stuff not adding up."

"Oh, Lord," Liz said. "Not another one."

"Not another what?" Sierra breezed into the room and took a bite of a granola bar.

"Another one of *you*, Nancy Freaking Drew."

Sierra held Liz's stony gaze and took another big bite of her granola bar as she grinned and chewed simultaneously.

Taylor looked back and forth between them, but couldn't figure out this weird unspoken language the women had. "I don't know what that means."

"It means Sierra's like a dog with a bone when something's fishy, and she gets her ass in trouble when she can't let shit go."

"What she means is I'm good at solving mysteries," Sierra said. "Eventually. What's your mystery?"

"No mystery. Just something weird about Austin's uncle's death. Or there might be. Some of Tink's stuff is missing."

Sierra wrinkled her nose. "That sounds boring."

"Know what's not boring?" Liz chimed in. "She's having dinner with *his mother* tomorrow night."

"Damn, girl, you move fast!" Sierra crumpled her empty wrapper and gave a golf clap.

"I'm not moving anywhere at any speed," Taylor insisted, more to remind herself than anyone else.

Sierra shrugged. "I'm not judging. Have some fun where you can."

Liz nodded. "Especially if you're going to be working here."

Taylor didn't know what that might mean, and her brain was already busy trying to convince her heart and other traitorous parts that this dinner was nothing more than a thank you and was definitely not a *real* date.

She decided to change the subject. Sort of. "Do either of you know a good chiropractor?"

---

8

*L*ight sprinkled in from around Taylor's blinds as the setting sun hit her west-facing second-floor bedroom window. It was just bright enough to see without needing to flip on the ceiling fan light.

"Hey there," she said in a soothing voice as she shut the door behind her. "Did you miss me?"

She knew the answer to that, but felt inclined to ask, anyway. Since she wasn't keeping this cat, she didn't need him to be her best friend. But she wanted to make Tink feel safe and welcome here and help pave the way for his adjustment to whatever new family he ended up with.

A quick check of his food and water dishes and his litter box in the opposite corner of the room had confirmed that everything was fine in those departments. She just needed to work on his fear. That would take time and patience.

The good news was that, besides him being in great health, he wasn't reactive. No hissing. No swatting. No growling. And definitely no biting. No aggression, as long as Taylor remained respectful and gentle with him.

She put her hand up to the carrier opening and held it still, just in case Tink felt a little braver today and wanted to sniff her fingers. He didn't. But he could get used to her smell and recognize her. Cats weren't serious sniffers the same way dogs were, but they still used every one of their senses to take in their surroundings and get to know new creatures.

After a few seconds, she removed her hand from the opening and slid away from him, closer to the box Austin had brought in that morning. "Let's see what we've got here, Tink."

The first thing she grabbed was a purple fleece blanket with images of Tinker Bell all over it. Adorable. And exactly what she was hoping for.

Taylor folded it neatly just outside of the carrier entrance. Later, after he got a good sniff of home, she'd put the blanket in a quiet corner and hope he'd go looking for it. Then she could use it as his home base and encourage him to try out new spots in the room or in other areas of the apartment.

The box also contained a few toys, a bunch of cute ceramic bowls, and a couple of small beds. She couldn't wait to see Tink comfy and curled up tight to fit in that tiny bed while half his body spilled over the edges.

A soft knock rapped at the door in a familiar rhythm. Ellie had played on her high school snare line and often tapped out old cadences on her thighs, doors, and whatever else was within reach.

"Come in," Taylor said, just loud enough to be heard through the door. A second later, it opened slowly. Ellie frowned at Taylor sitting between the box and the carrier.

"Still hiding, I guess."

Taylor nodded. "But he's coming out while we're gone, so I think he'll be okay soon enough. Austin brought some of his things, so having familiar scents should help."

"Austin, huh?"

Taylor sighed. Might as well get this over with.

"I went to the shelter site to let them know I want the job and to fill out paperwork, and he showed up with this box." Taylor sighed again. Not because she was regretting the next part, but in anticipation of Ellie's reaction. "He asked me out. Tomorrow night. I said yes."

Ellie sucked in a breath and raised her hands, but caught herself before she squealed. Instead, she tapped her fingertips together in a silent clap and gave a big, toothy grin.

"There's nothing to be excited about. It's just a thank-you for taking in Tink."

"I don't care, I'm planning my maid of honor dress, anyway."

"Don't I get to pick that?"

"Not in my future fantasy," Ellie said. "Where is he taking you?"

Taylor cringed. If people kept asking her about Austin, her face would eventually stick like this. "His mom's house."

Ellie blinked and craned an ear. "I'm sorry, I didn't hear correctly. Could you repeat that? Because surely you aren't having a first date with this dude and his *mom*."

"Not a first date. The *only* date. This is not a *thing*. And there might be other people there? I don't know. She's cooking dinner."

"Oh my gosh, Taylor. That does not make it better!" Ellie shook her head, and her eyes widened even more. "How on earth did he con you into agreeing to this?"

"He was very charming," she said. "You know I have terrible judgment. Especially with charming men."

Ellie grunted. "Your judgment isn't the problem. Shitty, deceptive men are. Maybe this guy isn't one of those?"

"How do I know the difference?"

"Hell if I know. Another reason I'm glad I'm not attracted

to them." Ellie frowned. "Also, I assume everyone is shitty and deceptive until proven otherwise. Which I don't recommend as an alternative to your wide-eyed optimism."

Pattering on the roof interrupted them, followed by rain splattering against the window as a gust of wind blew in with the storm.

"At least your date isn't tonight," Ellie said with an uncharacteristic silver-lining viewpoint.

"Right," Taylor said. "But it'll be cold tomorrow night. I have no idea what to wear."

"My brain isn't prepared for a dinner-at-the-mom's-house outfit suggestion. Where does she live? Maybe we can gauge formality that way."

"I don't know. He's picking me up." When Ellie gave her a side-eyed look, Taylor added, "He already knows where I'll be working. It's not like he couldn't follow me home if he was a dangerous stalker." Ellie's frown set in deeper, so Taylor said, "Fine. I'll have him pick me up in the parking lot, so he won't know which apartment I'm in. Happy?"

Ellie thought for a second. "Good enough."

"But I was kind of hoping to let him see Tink. Maybe he could get the cat to come out of the carrier and see that I'm okay if Austin's here."

"Nope. You want to invite a random dude you met a day ago into your apartment *and* your bedroom before or after a first *mom date*? Veto."

"You can supervise!"

"I won't be here," Ellie said. "I've got my own date. That barista from downtown I asked out last weekend. Remember?"

"Oh, that's right!"

Ellie had taken Taylor out for coffee last Sunday when Taylor was distraught over what to do about work and couldn't imagine facing everyone this week. Ellie had flirted with the adorable redheaded barista and got her number. Apparently, between her misery and nerves concerning the interview, Taylor had forgotten all about Ellie bringing home celebratory cookies Tuesday evening when the woman had agreed to a date Friday night.

"So no getting murdered on my night out," Ellie insisted.

"I'm not getting murdered."

Taylor's mind wandered back to her conversation with Austin about his uncle. With those developments and family involved, this dinner might be extra interesting.

"So back to the outfit," Ellie said. "Do you know anything about him or his family? Anything at all about this weird-ass date to help us plan proper attire?"

Taylor shrugged. Then she remembered something else he'd said that had appalled her and should have factored more into her decision. "He said his family's awful and referred to her as some sort of *Real Housewives* of Lafayette type person."

Ellie's jaw hung open as she stared at her roommate for a long while, like Taylor had lost her mind. "This is not good."

"But... it kind of sounds fun? Maybe? Interesting, at least?"

"You really like to punish yourself, don't you?"

"It'll be fine," Taylor insisted. "Just help me pick an outfit."

Ellie frowned deeply. "Okay, but I'm not even playing with what's in your closet. We're going straight to mine. If you're doing this, you'll need to borrow something. Come on. Let's go."

AUSTIN SAT on a bright red bar stool at the center counter in his uncle's kitchen. While the living room aesthetic had been

Jeff Goldblum in a psychedelic field of wildflowers, the kitchen aesthetic was a smoking hot trip to flavor town.

The color scheme was red, orange, and black. Even the cabinets were red and the countertops were dark granite. Everything in here had flames or an image of Guy Fieri on it.

He would never be able to sell this place. Not without hiring a reality show makeover crew.

Austin waited while the number he called rang. It was day three of tryouts back home, and he needed to check in to see how things were going. Just as his assistant coach answered, a streak of lightning lit up the house, followed by a rattling crack of thunder.

"Glad that isn't here," Mike said.

"It'll be in your neck of the state in a little while. The kids all got picked up?"

"Yeah, last one left twenty minutes ago. Josh was gonna walk home, but Brady gave him a ride."

"How'd it go this afternoon?"

"Great," Mike said. "It's been a good week. You'll be proud of them. The returning guys have kept up with their workouts and skills, and the new guys look great, too. Eager kids. Hard workers. It's gonna be an impressive lineup."

Austin hated not being there, but he was glad the guys had Mike. They were in expert hands, but Austin missed the beginning of the season's excitement. It was usually accompanied by painful anticipation since he couldn't wait to get things going and get the team in a game, but this part was important, too.

He was a coach, not a manager, and the bulk of his job revolved around developing these boys' skills and minds. He took that responsibility seriously. But he still itched every year to get things rolling.

"Glad to hear it. Can't wait to see them," he said. "Well, I'll let you go so you can beat this storm home."

"I'm fine," Mike said. "What about you? Riding out the storm at your uncle's for the night?"

"Yeah, I'm staying put. I'm meeting with the accountant tomorrow. We *still* haven't gotten the will yet, but I'm already listed on the accounts. He's going to give me a list of everything so I can make a plan for things that need to be taken care of."

He left out the other thing he had tomorrow evening. The thing he didn't want a second opinion on right now. Although Mike would definitely be in favor of this development with Taylor.

His phone beeped, and Austin sighed when he saw the caller flashing on his screen.

"I've gotta go. Got another call coming in. Be safe and go home before the storm gets there."

"Will do. You take care too. I'll call you this weekend to talk more about the lineup."

"Sounds good."

Austin paused a couple of seconds to let his finger hover over the button before switching to the other call.

"Hello, Mother."

"You're still coming for dinner tomorrow evening, yes?"

He sighed loud enough for her to hear. "Yes."

"Good. Then I need to know what you'd prefer. I can make that prosciutto-stuffed chicken and mushroom sauce you love so much or a new recipe I'm quite fond of. It's pork tenderloin with a date and cilantro relish."

"Whatever you want to prepare will be delicious." Food was the one thing Austin trusted her to not mess up. This next part, however... "You'll be happy to know, I'm bringing someone."

"Oh?" Her voice rose with interest. "A woman or a man? I hope you know I'm fine with either, darling."

Some days, he regretted telling his mother that he was

bisexual. She'd responded with grace and love, which was more than he'd expected, but she still didn't completely get the cluelessness of her comments sometimes. Like, in this case, that it didn't matter what gender his date was, except to satisfy her curiosity. Never mind the fact that she was excluding the possibility of him dating someone nonbinary.

"Her name is Taylor, and I expect you to behave."

"Behave? Of course. What do you think I might do?"

It wasn't her so much as her insufferable boyfriend that worried Austin. "Just tell Zeke to behave too."

"A new companion changes the menu. Does she have any dietary restrictions?"

"I honestly don't know. But I'll text to ask."

"If she's a vegetarian, I can make the herb-crusted cauliflower steaks with white beans and tomatoes. Leela said it was delicious when she was over last month. And I don't think any of those are a problem with dairy. I'll make a note for side dishes though if she has an intolerance. What about gluten? I can use gluten-free bread crumbs for the cauliflower crust if both are an issue. If meat is fine, I can't very well serve *chicken*. How about scallops? Make sure to ask her about shellfish allergies."

"Mom, really, please don't make a big deal out of this. Make the chicken."

Sure, it felt like a big deal to Austin. He hadn't been on a date in almost a year, and he hadn't brought anyone home for a meal or to meet any of his family since his first year of college. But he didn't want his mother to make this a bigger deal than it was. He was already struggling to keep his own expectations in check.

This was a one-and-done situation. A fun evening. A thank-you dinner. This wasn't going any further than that. It couldn't.

He would be returning to the Northshore in a couple

of weeks, so he couldn't start something here with Taylor that he knew he wouldn't be able to follow through on.

Although it felt like he was already doing exactly that.

"Of course, it's a big deal," his mother insisted. "A new guest is always a big deal. Who is this Taylor woman, anyway?"

"She's the new vet tech at the rescue that took Tink. She's fostering him while they finish building the shelter and until they find him a permanent home," Austin said. "I just want to do something nice for her, so *be nice*."

"Of course, I'll be nice. Dinner will be nice. Everything will be *nice*, Austin."

Austin was one of the few people she let down her mask with to hear that tone of annoyance unless she was verbally eviscerating someone for a perceived slight. It was fake veneer or verbal beatdown with her. There was no in-between.

Except around Austin. He got to see the in-between on rare occasions. He doubted she ever let her mask down with Zeke.

"Oh, I invited your cousin to dinner."

Austin's stomach sank to his toes. "Which one?"

"Does it matter?"

"I suppose it doesn't." Whichever one it was, the idea of a *nice* dinner was now out the window.

"Honestly, Austin, they're your family. You should be glad to see any of them for the brief bits of time you're in town. At least they're a pleasant alternative to those monsters on your father's side."

She wasn't entirely wrong. But being marginally better didn't erase the fact that the people on his mother's side were also monsters. Just a different breed.

Now he was beginning to regret inviting Taylor to this

mess. He'd promised her entertainment, but this felt more like feeding her to piranhas.

And yet, he couldn't bring himself to rescind the offer. Part of him was afraid that if he rescheduled or changed the conditions of this non-date, the whole thing would fall apart, and he'd never see Taylor again.

"Speaking of family," he said. "Are you sure no one saw or heard from Uncle Kenny the day he died? Before he missed his meeting."

"I wouldn't know."

"What about his friends? I have all of his contact information, but there are so many names, I'm not sure who he was closest with."

"Your uncle spoke more to me than with his own brother, when your father was alive, but I assure you he didn't share the details of his personal life with me. And we haven't been in touch much the last couple of years, so any names I remember hearing have probably already disappeared through Kenny's revolving door of friendship."

He bit down on his tongue to hold back a snipe about her own revolving door of "friendships."

"Could you write a list of names for me that you do remember?"

He knew better to share his questions and suspicions. His mother would try to talk him out of thinking anything happened other than the widely accepted story of Uncle Kenny falling down the stairs. Half of the stories also included him tripping over Tink as a cause of death. Ridiculous. The cat didn't move quickly and was too big to go unnoticed. Austin never bought that theory for a second.

He didn't have a solid suspicion, but something was off. And he needed to know where to direct his questions.

"Austin, what are you up to?"

"Nothing," he assured her. "I just want to know who to

contact if I find any items that should go to someone in particular."

His mother was silent for a moment, while heavy rain fell steadily outside. He could see her face in his mind, her narrowed eyes and pursed lips, judging him and weighing her response.

"I'll write the names I can remember."

"Thank you."

"I should go," she said. "I have a menu to plan. Let me know about any restrictions, though. Tonight, if possible."

"I'll text her as soon as I get off the phone with you, but if she doesn't have any, the chicken will be fine. Don't forget to write down those names for me."

"Yes, yes. I'll see you tomorrow."

Austin ended the call and immediately sent a text to Taylor.

My mom wants to know if you have any allergies or food restrictions?

She quickly replied with the word *no*, followed by a photo of Tink still lying in his carrier but with his head in the opening and one paw resting on the Tinker Bell blanket Austin had sent that morning.

Progress?

Baby step, Taylor replied. *What time tomorrow?*

Pick you up at 6? He hesitated with whether to add more information, but he felt he owed her a heads up. *I was just informed that one of my cousins will be there also.*

Three dots danced on the screen for what felt like three hours before he received her reply.

Should I be afraid?

Only because I'll definitely win the whose family is more awful contest, Austin responded.

She sent a laughing emoji followed by, *I haven't even had a chance to present my case!*

Before he could stop himself, he typed, *That can still be arranged...*

Three more dots.

Three more excruciating moments-that-felt-like-hours.

See you at 6 tomorrow

*a*ustin made a few quick turns and pulled into the apartment complex a little over a block from his uncle's house. He noted it was on the other side of a long park where Taylor could have absolutely run past his uncle and Tink on the weekends.

Not that he'd doubted her story. It's just that there'd been so many out-of-place things lately that it was nice to find a puzzle piece that fit where it should.

He found her building and parked in an empty spot. His foot jerked on the brake when he spotted Taylor standing on the sidewalk, flashing a reserved little wave at him.

She was stunning.

Taylor's long blonde hair was brushed sleek over the shoulders of a cropped forest green jacket open to reveal a tight black tank top. Matching green pants cropped just above the ankle hugged her legs, and short black heels and a black clutch completed the outfit.

She looked incredibly chic. His mother would adore her. Not that his mother's opinion mattered. Not of Taylor. Not of anything.

She sat beside him before he could get out to open the door for her.

"You didn't have to wait outside for me," he said while she warmed her hands. "It's freezing."

She clicked her seatbelt into place. "Didn't make sense to have you walk all the way up the stairs and back. I figured you'd be on time. You seem the type."

"The type?"

"Responsible."

He *was* responsible, since he was taking care of his uncle's entire estate when no one else lifted a finger to help. But he wasn't sure he liked the idea of someone being able to know that about him instantly.

Was that the vibe he put out? Responsible? That sounded boring.

Great. He was boring *and* said things like "vibe." Even if just in his head.

"I could have texted you when I got here so you didn't have to wait outside in the cold."

"I wasn't out there more than a couple minutes." She held up a gift bag and pulled out a small pink box with a white bow tied around it. "My roommate said this would be appropriate."

He examined the box and noticed the name of the sweets shop printed on the side. "Your roommate knows my mother?"

"No, but she grew up around dinner parties and people with estates to handle."

Her playful smile put him at ease. Austin wasn't ashamed of his family's money, but it made him uncomfortable. Mostly because he didn't want it to make other people uncomfortable.

"Anyway, she said fancy chocolates would be best since we didn't know if alcohol would be appropriate."

"Your roommate knows her stuff. That's perfect," he said. "But you didn't have to bring anything. You're my guest."

"Ellie disagreed when I explained that."

"Are you sure Ellie doesn't know my mother?" He smiled at Taylor, then backed out of the spot and exited the complex. "Sorry I didn't get to meet her."

"She's on a date," Taylor said. "Curiosity about you didn't win out over the hot red-headed barista."

"Understandable." He laughed a little, then turned serious. "Actually, I kind of hoped to maybe get a peek at Tink."

"Sorry." She rubbed her hands together in her lap, although now it looked more out of nervousness than for warmth. "He's doing fine. Still hiding mostly, but I can feel him hop on the bed at night, then circle me early in the morning." She paused. "Do you know if he normally has hairball issues?"

"Not that I know of. But I only had him a couple weeks."

"Did he have any problems with vomiting that you forgot to mention?"

"No. Why? Is he okay?"

"Yeah, fine," she said. "Just checking since he threw up a little this morning. It's probably just a hairball, but I wanted to check if you knew anything before we ran a blood panel."

"A blood panel?" That sounded serious. Austin's heart raced while his brain ran through a million things that could be wrong with the cat. He didn't know what any of those million things might be, just that they were all scary and he felt guilty for them even though he knew he didn't cause them or could have prevented them. Whatever they were.

"Normal senior cat blood work," Taylor said in a reassuring tone. "Vets run them annually at a certain age. It's common for older cats to develop diabetes or thyroid conditions, so we want to catch any problems early on."

"You think Tink has one of those?"

"Not necessarily," she said. "I was just checking if you noticed other symptoms or anything else we should look out for. It's nothing to worry about. And it's probably a hairball. I think out loud sometimes. Sorry."

Austin smiled. "No need to apologize for that. It's nice to see that someone else cares about the big guy."

"He really is a great cat. And I can tell he was well-loved. It's part of why he's so hesitant around us. He had a lot of good years with your uncle."

Austin couldn't help thinking how unfair it was that they wouldn't have even more years together. Uncle Kenny was supposed to outlive Tink. Although losing that cat probably would have killed him, anyway.

"So." Taylor clapped her hands. "What should I be expecting this evening?"

"Um… I'm not sure?" He never knew what to expect with his family. They weren't exactly predictable.

"How about food?" Taylor asked. "What's on the menu? Besides me."

Austin laughed at that. "I said they were awful people. I didn't say they'd carve you up."

"Well then, what are we talking about? Deep, uncomfortable questioning?"

"More blunt and thoughtless. Nothing is off the table. Feel free to make up answers. It's more fun that way."

"Ooh, improv! That sounds like fun. I've never been in any drama classes or plays or anything."

He turned off the main road and into a neighborhood with enormous houses crammed into tiny lots. "Knock yourself out and have a blast. My mom will never know the difference."

"I'm excited now!"

To his complete surprise, he was, too. He was already happy to spend the evening with Taylor, but getting a front-row seat to watch her drum up random stories and facts about herself to mess with his mom sounded fun.

But then he remembered he didn't really know her at all. That kind of threw a wrench in this little plan of theirs. "Wait, are you planning to fabricate all of your stories, or will I have to guess what's the truth and what's made up?"

"I don't know yet." She tapped a finger to her chin as she considered the idea. "I'll have to play it by ear. I don't even know how well I can improvise at all."

"Fair enough."

"Okay, so this is going to be your mom and her boyfriend, right?"

"We can call him that, I guess."

"What do you call him?"

Austin had a lot of names for the guy, but he wasn't telling Taylor all of them right now. "Zeke."

"And you said someone else will be there?"

"My cousin," Austin said. "Although I'm not sure which one."

"She didn't tell you?"

"They're all basically the same."

"Interesting." Taylor looked out the window and gawked. "These places are *huge*."

"Mom's also supposed to give me a list of my uncle's friends that she can remember. People I can ask about who might have seen him that last day after you saw him and Tink."

"Wait, so this is an investigative type thing? Like… a full-on mystery dinner theater? Complete with improv?"

"Not really," he said. "I'm just getting the list. Trust me, my mom and Zeke aren't ambitious enough to pull off anything deceitful. They're mostly designed for gossip and verbal backstabbing."

"But you really think someone hurt your uncle?"

"I don't know. I just know things are... off. And someone took that leash and harness. I don't know who or why, but the items aren't in that house. So someone was there that day after you last saw my uncle and Tink. And if someone was in the house with him, I have to question if he fell."

That idea had never sat right with him. Tink wasn't an underfoot kind of cat, and his uncle always knew where Tink was. Plus, in the time Austin had been in that house, he'd never seen Tink hanging out on those stairs. He was a downstairs-only cat, unless Uncle Kenny carried Tink to the second floor for bedtime.

Plus, Uncle Kenny was in good shape. No health problems. A random fall down those stairs made absolutely no sense.

"Did they do an autopsy?"

"We haven't gotten the results yet," he said. "But again, no one you'll meet tonight would—"

Austin stopped mid-sentence when he turned onto his mother's road and approached the large, semi-circular driveway.

"Um... why are we stopping here?" Taylor asked. "*Here* with all of these cars. I thought you said your mom invited one cousin?"

Austin parked his Prius behind a silver Audi he didn't recognize and turned off the engine. His stomach twisted as they got out, and Taylor stared in disbelief. There had to be six or seven cars lined up in front of them.

"That's what I was told," he said. "Want to get back in the car before it's too late?"

Taylor looked at the row of cars and back at the house. Then she turned to Austin with a slight twinkle in her eye. A twinkle that spelled mischief and *fun*. Austin liked the look of it.

"Nah," she said. "Let's do this."

———

Taylor swore the cars multiplied as they passed them on the way to the front door. Like a long line of reproducing car bunnies.

The simple little dinner she'd agreed to had exploded into a full-blown, most-likely dysfunctional, family reunion.

Austin held his finger over the doorbell and let it hover there. "Last chance to bail."

Her initial instinct when they'd arrived had been to turn right around and forget all about this. Gift cards would definitely be the preferable option. And since this was not the deal she'd signed up for, surely Austin would have agreed to take her home. Or somewhere else.

The somewhere else part sounded surprisingly appealing. Because as much as this party terrified her, she also didn't want to leave his side yet. The inside of his car had smelled like *him*. All woodsy and crisp and yummy.

She put her hand on his and pressed his finger against the button. "Let the games begin."

He laughed as a loud chime rang out from inside of the house.

"Just remember," he said, "I offered you an out."

She turned to say something snappy. Something clever. Something… anything. But she got trapped in his gaze and forgot how to form words as he stared at her with amusement dancing in his eyes. She found herself lost in those blue-gray irises for a moment longer, then remembered where she was and what she'd just agreed to.

"Noted."

Had she lost her mind?

No. Losing her mind had been sleeping with her married boss. *That* had been a bad decision.

This had the potential to be very interesting. Amusing

even. Especially since this wasn't her own family minefield she was walking into. Here, she had the chance to be whoever she wanted to be. Whoever she could imagine herself as. Free of expectations or obligations or past mistakes.

The door opened, and a man about their age stood over the threshold. His nearly black hair was neatly trimmed and slicked back. He wore a fitted white dress shirt with navy pants and a light brown belt and pointy brown dress shoes.

"There he is!" The man held a rocks glass in one hand and threw both arms out wide, sloshing dark liquid out onto the tile floor of the entryway. "About time. You know Melinda wouldn't let us eat anything until you got here."

Austin pointed at a clock hanging nearby behind the man. "We're early."

"Tell that to my stomach," the guy said as he rubbed his belly. He finally noticed Taylor, and his gaze landed just above her tank top, making her grateful she hadn't gone with the v-neck. "And who is this doll that's obviously too good for you?"

Taylor could feel Austin tensing beside her, along with the rage-heat radiating from beneath his dark sports coat and gray dress shirt.

He'd been sitting in the car since he'd picked her up, then she'd been shocked by the cars out front, so she hadn't gotten a good look at him until now. Unlike Zeke, who appeared to be trying hard to fit in here or on some influencer's social media, Austin had an air of effortless style. Not to mention the fact that she could still see the outline of his well-toned body beneath the fabric of his shirt and those tight slacks.

In a word: yummy.

"This is Taylor," Austin said.

Zeke narrowed his eyes in confusion, then widened them as his brain caught up. "Oh, cool. When your mom said a date named Taylor, I assumed dude." He let out a sheepish, embarrassed giggle. "My bad. Nice to meet you."

Taylor ignored the clumsy revelation and held out her hand, which the guy mistook for an excuse to kiss the back of it. Before she could pull away, Austin slipped his hand around her wrist and freed her from the man's grasp.

"Taylor, this is *Zeke*." The name came out like a low growl.

She turned to him with a raised brow. "Zeke?"

He answered her confusion with a curt nod.

Zeke. His mother's boyfriend. The man couldn't be more than a year or two older than Austin. If that.

"The one and only," Zeke said.

"Zeke..." Austin paused for what looked like dramatic effect. "What was it you do again?"

"Besides your mom?" Zeke snort laughed and playfully elbowed Austin.

Taylor was sure Austin would deck him right there in the doorway, but Austin just stretched his neck slightly and kept his cool.

"I mean the scam."

"No scam," Zeke insisted. "I sell natural supplements. Have you heard of celery essence?"

"We should get inside," Austin interrupted. "Don't want to hold up dinner, do we?"

"Right." Zeke looked over his shoulder. Then he leaned in close to Taylor, whispering in her ear with hot bourbon breath. "Don't tell Melinda. I'm going to fire one up while you make the rounds."

He stumbled forward and pushed his way between Austin and Taylor. She watched as he disappeared around the side of the building and into a set of over-sculpted hedges.

"How old is he?"

"We went to school together."

Taylor physically flinched at that. She couldn't imagine

how that must be for Austin. But she didn't feel it was appropriate to ask anything else about the situation right now. She'd been nosy enough already. "That explains the way you say Zeke's name."

Austin stared at where Zeke was a moment ago, as if to make sure he didn't reappear and sneak up behind them. Satisfied he was gone, Austin turned back to Taylor. "Sorry about that."

"You don't have anything to be sorry for." Zeke wasn't his fault or his responsibility. The last thing she would do was judge him for his mother's hot mess of a boyfriend.

"And spoilers, I guess," he said lightheartedly but with an edge of lingering annoyance. "I'm bisexual."

"None of my business," she said. "But since we're sharing, I'm... I don't know. Not that I haven't thought about it, but because I overthink things, so I triple guess every potential label that feels like it might be right. And then I decide not to decide yet."

A smile found its way to the corner of his mouth, and she felt glad to have had a part in its appearance.

"Makes sense. Thanks for sharing that with me." He nodded inside. "Ready to go in?"

He placed a hand against her, radiating heat across her lower back, so she could only nod. Then she followed him inside.

They walked through what she guessed was the foyer. She didn't grow up with a foyer or have any childhood friends who had one, so she was totally guessing here. Ellie's family probably had one, maybe two. Did people have multiple foyers?

They passed an open doorway, and Taylor peeked into a room containing a long, gigantic table complete with stacks of plates, a variety of glassware, and rich, red napkins at each place setting.

She was suddenly very glad Ellie had made her borrow this suit. Nothing in her own closet would have been appropriate for this. Certainly not her standard date night ensemble of black skinny jeans and a bold blue tunic.

They rounded the corner and stepped into a massive room with ridiculously high ceilings, a spattering of furniture, and more people than Taylor had been prepared to mingle with that evening.

There was no way she could improv her way through this.

But they were here, so she might as well give it a go. Right?

Besides, this wasn't a real date. This was a thank-you dinner. She didn't need to impress these people. Heck, she'd probably never see any of them again. Even Austin.

She ignored the searing pain that last thought brought with it and plastered a smile on her face as every set of eyes turned toward them.

Through her smile, she said softly, "I was totally joking about the mystery dinner theater thing, but this really feels like a movie dinner party where someone gets murdered and none of us can leave." She struggled to keep her internal cringe from showing on her face. "Except I'm not sure if I'm going to be the one murdered or trapped and interrogated."

"Well, if it's that first one, it'll be a double murder, because they'd have to go through me first."

Taylor didn't have time to process that statement, much less how she felt about it. A woman in a soft gray turtleneck and wide-leg burgundy trousers manifested in front of them. She held a deep-cut crystal rocks glass in one hand, her wrist propped at an elegant angle perpendicular to a pale, slender arm.

"So glad you decided to grace us with your presence, Austin."

"This is exactly the time you told me to arrive." There was an air of exasperated history in his tone.

The woman looked down her long nose at him with searing judgment before turning her attention to Taylor. In an instant, she flipped to a pleasant, welcoming demeanor. "You must be Taylor. That green is *stunning* on you. I'm Melinda, Austin's mother."

"Thank you. Pleased to meet you," Taylor said. "And thank you for inviting me this evening. This is for you."

Taylor held out the small gift bag containing the chocolates, which Melinda took and investigated more carefully than Taylor had expected. Once again, she was grateful for Ellie's input.

"Thank you, Taylor," Melinda said. "And from my absolute favorite shop. This is very thoughtful of you."

Austin leaned in close to his mother. "I thought this was just dinner?"

"It is," she insisted. "And I told you others were coming."

"You said Zeke and my cousin. *One* cousin. Not the whole clan."

"We are not a clan." Her voice was low and growly, making it clear where Austin got that little quirk from. "What difference does it make? They're family, and they wanted to see you. You almost never come home. I couldn't be *rude*, now could I?"

Taylor fought back a giggle at the hypocrisy. Mainly because it wasn't her own family's hypocrisy for once.

"Of course, you couldn't," Austin said in a mocking tone.

"Do introduce your lovely guest to everyone. I'll make sure they're ready in the kitchen to serve soon." She placed her hand on Taylor's arm. "I look forward to chatting more with you in a bit, dear."

Once she breezed away out of earshot, Taylor leaned toward Austin. "I thought you said she was cooking dinner?

I'm pretty sure I was promised a fabulous meal made by your mother. Did she bail once all these people came?"

"No way. She made the dinner. Well, most of it, I'm sure. But she has staff to serve the courses."

"Of course, she does."

She hoped that didn't sound as snotty as it did in her head. A quick check revealed an amused expression from Austin, and she breathed a little sigh of relief. Although she wasn't sure what she was relieved about.

This was not a date.

Right?

He slipped that hand behind her back again. This time, she leaned into it.

With his mouth close to her ear, his breath sent warm tingles down her spine. "Let's get you a drink before we face the rest of the firing squad."

AUSTIN HAD WOVEN through two of his cousins and their second or third spouses with minimal conversation. They were both from his mother's side of the family. Both equally insufferable but polite. The fake nice being part of what made them insufferable.

When they'd asked if she was from Lafayette, Taylor had told them that she'd been born in Alaska and that her parents had been traveling nurses. At first, the ease with which she told the tale impressed him, but he quickly realized the back-story could actually be true. He knew nothing about her family or where she was from except that she had a sister.

At the wet bar, he grabbed a glass for himself, then realized he didn't know what kind of glass to grab for Taylor, much less what to pour into it.

Over the years, he'd avoided subjecting people he liked to

this circus, so if he brought anyone near this place, he at least knew what kinds of drinks they preferred.

But he barely knew Taylor at all, much less her favorite… well, he didn't know her favorite anything.

She leaned against the bar with that twinkle in her eye again. None of this had shaken her so far, although he wasn't sure how. He'd fully expected her to be horrified and ready to leave by now.

Instead, she asked, "Want to make this really fun?"

He raised his brow. "As soon as you tell me what you're drinking."

"What do you have?"

"Anything you want."

She scrunched her face, giving it some serious thought, like it was the most important decision in the world. "I guess white wine. No, wait, vodka soda. No, wait…" She thought for another moment, then gave him an inquisitive stare. "Can you make a lemon drop?"

"Can I? I'll make you the best damn lemon drop you've ever had."

He grabbed a martini glass, lemon, and sugar, then went to work on the sugar rim for the glass. Next, he found the vodka, Cointreau, and his favorite secret ingredient for gentle sweetness and a nuanced undertone: maple syrup.

"I would ask if you were a bartender in college, but I guess, based on you growing up here, you didn't have to work your way through school." She waved her hands in front of her. "Not that I'm judging. Just guessing. Assuming, really, I suppose."

"You assume correctly." He poured the shaker's contents into the glass and grabbed the paring knife to create a perfect twist of lemon peel for the garnish. "It was more of a hobby than a job. And it impressed the hell out of a date or two."

"I'll be the judge of that." She took the drink he handed

her. After a slow, seductive sip that drove him wild in a way no gesture that small had in a long time, Taylor winked. "Okay. Fine. I'm impressed." She held the drink in the air. "Thank you."

He winked back at her. "My pleasure."

Wait a minute.

Was he flirting with her?

Was she flirting with him?

He was pretty sure she had been the one to start this whole flirting thing, but his brain was so shot from that wink he couldn't tell up from down.

Austin took a slow sip of his whiskey on the rocks, then played along. "How are we making this fun?"

"First," she said, "I need the dirt. Which of these people are we suspecting of shenanigans in this mystery dinner theater."

He set his glass on the bar. "You realize we're still talking about my beloved uncle's death, right?"

Her back straightened sharply, and she placed her glass beside his. "I'm sorry. I didn't forget, I just—"

"No, it's fine." He waved off her discomfort. "These people are ridiculous and deserve every amount of screwing with them you want to dish out. I just want to remember what the actual mystery is. And what's at stake, I suppose."

"Money?"

"Justice," he corrected.

"Right. For you," she said. "I meant, is money at stake for them?"

Austin surveyed the room. The guests were mostly relatives from his mother's side, but his father's sister was also here, along with her brat of a daughter, who should have outgrown her brattiness two decades ago.

He suspected his mother hadn't sincerely invited them all. Especially not the "monsters," as she called them. The odds were that they invited themselves, and family politics dictated that she not snub them.

And yes, money was always at stake for these people. Regardless of how much they already had.

But her question was really about who had money to gain from his uncle's death.

"Just two of them."

His Aunt Nadine and her grown brat, Melody, his uncle's only remaining direct relatives, and the only people besides Austin and his mother who might benefit from whatever was in that will. Although he couldn't discount the opportunistic vultures who had to know that Austin would soon hold most of the purse strings.

"So we've narrowed down our suspicious suspect pool. Any chance they could have pulled in some other relatives to be being shady with? Like a collective heist?"

Austin laughed and took another sip of whiskey. "Not likely. They can all barely stand to be in this room together."

"Then why come?"

"Like you said, money." He waved his glass to gesture at them all. "I'm the little red hen who did all the work. Which means I'm in charge of the bread."

"Nice analogy."

"Thank you," he said. "Well, until they release the will, which should be in a week or two."

He hoped it wouldn't be longer than that. The sooner the will was released, the sooner he could settle the entire estate, and the sooner he could get back to his life on the Northshore.

He flinched at that thought and watched Taylor take another thoughtful sip of her lemon drop, while he tried desperately not to think about how that life didn't have Taylor in it. She sparkled in a way that brightened whatever room she was in, making him realize how devoid of sparkles his life had been until now.

"So you can't really know anything yet. Until the autopsy and the will release, right?"

"Correct," he said. "I'm just keeping my eyes open."

She picked up her glass again and held it in the air. "Then my eyes are open, too. Consider them your assistant eyes."

The look in those eyes was sincere. Austin's blood raced through his veins with the extra pounding of his heart. He raised his glass to clink it against hers, sealing the deal.

"But this is supposed to be a thank-you dinner. Not another job for you."

"We need to work on your concept of 'thank-you dinner.'" She rolled her eyes toward the people gossiping behind her, then took another sip of her drink. "But really, this is kind of fun. I am truly sorry about your uncle, though. I don't want to make light of that."

"I know. And I appreciate it." He took a deep breath and exhaled. "Thanks for coming with me. You're making what would have been a miserable experience something enjoyable."

Her cheeks flushed a rosy color. It was downright adorable, and he wanted to find as many ways as he could to make her blush again.

"If everyone would please move into the dining room," his mother called out from the edge of the room. "Dinner is ready."

That twinkle of mischief sparkled in Taylor's eyes again. He never would have expected to see that from her, based on her work-mode persona the other day, but he was realizing there was a lot more to this woman than she let most people see. He looked forward to finding out what else she had to reveal.

Taylor slipped her hand around his arm as he met her on

the other side of the bar. She looked up at him with a wide grin. "Ready to keep our eyes open and have some fun?"

Austin felt weak at the sight of that grin, realizing he would follow this woman he barely knew just about anywhere. Even into that pit of vipers in the dining room.

Date or not, he was definitely in trouble.

10

*I*t wasn't lost on Taylor that Austin strategically placed himself between her and his mother seated at the head of the table, despite her offer to have Taylor close so they could get acquainted. That move also put him, not Taylor, directly across from Zeke.

In the time since receiving that perfectly crafted lemon drop, Taylor had introduced herself to various members of Austin's family as someone who loved white water rafting, once had a drink with a Rockefeller heir, and had a cousin in the rodeo circuit. That last one wasn't so far-fetched, and she regretted not putting more thought into her stories beforehand. Improv was obviously not her strong suit.

There was only so much she could make up since Melinda knew she was a vet tech. Everyone Austin introduced her to had already received that tidbit from her resume.

Now that the plan was to scope out his relatives for motives, however, she had too much to keep track of. If she kept making up stories about herself on top of that, she'd inevitably mess something up.

The first course was a salad of arugula, hearts of palm, and a sprinkling of goat cheese topped with a light, lemony dressing. Simple, elegant, and delicious. Austin was right. His mom knew her way around food.

Next came the main course. Taylor was surprised to see chicken on her plate, only because Melinda seemed like the kind of person who might turn her nose up at chicken as a showpiece. But Austin explained that this was his favorite dish, and he'd requested it specifically.

The chicken breasts were stuffed with prosciutto and spinach and topped with a rich mushroom sauce. After one bite, Taylor decided she could eat this every day of her life and never be sad about it.

The rest of the table ate and complimented the food. They all seemed relatively pleasant on the outside, but she knew appearances could be deceiving.

Well, they all seemed pleasant on the outside, except for Zeke.

Taylor couldn't figure out what Melinda was doing with that clown. From what Taylor understood, Austin's mother had plenty of money, so even if Zeke's supplements business was legit and wildly profitable, a money-motivated relationship didn't seem reason enough to tolerate the guy. And it couldn't be his personality. The only other reason Taylor could think of was...

Nope. She didn't want to think about *that* at all.

Normally, she'd think good for Melinda, but this was her date's mother and the guy that had practically licked Taylor's hand in greeting.

"So, Taylor," his mother began, "I understand you work for the rescue that took in my brother-in-law's cat?"

"Yes, I just started working for the new St. Martin Animal Sanctuary. The shelter itself is currently under construction." She left out the part where she was still technically working at another veterinary office. She hadn't even put in her two weeks' notice yet. That was an in-person task for Monday. A task she was dreading. "I'm fostering Tink in my apartment until we find a new home for him."

She wanted to give them all a stern lecture. Someone at the table surely could have taken in that poor cat. That fact alone put them on her list of suspect humans, even if not a single one of them had anything to do with the death of that cat's owner.

She stared them down, one at a time, allowing her gaze to pass slowly over each person at the table. But not one of them expressed an ounce of guilt. No discomfort at the mention of the cat. Tink was simply someone else's problem.

Taylor shoved half a green bean in her mouth instead of saying all the things she wanted to say to these people.

"Well, that's just lovely," said one of Austin's aunts. Nadine. The aunt from his father's side of the family.

A woman who would likely financially benefit from her brother's death.

Taylor added Nadine to the top of her mental list of people with motives. Not suspects, because there wasn't a definitive crime yet. But if the autopsy results came back suspicious, they'd have a list of people to look into ready to go.

What are you doing?

This wasn't her fight. She wasn't even sure yet if there was a fight to have.

Taylor needed to pump the brakes. Big time.

But making a mental list wouldn't hurt anything. Right? Especially since she was already here.

"So, Taylor," Zeke said before swallowing a huge mouthful of chicken. "Do you juice?"

"Excuse me?"

"Juice. Like celery, cucumber, carrot… that shit."

Taylor gave him a hesitant, "No."

"Good, because it's such a fucking waste of money and time." He laughed and held up his water glass. "This shit will hydrate you better, anyway."

Taylor glanced sideways at Austin, whose jaw was clenched with his eyes lasered on the man across from him. Whatever this was, Austin was intimately familiar with the pitch.

He took a sip of water. Taylor realized now that he had switched to water from his cocktail some time during the meal.

Jason, her not-for-long boss and the guy she should have had the good sense *not* to sleep with, would never have quit drinking early enough to drive her safely home. Heck, he'd never have thought to drive her home in the first place unless he thought she'd sleep with him.

But Austin barely knew her, and he didn't seem to expect anything from her either.

Was he this responsible with everyone? With everything?

As flattering as it was to think he was being especially considerate of her, it was also refreshing to imagine that maybe he was just wired that way. That it was simply in his nature to be considerate. The idea of that was downright charming.

Damn it.

Was she falling for someone's charm *again*? Or was this something new? Was she legitimately falling for *responsibility*, of all things?

"It's much easier to get those antioxidants and shit another way," Zeke continued. "What if you could get all the good essence from that celery juice in a capsule?"

"Like... celery seeds?"

"No, like the *essence* of the celery. All the good stuff. I've got these capsules that heal your gut and fight inflammation. They make you all alkaline and shit. I don't understand it, but the scientists and doctors in the lab say it's for real."

Taylor could feel Austin's rage simmering beside her, but Melinda spoke up, calmly heading off the impending eruption.

"Let's at least hold off the business talk until after dessert, please."

Zeke frowned in disappointment like a little kid, but he fell in line, anyway. "Right. Sorry. I'm just excited about it and want to *help* people."

"I know, but I'd like to get to know Taylor a little better," Melinda said. "Are you originally from Lafayette?"

Taylor scrambled to remember what stories she'd already told that evening. "I grew up here, yes."

Taylor tried to focus on Melinda, but her brain spun in the background, wondering what Zeke's connection to Austin's uncle might have been. He wasn't an heir or a relative, but could he have some monetary stake in the man's death?

Nobody could be buying this crap he was selling. Celery *essence*?

Maybe Melinda had thrown some startup cash his way. He couldn't possibly be getting rich off of this. It was a total scam, but he wasn't very good at the con. He wasn't subtle, and he certainly wasn't charming. There was no way this would be his get-rich-quick scheme. So he'd need more money, eventually.

Taylor added him to her list. He wasn't a direct descendant and Melinda didn't need the money, but Melinda having the uncle's money might give Zeke access to it.

Maybe Zeke was running a long con here. Maybe Taylor needed to give him more credit.

"So you two met when you dropped off the cat?" An older

male cousin whose name Taylor had forgotten cast a judgy look at them from across the table.

"Yes," Austin said.

"And when was that?" The guy would not let up. His wife gently elbowed him, but he ignored her.

"Wednesday," Taylor answered in a cheerful tone.

The cousin chuckled with an ugly edge to the sound.

"Got a problem, Lance?" Austin had clearly had enough of everyone's crap.

"That's what, three days?" This time it was his Aunt Nadine poking the situation. "Dating sure moves fast these days, I guess."

Taylor was prepared to step in again to diffuse the situation before Austin completely lost his patience. But she didn't have to.

"Don't worry, Nadine." Melinda dabbed at her mouth with her napkin and returned it to her lap. "I'm sure you'll eventually find *someone* to show you how it's done these days."

Taylor choked down a laugh. His aunt's face turned an unflattering shade of red as people emerged from the kitchen to take the last of the plates away and whisper something to Melinda.

"Ah, fantastic," she said in a commanding voice. "It's time for dessert."

———

"So did I win worst family?" Austin turned into the same spot where he'd picked her up earlier that evening and put the car in park.

"Yes, I think that's pretty clear." Taylor laughed and unbuckled her seatbelt. "Although that isn't quite fair, since you haven't met my family yet."

"Yet?"

Her cheeks turned red again. Gosh, he loved the sight of that.

With a shy smile, she said, "Thanks for inviting me. Your family's a mess, but I had a good time." She hesitated and stared down at her lap. "I had a good time with you."

Those cheeks reddened again.

How the hell was he supposed to unsee that and go about his life pretending this wasn't a date?

Because it wasn't. That had been the arrangement.

Then again… she'd said she had a good time *with him*. That felt like an important distinction.

Still, it didn't matter how much fun either of them had or how many times he made her blush. He was leaving in a few weeks. His life was on the Northshore, back with those kids and that team and his classes. He couldn't afford to start anything with this woman. He'd probably already started too much here tonight. At least on his end.

"Thanks for coming with me. I had a good time with you too." Then he changed the subject. "Am I biased or do you think any of them could be awful enough to have hurt my uncle?"

"I don't know. Most of them could have money motives, and I wouldn't put it past any of them." She paused. "Even Zeke."

"Especially Zeke," he agreed.

"What's up with that guy? Seriously, what does your mom see in him?"

"Do not ask that." The last thing he wanted to do was give the obvious answer that haunted him ever since he found out about the relationship.

Taylor laughed. "Okay, okay. We don't have to talk about that part."

"Aside from that, I just don't like the guy. Never did. Even back in high school."

"I can see why," Taylor said. "But he seems like…"

"Not a criminal mastermind?"

"Yeah," Taylor said. "Like, I can't imagine him committing any crime, much less a *murder*, without leaving any evidence."

"We didn't get the autopsy back," Austin said.

"Right, but I'd expect him to leave a shoe behind, Cinderella-style, or something equally clumsy."

She wasn't wrong. That was his exact impression of Zeke as well. Always had been. "I see what you mean."

"Do you think your mom would be clueless enough to include him in her will or give him access to her assets?"

Austin sighed heavily. "I know where you're going with this, and I can't imagine a scenario like that. My mom didn't get her money by being careless. Some of it was her family's money. Some of it was money my father made. But whatever my father earned came from my mother whispering in his ear and guiding his decisions—business, investment, everything. He was a good man, but shrewd, he was not."

Taylor nodded. "Your mother definitely seems shrewd. In a good way."

"Sure. In a good way." He cracked a small smile. "If you say so."

"I'm giving credit where it's due."

"Fair enough," Austin said. "Did you enjoy the meal? Honestly?"

"The food was excellent. Your mother is a fantastic cook."

"I'll be sure to pass that along."

"Please do." There was an awkward pause, then she tilted her head and looked sideways at him in the driver's seat. "Would you like to see Tink?"

Austin choked up. If someone had asked him a couple of

months ago if that cat would leave him utterly speechless, he'd have called the idea laughable. But there he was.

"Yes, please. If you're okay with that."

Taylor nodded at her window and exited the car. He followed her up the stairs, keeping his eyes on the railing so as not to catch sight of her backside in those tight green pants with the cropped jacket riding up with every step she took.

She dug the keys from her clutch, then opened the door while Austin followed her into the apartment. The place was uncluttered and clean. A couple of bright, impressionistic prints of a cat and a dog hung above a couch. That couch was the only furniture besides a TV stand and a small dinette table near the kitchen entrance. The apartment was cute and functional.

Taylor hesitated in front of a closed door.

"I can wait out here," Austin said.

"He doesn't like to leave this room," Taylor said. "But maybe seeing you right outside might make him feel safe enough to come out."

"If he recognizes me."

"It's only been a few days."

Taylor opened the door and turned on the light. The bedroom was like the living room in its minimalism. A fluffy comforter with red, orange, and pink stripes was stretched neatly across a twin bed, and a white nightstand and short white bookshelf beside a closed closet door were the only other items in the room.

Austin sat with his back against the closed bedroom door, far from the carrier so as not to crowd Tink. Taylor sat on the floor beside the open carrier and softly patted the purple fleece Tinker Bell blanket that lay folded in front like a welcome mat. She held her hand palm up in the opening so Tink could sniff her fingertips like a dog.

"Hey, buddy," she said in a soft voice. "It's me. And I brought a friend who's pretty excited to see you."

When she nodded, giving him the go-ahead, Austin said, "Hey Tink. Remember me?"

Taylor moved her hand out of the way, and a second later, a pink nose poked out from the dark interior of the carrier. Tink sniffed the air for a moment, then let his head drift from side to side, scanning the room for confirmation. When his eyes landed on Austin in the doorway, he let out a low, timid howl.

"Yeah, it's me."

Taylor gestured for him to move closer. He scooted across the carpet until his knee was touching Taylor's. When he was close enough for Tink's old eyes to confirm his other senses' messages, Tink walked out of the carrier and went right up to Austin, rubbing his face against Austin's hand and knee and anything else he could mark his scent on.

"Damn it." Austin wiped at his eyes with one hand and pet Tink with the other.

"Told you he'd remember."

Austin looked up to see that there was no smugness in her eyes. Only happiness and compassion. His heart swelled knowing that this was the woman caring for Uncle Kenny's beloved pet. That she was giving all of her expertise and caring to Tink as if he were her own cat.

"Thank you."

Tink toppled his gigantic body over Austin's leg to snuggle in his lap, his warm purrs vibrating over Austin's crossed calves. He didn't care how much hair that cat left all over his dress pants. He was just glad to be reunited with the old guy again, even for a little while.

"It's no big deal. I'm just giving him a quiet room and time to adjust."

"It *is* a big deal though." Austin put his free hand, the one not on top of Tink, on Taylor's knee, and leaned in closer. "To me, it is."

She stared back at him, her big brown eyes locked onto him from beneath her thick, dark mascara and intense green eyeliner. Those eyes mesmerized him. Everything about her was mesmerizing, like he was another stray animal she'd lured into her orbit of safety and magical goodness.

Austin was so mesmerized he hadn't noticed she was also leaning closer until their faces were inches apart. He moved his hand from her knee to the side of her face and closed the remaining gap between them. His eyes shut as their lips met, setting off fireworks behind his lids and heat racing through his body. She tasted like lemon and sugar, and he wanted to drink up every bit of her.

What the hell was he doing?

He draped another kiss on her soft lips and pulled back slightly, still holding her face in his palm. He found his own excitement and uncertainty reflected in Taylor's eyes.

This was all too fast. He'd known this woman… three days?

Heck, this shouldn't be happening *at all*. He would be leaving soon. He had a life on the Northshore that he needed to get back to.

"I should probably go," he said.

Taylor gave a small smile and nodded. Then she laughed softly as she looked down at the gigantic furball in his lap. "Let me help."

She pet Tink's head a few times, then slipped her hands underneath him, gently nudging him up and out of Austin's lap. Tink didn't seem upset at all by the disturbance. He simply traded locations and fell into contended sleep on Taylor.

Magic.

The woman was true animal magic.

"Thanks for letting me see him."

"Of course," Taylor said. "He was glad to see you too."

Austin smiled. Then, because he couldn't help himself, he kissed her forehead. "I'll lock the door behind me on my way out."

11

Taylor arrived at work fifteen minutes early, and she'd finished her entire travel mug of coffee before pulling into the veterinary clinic parking lot. Her hands were shaking, but she was ready for the day ahead. Armed for battle with caffeine.

Things had been pretty quiet after Friday night. Liz and Sierra had told her to take the weekend off and that they'd be in touch during the week to order clinic supplies. They'd said not to worry about them and to rest up for her last couple of weeks at her other job.

Little did they know, she needed over two days or even the whole last week to prepare for this.

Her hands weren't shaking just from the coffee, but she wasn't having second thoughts about quitting or about working with the rescue. She was shaking because she didn't want to face anyone in that building. Didn't want to face how they'd inevitably make her feel. Definitely didn't want to face how she might make *herself* feel.

Guilt sucked.

Austin had texted her on Saturday to check how she was

doing. She was used to charming, but she wasn't used to genuine kindness.

When he checked in again on Sunday, she'd told him what she had to do on Monday. She was dreading it all weekend and needed to tell someone, and Ellie was spending a park day with the barista.

To her surprise, Austin texted again first thing Monday morning with a GIF of a cartoon cat opening its arms to spread a sparkly rainbow with the message, "You've got this."

It was the most adorable little pep talk she'd ever received. She wasn't into baseball—she wasn't really into sports at all—but she imagined he was the best kind of coach. Those kids were lucky to have him.

But the fact that he even thought about her and remembered that she was about to face a tough day made her feel things she wasn't ready to feel. Heck, that whole Friday night, despite the awkwardness of the dinner itself, had made her feel things about Austin that she wasn't ready to feel.

She couldn't deny he was charming, and history had proven she couldn't trust herself around charming men. So the charming man with the adorable GIFs was a problem for another day.

Today, she knew exactly what she needed to do. She'd made her decision, and she could trust herself enough to follow through on it. She could do this.

Taylor pulled open the glass door and forced a smile as she walked inside. She waved to Danielle as she breezed past the reception desk.

"Good morning."

"Well, hey there," Danielle said with the widest, fakest smile Taylor had ever seen. And on Danielle, that was saying something. "Welcome back."

"Is Jason in his office?" Taylor barely slowed to wait for the answer.

Danielle gave a worried look. Of course, she hadn't been worried enough to warn Taylor about the guy before this total mess. But now she was worried Taylor might cause a scene.

"In his office."

Taylor thanked her and hurried down the hall past the exam rooms. Then she stopped at the last door on the left, held her breath, and knocked.

"Come in," said the deep voice with a sleepy drawl.

Taylor entered the office where her boss, Jason, sat behind a too-large-for-the-room desk. He held his phone in both hands, typing who-knew-what to who-knew-who. A few moments later, he looked up at Taylor standing across from the desk.

"Oh, Taylor. Good morning."

She didn't return the greeting. Instead, she sat silently in the chair opposite him, momentarily forgetting everything she'd planned to say. Everything she'd practiced saying on the drive over that morning.

Jason placed the phone face down in front of him. His dark, curly hair looked like he'd gotten it trimmed while she was out last week. "Can I help you with something?"

Taylor clasped her hands in her lap, squeezing them tightly. She didn't know what she'd ever seen in this man.

She could chalk the mistake up to a lapse in judgment. Maybe loneliness. It didn't matter what had caused her to fall for this guy and temporarily forget her own moral compass. The spell had worn off now.

"I'm here to put in my two weeks' notice."

He looked surprised, but not upset. Like, not at all upset, which, of course, added insult sprinkles on this whole insult turd cake. "Are you moving?"

Jerk.

He couldn't think of any other reason she'd leave this job

than because she might be moving. He couldn't possibly fathom that she might want out of this hellhole and the miserable situation he'd put her in.

Why did he think his last vet tech left? And probably one or two before that one as well?

"No," Taylor said firmly. "I was offered a job with an animal rescue. It's a new one. They're just starting up, and I've been offered a position to run their clinic."

She was continuing to talk and explain herself for no other reason than she was excited about the rescue. She didn't owe him an explanation, and he surely wouldn't have asked about it. He didn't care. About her or the inconvenience of having to fill her position. She was *replaceable*.

"Well, good for you."

Completely unbothered.

She should have expected this. He was probably glad she was leaving, especially once he realized he wouldn't be getting anything else out of her.

She felt sick, suddenly regretting all that coffee. Now she had an entire day ahead of her with extra caffeine and an upset stomach. Great. Just another poor decision on her part.

"Was there anything else?" he asked.

Taylor wished she had something more to say. She wished that she'd spent the weekend preparing a better speech. Something scorching that would put him in his place. Something to make him think twice about doing this ever again to another employee. Something that would make him afraid he might get caught.

But no. She'd lounged on the couch and watched *Murder She Wrote* for two whole days with a brief vacation with *The Golden Girls*.

"No, that's all," she said. "I'll be here for another two weeks, then I'll be working with the rescue."

"Well, thanks for letting me know." He picked up his phone again and resumed typing.

Taylor balled her fists, resisting the urge to toss everything off his desk, slam her palms on it, and yell in his face.

Instead, she stood and calmly walked out of the office, closing the door behind her.

The good news was that as small and angry as the interaction had made her feel, it also made her even more confident she was making the right decision. Now, with that business done, she couldn't wait to get started in her new job.

Her first instinct was to text Austin.

Why? She didn't entirely know. Maybe just because he cared. Jason sure as heck didn't care that she was leaving. Deep down she'd always known he never would, and it didn't matter if he cared or not.

Austin, however, continued to surprise her with his care and concern and cute cats.

But she'd text him later.

She sent a quick message to Ellie that just said, *it's done*.

Almost immediately, she got a reply with a middle finger and party popper emoji.

Taylor smiled at the text, tucked the phone into her scrub shirt pocket, and headed to the reception area to meet her first patient of the day.

AUSTIN PLACED the last of the framed photos in the cardboard Bankers box. Every photo was a version of the same: Austin's uncle wearing a white button-down short-sleeved shirt with a flames pattern all over it, cargo shorts, sunglasses, a floppy hat, and neon green sandals with his arm draped around a short woman about his age with messy, cropped gray hair and a similar outfit, minus the flames.

The box was also loaded with pins, programs, and other keepsakes from various festivals Uncle Kenny had attended with his oldest friend. Patricia was one of the few people in his uncle's circle that Austin recognized by sight and name. The rest came and went fairly quickly. His mother hadn't been wrong about that.

Friends went in and out of Uncle Kenny's life so often that Austin hadn't recognized any of the names on the list his mother had handed him as he left Friday night. His mother hadn't been sure she was remembering the names correctly, but perhaps Patricia could help him with that.

Uncle Kenny and Patricia had been close for as long as Austin could remember. He was never sure if there was anything other than friendship between them, but that didn't seem to matter. Patricia and his uncle didn't bother with defining themselves by labels. Patricia had been Uncle Kenny's perpetual festival companion. A kindred free spirit who loved music, dancing, and enjoying life.

Austin picked up a big, floppy sun hat covered in enamel pins. There was one pin from each year of the big local festival, and it was the same hat he wore in all the photographs of him and Patricia. He placed the hat on top of everything else in the box and carried it downstairs.

This part had been a fairly effortless task. None of these things were items that Austin wanted to keep for himself, nor would anyone else in the family want them. The vultures weren't clawing for anything that didn't have immediate monetary value. So it had been a straightforward decision to call Patricia to pick them up.

Besides being an effortless task, it also made for a useful distraction.

He'd been worried about Taylor giving her two weeks' notice, and he hadn't heard from her since texting some encouragement first thing that morning.

He probably wouldn't hear from her until lunch or later after work. But that didn't stop him from worrying.

He wasn't sure how they'd gotten to this point so quickly, but he genuinely cared about her, even though he'd met her less than a week ago. And he couldn't stop himself from thinking all weekend about how great Friday night had been.

Looked like despite his insistence that Friday night was more of a fake date than a real one, he'd started falling for this woman already. Falling for those big brown eyes. That playful sense of humor. That magical compassion. Those lips...

All of that falling, however, meant he was starting something he had no intention of finishing.

No matter how wonderful Taylor seemed, Austin's life was still two hours away. Plus, his schedule was completely booked with baseball for the next several months. He couldn't put Taylor on a shelf, like a toy he might take out to play with for the summer, only to put her back on the shelf again once school started.

He needed to cool it with the texts. And the cat GIFs.

Right after he heard how today went for her.

And maybe one more cat GIF if it turned out she needed cheering up. But just one.

While he waited for Patricia to arrive, Austin pulled out the sheet of paper he'd printed earlier that morning. The final team lineup.

During tryouts last week, Mike had sent several videos of the new kids so Austin could evaluate their skills. It had been a fairly smooth process, although it was never easy to tell these kids that they didn't make the team or that they weren't getting the position they wanted. But at least on the management end, the decision of who went where had been clear this year.

Still, he hated not being there. Hated not being the one to

bear the responsibility of pulling those kids aside and giving them a bit of encouragement. Sure, Mike was great at that too, but it was Austin's job. A job he took seriously.

Maybe he'd go out there on Wednesday for the first practice. It was only a couple hours away, so he could go out there, give them a big pep talk, attend practice, then leave around dinnertime when the kids all went home.

He didn't anticipate being in Lafayette too much longer. He had an appointment set up next week with his uncle's attorney to go over the will together, but once Austin understood everything, the attorney could handle the distribution and notifying any other beneficiaries.

And then there was the autopsy. He was told the results should be in any day now. Then he'd have some answers. He still had nothing legitimate to go on, so maybe this was just grief manufacturing an idea for him to focus on.

His phone buzzed, and he smiled at the message.

Went great. Thanks for the pep talk! *thumbs up emoji*

He sighed in relief. Not that he was worried anything would happen. He didn't even know what the real reason was for her leaving that job. He just knew she'd seemed upset about it, and he was glad that stress was over for her.

The doorbell rang out through the kitchen. Not a regular chime, of course. The doorbell version of the "Funky Town" melody.

Austin found Patricia standing on the other side of the kitchen door. The door that only Austin and his uncle's close friends ever used. She wore an oversized, long-sleeved black T-shirt with the white outline of a cat on the front with brown linen pants and hiking shoes instead of her typical summer sandals. Redness rimmed her eyes like she'd been crying on the way there.

Without a word, she held out a glass dish with a blue plastic lid. Austin took the dish and gestured for her to come inside, not bothering to go through the whole, "You didn't have to do that," of it all. It was Patricia. Of course, she had to. He knew her at least well enough to know that.

She shuffled in while he placed the food on the nearest counter. When he turned around, he realized she was staring through the kitchen into the next room. The large entryway. The location of the main staircase.

Austin put a hand on her arm and gestured at the center bar with his other hand. "Why don't we sit for a bit."

She nodded and shuffled toward one of the bright red, vinyl stools.

"Can I make you some tea?" he asked. "Coffee? Water?"

"No, thank you. I can't stay long. Meeting my niece for lunch in a little while. I just wanted to bring you some lasagna."

"That was very thoughtful. Thank you."

There was a long, awkward pause while he sat on the stool beside her, wondering what to say next. He felt compelled to tell her about his call with the police. About his questions. But he didn't want to burden her with all of that. Not until he got solid answers.

"How have you been?" she asked. "I know it must be hard dealing with all the details. But Kenny knew you were the best person to handle everything for him. He always spoke so highly of you. He was incredibly proud of you. I hope you know that."

"I do." His voice cracked with the answer, and he cleared his throat to gather himself. "He really loved you, too. Always lit up when he talked about your adventures together."

"Did he tell you we were planning a trip to the Grand Canyon?"

"No, he didn't." Although the idea didn't surprise him.

His uncle had always wanted to travel, but he'd been too busy with his restaurants. He'd already been a successful advertising copywriter when he and Austin's dad and aunt all inherited their father's estate, so he'd invested his share of the inheritance in a few local restaurant ideas. One of those hit big enough to retire early from his job, but running a restaurant had meant he kept his adventures local. He'd sold the restaurant a couple of years ago, and Austin knew he wanted to plan all the trips he couldn't before. Austin just hadn't heard any specific plans for those travels.

"We were planning to go this fall. Rent a big, fancy RV."

Austin smiled. "That sounds like it would have been a blast."

"Yup. Maybe I'll find a way to go, anyway. You know, in his honor and all." She looked around the kitchen and into the other room again, then back at Austin. "Tink?"

"He's fine. In a foster home until the rescue finds a place for him."

"That sounds good, I suppose."

She looked upset. Patricia had been one of the first Austin had asked about taking Tink, but she had two dogs of her own who didn't tolerate feline roommates. She'd been as concerned as Austin was about making sure Tink found a good home.

"He's staying with a vet tech," he said. "I met her myself. He's in excellent hands."

Patricia perked up at that. "That sounds good for him."

Austin held back all the flattering things he wanted to say about Taylor. Those things weren't important now. Well, they were important to him, but not to Patricia or this situation.

"While you're here, I have a question for you." Austin dug the paper his mom had given him from his back pocket and unfolded it on the counter. "Do you know any of these people? I'm collecting contact information for anyone I might need to get in touch with or send items to as I go through the house. These are names my mother mentioned, but she's not sure it's accurate and doesn't remember last names."

That sounded innocent enough. Nothing that would make Patricia think he was snooping on his uncle's personal life to hypothetically track down a potential murderer.

"That's so kind of you to think of everyone that way. Let me see the list, although I don't have my glasses with me." She slid the paper closer and squinted at it. Then, a deep frown set in.

"Do you know some of them?"

"A few. Mutual friends. I can get you their phone numbers."

"What's wrong? Does a name not belong on there? Someone he isn't in touch with anymore?"

Maybe someone he had a falling out with? Someone who might have pushed him down a flight of stairs?

She tapped her index finger on the list.

"Brandon? What about him?"

She rolled her eyes but tried to hide it. "Not really." She slid the list back to Austin. "Brandon Wiltz. I just never got a good vibe from that guy. And he seemed like he was kind of inserting himself in Kenny's life like he thought of himself as a boyfriend. Like he wanted to tell Kenny where he could go and what he could do and who with." She shook her head. "You know how your uncle was, though. Never wanted to hurt anyone's feelings. I don't have a number for the guy, though. Sorry."

That sounded right. People around his uncle sometimes got the impression they were closer than they were, but his uncle had never been one to hitch himself to any one person.

A jealous ex? That was a motive, right?

"Thank you." He grabbed a pen from a nearby drawer and jotted down the last name.

"I'd better get going. I need to take the dogs out before I meet with my niece." She hopped off the stool and wrapped her short arms around Austin, pulling him in tight. "It was so good to see you."

"You too. Hang on just a sec. I have something for you." Austin left to retrieve the box from the next room. "These all belong with you."

Patricia put a hand on the box and slipped her thumb under the lid as if she would lift it, but froze. She shook her head as a tear fell down her cheek. "I still can't believe he's gone."

"I keep saying the same thing." He laughed softly. "Unicorns are supposed to be immortal, right?"

Patricia laughed too and wiped her face. "Something like that. He was one of a kind, wasn't he?"

"That he was."

They both looked around the house, taking it all in. The flavor town kitchen. The Jeff Goldblum psychedelic flower-child-themed living room on the other side of one wall. The Britney Spears tribute table in the hallway outside the guest bathroom.

Austin would have to get rid of everything in here. He'd probably hire someone to run an estate sale. Hopefully, he could arrange that from the Northshore.

"I'll carry this out to your car."

"Thank you," Patricia said.

He followed her out the front door while she shuffled down the walkway to her Subaru in the driveway. Once he'd placed the box on the back seat, Patricia gave him another big hug and took one last look at the house behind him.

"I'll get your dish back to you," he said.

"No worries. I'm sure there are a few of my other dishes in there already."

She told him to take care and to send that list so she could give him phone numbers for the ones she had.

Austin waved as she drove off, then walked back toward the house. When he grabbed the door handle, he saw a rough patch in the frame. Something he hadn't noticed before. It looked like it had been chipped. Maybe he was paranoid, but it looked like someone had clumsily tried to pry their way in.

He didn't know when it could have happened since he'd been home all weekend. But it could have happened overnight. He slept upstairs and didn't have an animal to alert him if someone tried to break in. Maybe someone knew his uncle was gone and thought the house was empty. But his car was always in the driveway.

Except for last Friday night.

12

"Nice hit, Steven," Austin shouted from the dugout. "Blake, let's tighten up that pocket a little. You're leaning outside with most of those throws."

Beside him, Mike clapped while the team trotted off the field. "Good job this afternoon, guys!"

The sun hung low on the horizon that Wednesday and gleamed off Mike's dark shaved head when he lifted his red cap, allowing the crisp late January air to dry off the sweat.

"Good to see y'all." Austin patted his senior pitcher, Blake, on the head as he walked past. "Great work out there! I'm excited about this season. Can't wait to get back here again and see what you guys do while I'm gone."

The kids filed into the locker room to grab their things and head home. Austin and Mike hung back, strolling toward the school.

"So, what do you think? Honestly."

"Looks good," Austin said. "I think we've got a talented team this year."

"Yeah, same," said Mike. "Hardworking guys too. I'll have them in shape for you when you get back for good."

Austin patted Mike on the back. "I have no doubts about that. I can't wait."

He didn't know where the hesitation in his voice and in his gut were coming from. Austin genuinely missed being here. He loved his job at Northshore High. He loved working with these kids. He even enjoyed teaching his classes, not just coaching.

But for some reason—a certain adorable blonde reason, if he had to guess—he wasn't looking forward to coming back so much lately.

Mike also noticed the hesitation. "Something wrong? Did something happen back home that you haven't told me about yet?"

That "yet" was there, because Austin normally told Mike everything. They weren't just coworkers. Mike was his best friend.

"No," Austin said. "I mean, everything's a mess, but that's normal family mess stuff."

"But you sound... not ready to come back. Feeling some burnout? Pre-season anticipation anxiety?"

"No, no, nothing like that." Austin considered whether to tell Mike everything. Not that he didn't trust the guy. Austin just didn't want to admit what he'd landed himself in, despite knowing better. "There's someone."

"Someone as in you met someone?"

Austin nodded. "Her name's Taylor. She's the vet tech that took in my uncle's cat."

"You mentioned something about that cat. So you've got a thing for the vet now, huh?"

"Not a thing," Austin said.

Who was he kidding? It was definitely a thing. A thing with an expiration date. A vague date, but an inevitable expiration.

"Tell you what," Mike said. "Why don't you have dinner and a beer with me, my treat, before you drive back."

That sounded like fun. He could catch up with Mike, talk about something other than his family drama or baseball for once. Have one beer and hit the road a little later than planned.

"Sure, man. Let me just make sure nothing's on fire back home first."

Austin pulled out his phone to check his messages and peek at his security camera feed. After some debate, Austin had decided not to report the attempted break-in. There was barely any damage, and there didn't appear to be anything missing from inside the house.

But he bought two cameras Monday afternoon, right after he'd found the damage to his uncle's door frame. It took him most of yesterday to install them and set up the wireless feed, since tech stuff wasn't exactly his strong suit.

He couldn't believe his uncle didn't already have a security system for that big, expensive house, but he shouldn't have been surprised. Uncle Kenny trusted everyone. All someone had to do was ask, and he'd give them anything he could to help. Unless they'd burned a few bridges, like Austin's Aunt Nadine had.

Austin never heard the full story about whatever went down between the siblings. All he knew was they hadn't spoken in years. Which made her presence at his mother's dinner extra suspicious.

After a peek at the live feed, he noticed he had a missed call from an unknown number.

He listened to the voice message. It was a detective. They'd sent over a copy of the autopsy report but wanted to discuss it. The guy said he'd be at work late so Austin could call him back to discuss the results. It didn't sound like a polite offer either. From the tone, it sounded more like the guy wanted Austin to call him to discuss something specific.

"Something on fire?" Mike asked.

"Not sure."

Austin checked his email, and there it was. An email with an attachment. His uncle's autopsy report.

The surrounding field blurred, and his ears rang.

He closed the app without opening the email. He'd be thinking about that the entire ride home if he looked at it now. Heck, he'd already be thinking about it, but if he saw the thing, he'd be mentally running through every line of that report in his head instead of focusing on the road.

"I'm gonna have to take a rain check," he told Mike. "I've got some legal stuff I need to take care of."

"No problem. Anything I can help with?"

"Know how to read an autopsy report?"

Mike cringed. "Yikes. You sure you don't want to have that burger and a beer first?"

"I'd better not." Austin held out his hand to shake Mike's. "Thanks for the offer, though. Raincheck?"

"Definitely."

"And thanks for holding down the fort here while I'm gone."

"Of course," Mike said. "Take care, man. I'll keep in touch and keep you up to date on everything here."

"Thanks."

It really helped to know that Mike was handling everything with the team and that the school had his back. They had a great long-term sub in his classroom until he was ready to return full time.

Austin walked to his car and let it warm up while he connected the phone to the speaker. Then, he headed off-campus while he waited for the detective to pick up his call.

EVERY STEP UP to the porch of the St. Martin Animal Sanctuary seemed heavier than the one before. There were only three steps, but they felt like thirty.

Not that Taylor didn't want to be here. It was more that her other job had been sucking the life out of her all week. By Wednesday evening, her head throbbed, her shoulders ached, and she needed a very long nap.

Thankfully, she had tomorrow off. After taking off all of last week to sort out her life, returning to that draining job had worn her out more than she'd expected. And then there was Mrs. Melancon's seventy-pound golden retriever, Frank, that she had to lift onto the exam table this morning. Exhausted didn't cover her current state.

But the worst part was this mild nausea she couldn't shake. Ever since Monday, her stomach had been a wreck of nerves and stress. She'd expected to feel lighter by Wednesday evening when she headed to the shelter, but she still felt awful. Just worn out, she supposed.

Taylor stopped at the top of the steps and took another whiff of the passing breeze despite her stomach's protest.

Yep, definitely a skunk nearby.

She held her forearm over her nose, then knocked on the door. A few moments later, the door opened, and Liz stood in the entrance.

"Hey there. Come on in." Liz stood to the side so Taylor could enter. "And for future reference, you work here now, so no need to knock. Just come right on in."

Taylor froze once she stepped inside and gaped in awe at the changes. The walls were a cheery yellow and all the trim was up in crisp white. There were also two cute aqua-colored benches along the walls, and the metal chairs at the table had gotten a coat of aqua spray paint as well.

"Wow."

"Looks good, doesn't it?" Liz crossed her arms as she took in the sight of the front room alongside Taylor. "We've still got a bit left to do, but making progress."

Taylor put her arm down from her nose. "It looks great."

"Sorry about the smell out there," Liz said. "I think there's a family of skunks somewhere."

"Oh, gosh," Taylor said, hoping that "somewhere" didn't mean under this building.

Liz shrugged. "Comes with the territory out here. Along with other things. Don't worry, you'll get used to it. I did."

Taylor had lived her whole life in the city limits of nearby Lafayette, and while it wasn't a big city by any means, she'd always lived along busy roads where there were no skunks. At least none that stuck around long enough to make a family. Breaux Bridge was just a short drive away, but it felt like a whole other world. A beautiful, peaceful, and smelly world.

Liz took another good look at Taylor. "You all right? You don't look great."

"Yeah. My stomach's just been a mess this week, and the skunk smell isn't helping, that's all."

"You look worse than an upset stomach."

"Long few days at the old job."

Liz grunted and nodded. "Gotcha. Hey, do you want to see the clinic room?"

"Absolutely."

Taylor followed Liz down the hall, where the smell dissipated the farther they got from the front door. The other rooms along the way were still under construction, as was the clinic room in the back.

"How's that foster cat of yours doing?"

"Settling in," Taylor said. "Oh, would you maybe want to run a senior panel on him?"

"Problems?"

"Nothing major. He seems healthy, but he's been vomiting a little in the mornings." Taylor suddenly felt flushed. Was it hot in there? "At first I figured he was just working up a hairball, and maybe he still is. But it's weird, like it happens consistently early every morning. He'll come up to greet me before the sun's up—which is great because he's warming up and settling in and getting friendly—but I'll pet him and kind of ignore him while he meows for breakfast. I'm not making six o'clock breakfast turn into five o'clock breakfast."

Liz nodded. "Good plan."

"But maybe there's something else going on with him other than a stubborn hairball?"

"Maybe," Liz said. "Especially if it's persisted for that long." She tapped her chin as she thought. "You're the expert here, so we'll trust your opinion. Could be thyroid at his age. Any other issues?"

"Nothing else that I've noticed."

"We don't have the supplies here yet. Do you think it's serious? Like, do we need to pay for him to go somewhere else and have them run the bloodwork?"

Taylor shrugged. "It's certainly not an emergency yet."

"Tell you what," Liz said. "You make the call. If you think you want to wait until we get supplies in a week or two, we can do that. Then you can bring him in here for the blood draw, or have someone help you do it at home, and we'll send it off to the lab. Or if you want to take him into your veterinary clinic, you can have them do the panel and call me for approval, since we're listed as his owners."

Taylor didn't think anything was seriously wrong with Tink, but she'd feel much better if they had a clear picture of what was going on. And she'd feel guilty if something really was wrong, and she'd delayed his treatment.

"I'll think about it and let you know."

"We'll sign off on whatever you think is best," Liz said. "Speaking of those supplies and bloodwork." She motioned to a brand new counter in the back of the room. "Here's that supply list. Go ahead and place the order and have them bill us."

"Okay." Taylor took two steps toward the counter and felt weak. The room started going black, and her head felt like a sandbag.

This wasn't the skunk.

"Whoa." Liz grabbed a chair and guided Taylor into it. "You look pale as a ghost. Don't move." She disappeared and returned a minute later with a bottle of water and a wet dishrag. "Put this on your head."

Taylor sat as ordered and took a sip.

Sitting helped. Water helped.

"I've just had a long day."

"That doesn't look like a long day."

Sierra walked into the room and said, "Whoa. You look awful."

"Thanks," Taylor mumbled.

"One of us can give you a ride home," Liz said.

"No, no," Taylor stammered. "Like I said, just a long week, and I did too much today. Probably didn't drink enough water either. I'm sorry, I don't mean to worry you."

"Well, you did, but that's okay," Liz said. "You're part of our little work family now, and it's our job to look out for each other."

Taylor felt dizzy again, but this time from a rush of overwhelming emotion. She managed to squeak out, "Thanks."

"While you're sitting there, do you know a photographer?" A devilish grin spread across Sierra's face.

Liz looked resigned to whatever this idea was. A sure sign that if Liz wasn't standing in the way, that meant whatever this idea might be was a go at this point.

"I might." Her sister was an amazing photographer, but had never considered it a "real" career option. Taylor wasn't planning to offer this information, however, without knowing what this was all about. "What do you need them for?"

"We'll need one eventually to take website photos of the animals," Sierra said. "But for now, Liz says it's too cold for a dog wash, and I don't want to bake five thousand pupcakes."

Taylor's head spun again. "Pupcakes?"

"We're trying to arrange a fundraiser," Liz explained. "Got a line on a location downtown and someone to help with promo. We just need a photographer to take pictures for free."

"People would sign up for portrait packages as a donation?"

"That's the idea," Liz said.

"Do you know someone?" Sierra asked.

Taylor nodded. "Maybe. I wouldn't hold your breath on her doing anything for free though."

"Tell her it's for the animals," Sierra said. "You know, with big pleading eyes."

Taylor laughed. She was going to regret this once she felt better. The last thing she wanted was to talk to her sister, much less ask her for a favor, but she was suckered in by Sierra's rough-edged optimism. "I'll see what I can do. I'd better go."

"Are you sure you're okay to drive?" Liz asked.

"Positive." Taylor felt much better after sitting and drinking some water. She was probably just dehydrated. Working herself too hard, once again, plus the stress of the week. That was all.

"You be safe getting home." Liz handed Taylor the papers. "Do not touch this until you're feeling better. Understood?"

"Understood."

It was good to feel like she was a valued part of a team at a place where people actually cared about her well-being. She'd never felt anything like that at her old job. Heck, she couldn't even say she'd ever felt that way in her own family.

Family.

Crap.

What had she just agreed to?

Before she reached the front door, Sierra called out from the back. "Don't forget to let me know about that photographer! ASAP!"

*A*ustin pulled into his uncle's driveway and sat in the car with the engine off. The garage remained closed, with Uncle Kenny's strawberry red Mercedes-Benz hidden inside. Another item Austin would have to deal with soon.

He sure didn't plan to drive that thing around. It was way too flashy for his taste and horrible on gas. Then again, everything was horrible on gas compared to his own car.

With his head resting against the seat, Austin closed his eyes, processing what the detective told him during the drive back from the Northshore. It wasn't what he'd wanted to hear, but pieces were matching up. The puzzle still didn't make sense, though.

Part of his brain was telling him to let this go. Or to at least let the police handle it. But if his family was involved somehow, he knew them better than any detective. If something shady went down, Austin could connect dots for the police with his inside knowledge.

Austin picked up his phone to call Taylor. He might not put this puzzle together, but hearing from Taylor might ease that frustration. Or at least distract him for a minute.

"Hey there. How was the rest of your day?"

"Fine," she said. "I went to the shelter after work to pick up some stuff to do from home."

Her voice had a weakness to it. Like every word was a struggle.

"Are you okay?" he asked. "You sound... not good."

"I'm fine."

But she didn't sound fine. Not even close. "Did something happen at work?"

"No, nothing like that," she said. "I'm just not feeling great. It's been a long week."

He laughed softly. "It's only Wednesday."

"I guess it just feels like a lot after having last week off." She coughed. It was a wet, hacking cough. Definitely not a "fine" cough.

"You sound like you're coming down with something."

"Maybe I'm fighting off a cold."

He'd called looking for a pick-me-up for himself. And maybe to share the autopsy information he'd received. Only now he couldn't think of anything but that cough and what sounded like labored breathing.

"Can I bring you anything? Medicine? Soup?"

"I'm fine, really," she said. "I probably just need to rest."

Her positivity was, as usual, adorable.

And completely unacceptable in this case.

He considered his next move. He'd already grown too close to Taylor, considering he was still returning home soon. No point setting them both up for disappointment. *More* disappointment, that is. Because leaving would already hurt like hell.

That kiss had been a mistake.

No, it was *not* a mistake. Mistakes were things you regretted, and that kiss was not something he regretted.

Still, he should leave it at that.

"Is your roommate home?"

He'd feel much better if he knew someone else was there to monitor her. Another pair of eyes to tell her when she was being overly optimistic about her health.

"No, she's working a night shift at the emergency clinic."

There was no question about what he would do next.

"I'm coming over. If that's okay."

"You don't have to do that," she said. "I'll be fine. I just need rest."

"Great. I'll bring you soup. We can have dinner together. Then I'll leave, and you can rest."

"You really don't have to do that."

"I do have to," Austin said. "Even if I'm overreacting, we can still have some tasty soup, and you can help me make sense of this autopsy report."

"You got the report?"

"I can tell you all about it and my conversation with the detective over soup."

She was quiet for a while. In the end, her curiosity won out over her stubbornness. "Okay."

"Any requests?" He started his car again, already backing out of the driveway and knowing exactly where he was headed unless she had another idea.

"Honestly? I don't really like soup."

"The question is, do you *need* soup?"

She sighed. "Probably."

Finally. An admission that she wasn't well. Which meant she was probably near death's door if she was admitting she needed liquid meal assistance.

"Okay then," he said. "I'll bring you the best soup in town. If this stuff doesn't win you over, none will."

Taylor laughed, which transformed into a wet cough. He liked the sound of this cough even less than the last one.

She was probably right, and it probably was just a cold,

but he wasn't taking any chances. And he wouldn't feel better about it until he saw her for himself. Even then, he wouldn't feel better until she was well again.

Yep, this was going to hurt like hell when he left.

"Is this another challenge?" she asked. "Like the worst family competition?"

"That was no competition," he said. "But I have a good feeling I'm going to win this one too."

His text arrived a few minutes before Austin's knock landed on her door. He'd sent a warning that he was in the parking lot, giving her a heads up so he didn't startle her when he knocked, in case she'd fallen asleep on the couch.

The man was more considerate than anyone Taylor had ever met, and she found that consideration weirdly sexy. Not that she planned to do anything about the sexiness. Not in her current condition, at least.

Taylor draped her fuzzy blanket over the back of the couch and answered the door. Austin stood in front of her with a warm smile on his face and a large, stapled-shut paper bag held up in one hand.

"Your soup challenge has arrived."

She forced a smile that actually hurt. But everything hurt. Every muscle. Every joint. Even her *skin* hurt.

"Taylor, you are not fine." He entered the apartment and closed the door behind him. Then he pressed his free hand against her forehead and cheeks.

"Your hands are freezing."

"That's because you're burning up." He aimed the bag at her couch. "Sit. You're eating some soup, then you're going straight to bed."

This might have been the first time she'd ever found bossiness sexy. *Responsible* bossiness.

Damn. She must have a fever.

She led the way into the living room, and he placed the bag on the coffee table. Taylor sank into the couch, her skin and muscles protesting at both the touch and the movement.

Okay, so maybe she was a little sick.

Austin glanced at her bedroom door. "Maybe we'll have company?"

"Probably not. I leave the door open, but he mostly stays on my bed. He might wander out if he hears your voice, though. It worked last time."

He opened the paper bag and pulled out a carton.

Taylor was suddenly self-conscious of eating on the couch. After seeing his mother's house and how he grew up, Taylor doubted he'd ever eaten a meal in his life camped out in front of a TV.

"We can eat at the table," she said.

"Oh, no." His voice was gentle but firm. "I want you comfortable. Sit."

She did as he commanded, completely under his bossy spell. It felt nice to have someone taking care of her for once. She was usually the one doing the caretaking.

Austin removed the lid from the container and handed her a deep plastic spoon.

Taylor sniffed the contents, not expecting much of anything. She'd become progressively more congested as the day went on. Truth be told, she was glad Austin had come over. She didn't enjoy being alone when she was sick. Not that she needed him to do anything for her. It was just comforting to have another person in the house.

Austin had cuddly stuffed animal vibes. She wanted nothing more than to curl up against him and fall asleep with her head on his strong shoulder.

To her surprise, she could smell the soup. The clear broth smelled healing, and the big ribbons of basil woke up her tired, stuffy senses. Baby meatballs floated on the surface along with vegetables and tiny, round pasta pieces.

"It smells good," Taylor said. "Not that I thought you'd bring me gross soup. But I can actually *smell* it."

"Italian wedding soup. The best I've ever had," Austin said. "We used to eat at this local place all the time when I was a kid, Vitale's, and my mom would pick up this soup for me whenever I was sick."

"I don't think I've ever been there." Taylor's family was more into local seafood places, but she'd heard of Vitale's. It had always seemed way too fancy for her. Or, at least, too fancy for her to afford.

"I haven't eaten in the place in years," Austin said. "I took a date there once in high school. Thought it was a slick move back then."

Taylor laughed. "How'd that work out for you?"

"She liked the pasta better than the company," he said. "I was trying as hard as that restaurant to impress her. Just came off as pretentious."

Taylor couldn't imagine a pretentious version of Austin. But she could imagine him trying too hard to make sure someone else had a good time.

"Too many bad memories to go back there?"

"Nah," he said. "I just don't like the atmosphere. Give me a beer and a burger, and I'm good. I don't need Roman columns and statues hovering around my table while I eat. But they still make the best soup in the city. Hands down."

Taylor brought up a spoonful to blow on it. When the soup hit her tongue, her mouth exploded with flavor, and her eyes widened.

"You win again."

If he was going to continue introducing her to delicious things, she would happily lose every contest.

A smug, satisfied smile crept across Austin's face. She must be *really* sick because even that was cute.

"Told you," he said.

Taylor took another bite, this time with a meatball. She didn't normally care for meatballs either, but these were flavorful and comforting, just like the rest of the soup.

Unable to contain her curiosity any longer, she asked, "So, you got the autopsy report?"

"The detective called me this afternoon before I left Northshore."

"You drove back to work today?"

"Not officially. I decided to go to the first practice. The drive's just a couple hours, and it was totally worth it to see the team."

"How are they doing?"

"They look great," Austin said. "It was really good to see the kids, and Mike, the assistant coach, has been doing a great job with the tryouts and getting everything ready while I'm gone." He laughed. "They probably don't need me at all. I'm working myself out of a job here."

"I doubt that."

Taylor didn't know school employee policies or his school's attitude in particular, but what she did know was how good he must be for those kids. The way he was caring for her and worried about her, she was sure he must care for those kids the same way. Probably more so, since he barely knew her.

"What did the detective say?"

"The cause of death was definitely the fall, and they didn't find anything in his system that would make him dizzy or inebriated."

Taylor wasn't sure what to say. Even without the fever,

this would be a difficult discussion to navigate, and she wasn't sure if she should console him or interpret that as a good thing. "Does that mean he tripped?"

"Maybe," Austin said. "It's possible, but…" As his voice trailed off, his eyes drifted up and to the side, looking at the ceiling, lost in thought.

"But what?" she asked.

Austin brought his gaze and his focus back to Taylor. "He didn't have any major injuries to his hands or arms. Just the head injury and some minor bruising, but the detective said they expected him to have maybe a broken wrist or more serious bruising on an elbow. Especially at his age. Something to show that he put his arms down to block his fall."

"So he didn't realize he was falling? Is that what they're suggesting?"

"I don't know for sure," Austin said. "The lack of evidence of him trying to break his own fall *could* indicate that maybe he was pushed. That it could have happened too fast, or he was so shocked or surprised by a shove that he didn't have time for his reflexes to kick in. All they know for sure is it looks like the main blow to the back of his head took the brunt of the fall and probably knocked him out instantaneously."

Taylor suddenly felt queasy again through her chills, despite the soup doing an excellent job of warming her insides. "At least it sounds like he didn't suffer much."

Some people hated when she found the bright spot in everything, but she couldn't help it. She couldn't just sit here and swim in the grim details of a man's death without pointing out something positive. Something to hold on to with so much negative energy surrounding them.

Austin seemed to appreciate it, or at least wasn't bothered by her positivity. "They're pretty sure that first blow knocked him out, so even if he didn't die immediately he would have been unconscious and not in pain."

"I'm so sorry, Austin." Taylor put her spoon down and placed her hand on his leg.

"I'd hoped I was being ridiculous in my suspicions. That I was looking for some way to make sense of his death and seeing things that weren't there. That it was just a fall." He sighed heavily. The weight of the entire month was visible on his shoulders. "But if the detective is suspicious too, I'm right back to wondering who could have wanted to kill my uncle."

Taylor wasn't sure what to say. Last Friday night, she'd met plenty of people, all with the same motive to kill the man: money. But it didn't feel appropriate to run down that list right now.

"Are the detectives looking into it?"

Austin nodded. "The guy I spoke to said they would bring people in for interviews and maybe come by to collect more evidence. I think that's what he said. I was barely paying attention at that point."

"Understandable. That's a lot to deal with."

"And I know there are plenty of people who could profit from his death." There was a hint of resignation in his voice. "Or at least plenty of people who *think* they'll get a payout. No one knows for sure yet. I'm meeting with the attorney next week, then we'll notify beneficiaries. But even I don't know what's in the will. Uncle Kenny was private about his financial affairs."

"Wouldn't it also be somebody with access to your uncle?" Taylor took one last bite of soup and left the rest for tomorrow. "Someone who would have a reason to be in the house with him? And at the top of his stairs at that?"

"Yes, but Uncle Kenny didn't cut people off. If someone asked to come over, he'd let them in. And it's not just Zeke and my aunt and the cousins you met on Friday who are on the suspect list. Plenty of other relatives didn't weasel invites." He scoffed. "It would make more sense for anyone who had something to do with Uncle Kenny dying to *not* show their face around that house. Or anywhere around me."

Taylor still couldn't get the idea out of her head that pushing an older man down a set of stairs sounded like a very scummy, opportunistic thing to do.

A very Zeke thing to do.

She'd only met the guy briefly, but he hadn't left a great impression. Definitely seemed like the impulsive type too.

Those scammy business pitches came to mind.

"Was your uncle maybe loaning Zeke money?"

"Uncle Kenny and Zeke weren't exactly close, if that's what you're asking. But could he have loaned the guy money as a favor to my mom?" Austin shrugged. "Anything's possible."

"What about someone else? Someone that wasn't family?"

Austin ran a hand through his hair. "I talked to his best friend, Patricia, a couple of days ago. She came to pick up some things I set aside for her. Things I know uncle Kenny would want her to have. Photos & keepsakes. She was a wreck."

"I'll bet."

"She mentioned a guy I don't know. Said he came across as a bit possessive. She didn't seem to think he was a boyfriend in any official capacity, but who knows. Uncle Kenny wasn't into labels of any kind, but they still could have been close."

Austin seemed like a good judge of character, so if he was fond of his uncle, that meant a lot.

"He sounds like he was a really interesting guy. I'm sad I never had the chance to meet him."

A genuine smile formed on Austin's face. He was heart-broken, but obviously glad to have Taylor beside him. "I wish you could have met him, too. And he would be really glad that Tink's with you now."

Taylor didn't know if it was the sickness or being so close to Austin again that was making her lightheaded.

He took her hand and grabbed the blanket off the back of the couch and wrapped it around her shoulders. "I think you've had enough day." He put a hand to her head again. "Definitely a fever. Let's get you to bed."

Taylor wished she felt well enough to make some joke at that wording or to offer to take *him* to bed, but she was too exhausted to do anything but hold the blanket tight and let him care for her.

AUSTIN GUIDED Taylor into her bedroom. He left the light off and pulled back the bedsheets so she could climb in. She'd already been in her pajamas when he arrived, so he took the fluffy couch blanket from her, then pulled up the sheets and comforter.

She was obviously sick. Too sick and too tired to further object to his care or insist she didn't need his help.

"When does your roommate get home?"

"I don't remember." She slurred her words like a drunk, sleepy toddler as she settled her head on the pillow. "Two. Three. Something like that."

Austin looked down at her. She was both pale and flushed. There was no way he was leaving her alone like this.

He took a step back toward the door. "I'm getting a wet towel from the bathroom to cool you down. Then I'm camping out on your couch until she gets home."

"She'll freak if she finds a stranger in the living room."

"Then text her a heads up while I get the towel." He wasn't leaving wiggle room for her to argue anymore. She needed someone to monitor her, and he was already here and had nothing better to do. Besides, he'd be up worrying about her all night anyway if he left now.

"You don't have to—"

"I do have to," he said. "Text her. I'll be right back."

He dipped out of the dark bedroom and found the bathroom one door over. He dug around until he found a hand towel and ran it under the cold water before wringing it out and returning to Taylor's bedroom. When he approached the bed, he got a different greeting than he'd expected.

Howl.

Austin sat on the edge of the bed and placed the folded towel on Taylor's forehead. She was petting Tink, who sat against her side like a proper guardian. "You helping, big guy?"

Howl.

"He's such a good kitty." Taylor's words were even more drawn out than a moment ago.

"He is."

Austin gave Tink a pet on the head, too. Then he rubbed the damp towel gently over Taylor's forehead and cheeks and finally on her neck before flipping it over and returning it to her forehead.

Her eyes began closing.

"Sleep," he ordered. "You need to rest."

"Mmhmm."

Agreement. That was good.

Or a bad sign.

"Did you text your roommate?"

"Mmhmm," she said again. "Ellie."

"Her name is Ellie?"

"Tell her you didn't murder me and soup. She'll like you."

The words trailed off into silence as her eyes shut completely, and her jaw went slack.

Austin gave Tink one more scratch around the face. "Keep her company, buddy," he whispered. "I'll be in the living room."

Tink, as if he knew better than to wake his sick temporary person, settled in to lie down against her side and keep watch.

Satisfied the two of them were fine for now, Austin left the room to put away their soup and clean up. He planned to spend the night on the couch, or at least stay until Ellie came home, but he didn't expect he'd do much sleeping.

14

Howl.

Taylor woke to that familiar, deep-throated meow followed by gagging and retching beside her bed. She would never get her apartment deposit back after what Tink was doing to the carpet every morning.

She sat up, quickly realized she was still woozy, and paused for the room to stop spinning. Her congestion was worse this morning, and she was still weak, but she wasn't as achy as the day before. Her fever must have broken in the night.

Suddenly, she remembered.

Austin.

She tiptoed around the puke. It wasn't much, just a little liquid. Then she made her way out of the bedroom and into the living room. She was glad the fever was gone, but she still wasn't a hundred percent, and she was grateful to have the day off from work.

Instead of Austin, she found Ellie on the couch.

"Good morning, sleeping beauty."

"What time is it?" Taylor asked.

"9 AM."

Taylor scanned the kitchen and living room, then glanced down the hall. The bathroom door was open, and the light was off.

"He's long gone," Ellie said.

"He was here when you got home?"

Ellie gave a sly grin. "I can see why you would risk murder for that guy."

"There was no murder at stake."

"I know, he told me." Ellie laughed. "Apparently you told him to let me know that."

Oh, gosh. What else had she told him?

"He left after I got here," Ellie said. "I told him I could take it from here, and he could take the next shift."

"No one needs to take shifts with me."

"Austin seemed to think so. And the fact that you ate *soup* last night tells me he was right."

Taylor ignored that and sat beside Ellie on the couch. "What do you think?"

"About you eating soup?"

"About Austin."

"Definitely handsome," Ellie said. "*Definitely* charming. Definitely gets the seal of approval."

"I thought we weren't giving the seal of approval just based on charm and good looks anymore."

"Handsome and charming are side notes. The seal of approval is because he ran over here to take care of you."

Taylor couldn't help grinning. "That was pretty sweet of him, right?"

"Indeed," Ellie confirmed. "Did anything interesting happen besides soup eating?"

"He got to see Tink again." Taylor remembered. "Tink. He threw up just before I came out here."

"I got it. You rest." Ellie headed to the kitchen for paper towels and cleaning spray.

"Hey, can you hand me my laptop?"

Ellie grabbed the computer from the table and handed it to Taylor as she walked by. "Is it a lot of puke? Hairball?"

"Just a little liquid," Taylor said. "Liz told me I can take him in for bloodwork if I'm concerned."

"Might need to. He keeps doing it every morning, so we probably want to check that out. Although it's not an emergency if it's just a little bit."

Taylor opened the laptop and checked her email while she put her feet on the coffee table. Then she opened the search engine and typed a name. A name she couldn't stop thinking about since Austin told her about the autopsy last night. It was the one thing she remembered clearly from their conversation.

A few minutes later, Ellie returned to throw the paper towels in the trash can and put the supplies away. Then she sat beside Taylor on the couch and peered over her shoulder.

"Who's Zeke?"

Taylor stared at the search bar, trying to remember if she'd heard Zeke's last name mentioned. Champagne was Austin's last name. And his mom's. But she didn't know what Zeke's last name was.

"Austin's mom's boyfriend." Taylor remembered the local high school they went to and that Zeke and Austin had both played baseball. She took a chance and strung together what she knew.

"Sounds juicy."

"Yup." Taylor squinted at the screen and scanned through the search results. She found a list of players from a year when Austin was on the team. "Bingo."

She clicked the link and found a Zeke Fournet on the list. She copied the name and put it in the search bar.

When a photo of him popped up, Ellie asked, "Why are we looking at this guy?"

Taylor wasn't sure how to answer. She only knew Zeke was scummy as heck, and he was likely guilty of *something*. Knowing now that someone probably pushed Austin's uncle... well, Zeke seemed the most obvious suspect. "The detective thinks Austin's uncle might have been murdered. Or at least that he didn't trip and fall and die on his own. I was hoping to find something that could tie this guy to Austin's uncle. Something shady."

"But why are you looking up this guy like some kind of cyber crimes prodigy instead of the actual people who get paid to do this shit?"

"Because I'm sick and have nothing better to do today?"

Ellie narrowed her eyes and nodded in approval. "Fair enough."

"Does that mean you'll help me make sense of this? Because I'm still a little fuzzy-headed."

Ellie thought for a minute, then said, "Only if I get to watch you eat some of that soup. Because I don't believe it."

"It's actually really good," Taylor said. "Or maybe I was fever delusional."

"Only one way to find out." She stood and headed to the kitchen.

"For breakfast?"

"Why not?"

"Fine," Taylor said. "Promise you'll help me dig up dirt on this guy if I eat breakfast soup?"

"Promise."

Taylor nodded and looked back at the screen. "Then it's a deal."

AUSTIN SAT on the bright red bar stool in front of his laptop and typed the name of the man Patricia mentioned on Monday. Scoping this guy out was probably a waste of time, but he needed something to get his mind off Taylor.

She'd looked so awful the night before, and he worried about how she was doing. He knew her roommate would take good care of her. Ellie had seemed nice, and she was a vet tech like Taylor. That apartment was overflowing with caring capacity. But he still couldn't help wondering if Taylor had woken up feeling better or worse or if her fever had spiked even higher after he'd left.

It was midday now, but he didn't want to call and wake her if she was sleeping this off, so digging up dirt on Brandon Wiltz was a better option than checking his messages again for the five millionth time that afternoon.

Brandon Wiltz.

The most likely result was a local corporate attorney. After a quick scan of the guy's bio and some news articles mentioning companies he'd worked for, nothing leaped out at Austin as suspicious. The guy even looked like he had an honest face. Or maybe Austin was too trusting of honest faces. It wouldn't be the first time. In his defense, no one in his family had an honest face, so he jumped straight to trust when he found one.

But perhaps his credible appearance itself was the red flag. A corporate attorney was probably used to rules and order and things going expected ways. Not the chaos that was Uncle Kenny's retired life.

Austin did some image search scrolling and found a photo of Brandon and his uncle posing together at a Krewe of Apollo ball last summer. It was clear they'd at least known each other for a while.

Maybe Patricia was wrong about Brandon.

Or her instincts were right, and Brandon had grown tired of Uncle Kenny's noncommittal style.

Austin's phone rang beside him as his mother's name lit up the screen.

"Hello."

Austin tried to mask his anticipatory annoyance, but the last thing he wanted to do right now was fend off another dinner invitation. He'd actually enjoyed Friday night, but only because Taylor had been with him. And he didn't want to drag her back into that viper den so soon.

So soon?

This wouldn't be a dinners-with-the-family relationship. It wouldn't be any kind of relationship at all. It couldn't be.

Except he had a sinking suspicion it already was.

"Austin, I need you to go to the police station for me."

That got his attention.

"What for? Are you okay?"

"I'm fine." But her annoyance came through loud and clear. "I can't very well be seen at that place myself, now can I?"

Fear and panic morphed into situation analysis. He was used to interpreting his mother's underlying meanings, but he wasn't used to police involvement.

His mind immediately jumped to his uncle's case. But the detective would have called Austin first, not his mother, if they'd found more information.

Austin sighed. "What do you need *me* to go to the police station for?"

"I need you to pick up Zeke." It was her turn to sigh. "He's been arrested."

15

By noon, Taylor had enough of digging up Zeke dirt. Ellie had long ago called it quits and went to sleep off last night's shift, leaving Taylor alone to create a doc to capturing everything she could find about the guy since high school.

In the ten years since his "glory days" of high school athletics, there wasn't much to find. Then recently, he started showing up on Melinda's arm in society article photos. One photo even mistakenly captioned him as Austin.

Austin must have *loved* that.

Then again, maybe he hadn't seen it. Taylor doubted he kept up with articles on Lafayette's elite while he was living on the Northshore. It sounded like he'd moved there partly to get away from that stuff.

Crap. Austin.

She grabbed her phone and sent a quick text.

Thanks for the soup. It made an excellent breakfast. And I appreciate you looking out for me.

A few moments later, she got a text back asking how she was feeling today.

Better. Fever broke. Just tired and cruddy now.

He replied with one word, *rest*, and a heart emoji.

Taylor ignored her own fluttering heart, insisting that it could function without Austin for a day, and went back to organizing and analyzing her research. Zeke's company had started up not long after he showed up on the society radar with Melinda.

And Zeke wasn't kidding. The company sold celery *essence* capsules. That couldn't possibly be legit.

And she wasn't the only one who thought so. There were complaints, a lawsuit, and an FDA investigation. Taylor wasn't entirely sure how to navigate those legal searches, but it didn't look good for the future of Zeke's company.

Which kept him squarely on top of the suspect list. At the very least, the guy would need lawyer money.

Taylor put her laptop on the coffee table and turned sideways to lie on the couch. Okay, fine. She was still sick. Her core muscles refused to hold her upright any longer, even though she wasn't doing anything more strenuous than sitting.

She closed her eyes and tried to remember what else she'd done yesterday besides getting tucked into bed by Austin. That was the only fact her brain wanted to latch onto.

The shelter.

She remembered going to the shelter after her shift at the clinic. She'd met with Sierra and Liz. Got the supply list approved. Talked about Tink throwing up and made a plan to get him checked out if he continued.

Oh! The fundraiser. That's right. She had promised to help them find a photographer.

Taylor sighed and grabbed her phone again. She couldn't do much of anything else now, so she might as well get this over with.

She considered sending a text, but it was twelve twenty.

Right in the middle of Geena's lunch break, which she took at the same time every day, like clockwork.

"What's wrong?"

"Nothing's wrong," Taylor said. "Just calling to say hi."

"One, you never call me. Especially not in the middle of a workweek. And two, you sound like shit, so you're a liar with a problem. Spill it. Are you sick? You sound rough."

Geena was the one who was a little rough around the edges, but it was part of what made her good at everything she did. She was focused and driven, and if you needed stuff done, you wanted Geena in your corner.

"It's just a cold," Taylor said. "And I've got people looking out for me, so I'm good."

"People? Your roommate is a person. Who else is looking out for you? Tell me that asshole isn't over there."

Taylor had regretted telling her sister about the situation with her boss from the moment the words slipped out a couple of weeks ago. Geena had been right about him from the start, and she was right to worry about Taylor. Despite their differences, Geena seemed to care about her sister. Her bedside manner, however, wasn't spectacular.

"No," Taylor said. "I assume you mean Jason, and no. Absolutely not. You'll be happy to know I quit that job."

"I didn't think you'd go through with it. Good. I'm proud of you. He was the worst."

"Agreed." It was one of the few things they agreed on. In hindsight, at least.

"Did you find a new job yet?"

"Yes. I've got next week left at the clinic, but I've already started working for a brand new animal shelter in Breaux Bridge."

"In Breaux Bridge?" Geena sounded appalled, as Taylor should have expected from her snobby sister. "Couldn't you find anything locally?"

"It's less than half an hour from my apartment," Taylor said. "I like what they're doing. The people starting it are great. And I like the idea of helping them build something from the ground up. Plus, doing a lot of good with the whole rescue thing."

"That does sound very *you*." Geena at least tried to hide the disgust in her voice, but failed miserably, as usual.

"Speaking of the shelter..."

"See? I knew there was a reason you called."

Taylor ignored that comment and continued with her request, only because she'd promised Liz and Sierra. "They're having a fundraiser."

"Like a dinner? Auction? That could be fun. Sign me up for a plate or whatever. Just let me know how much, and I'll talk Ricky into coming with me."

"It isn't that kind of event," Taylor said. "You still have your camera, right?"

There was a long, agitated pause. "Yes. Why?"

"They're looking for someone to take portraits. Of dogs. And maybe their people with them."

"For promo for the fundraiser?"

"Um, no. That is the fundraiser," Taylor said. "They're selling portrait packages."

"Like a Sears studio?"

"Maybe? I don't know exactly. I just know they're looking for a photographer to help out, and I promised them I'd ask you."

"Oh my gosh, Taylor. What makes you think I would do this?"

Taylor channeled her most sympathetic voice. "Because it's for the *animals*?"

"Animals are smelly and dirty and *shed*. Animals are *your* thing. Not mine."

"So you'll consider it?"

"Taylor."

"Pleeeeaaaase. Do it for me, then. I like this place and want to help as much as I can to make the shelter amazing. Did I mention I'm going to head the vet clinic there? I mean, I'll be the only vet staff, so we'll be limited, but still. I get to set it up from scratch and run it myself."

"Really?" Geena's tone softened a bit. "That does sound good. I'm happy for you."

"So you'll do it then? For me? Pretty please?"

After another long pause, Gena sighed. "Fine. I'll *consider* it. If it fits with my schedule. Send me the date and details, and I'll see what I can do."

Taylor squealed, then fell into a coughing fit. Somehow, she forced out, "Thank you!"

"You sound awful," Geena said. "And you never said who 'people' referred to. Please tell me there's no new loser."

"He's not a loser."

Taylor closed her eyes and grimaced, but all that did was pop up an image of Geena grinning like an animal poised to lock onto its prey.

"Spill it," Geena said.

"His name is Austin. I think you'd like him." Austin was a sports guy who came from money. Actually, he was probably more Geena's type than Taylor's. "I met him at the shelter, and I'm fostering the cat he brought in."

"Jeez, Taylor."

That was not the expected response. Taylor thought she'd pitched this guy pretty well. "What's wrong with that?"

"You fell for a guy who needed something from you."

"He's not using me, if that's what you're implying," Taylor said. "He'd already signed over the cat before I offered to foster it. Austin didn't even know. And he asked me out after that."

Geena grunted. "What does he do?"

That was always Geena's question. Not *is he nice?* Not *does he treat you well?*

No. Geena wants to know, *what does he* do?

"He's a high school baseball coach."

Another grunt. "That doesn't sound awful. Poor, over-worked teacher isn't my thing, but definitely up your alley. What's the catch?"

"Why does there have to be a catch?" When Geena didn't take the bait, Taylor said, "He lives on the Northshore. He's only in town to handle his uncle's estate. His family is from here."

"Long-distance *sucks.*"

"I know. This isn't a long-term thing."

Immediately, her heart kicked up a notch, forcing Taylor to acknowledge the lie. She hadn't meant to fall for this guy, but here she was.

She blamed the soup.

"Have you told him about the boss thing yet?"

The thought sent a wave of nausea rolling through her body. "He doesn't need to know that."

"No, but you don't exactly have the best track record with picking winners," Geena said. "If you tell him about that and he gets weird, then you'll know not to waste time or energy on him. Certainly would save you the pain of dragging out the whole long-distance thing."

"I'm not telling him that," Taylor insisted. But as the words escaped her mouth, her brain caught up to the conversation and proposed that Geena might be on to something. Not that she was exactly on the mark, but that maybe she and Austin didn't know each other all that well, and a serious conversation was due. "Not now, at least."

The thought terrified her and filled her with embarrassment, but she couldn't evict the idea from her mind.

"My lunch is almost over," Geena said. "Don't go outside

today. It's freezing. Are you sure you're okay? I can swing by after work and check on you or bring anything you need."

"Thanks, but Ellie's here and off today. I've still got some of the soup left that Austin brought last night."

"*Soup?*" Geena cackled. "This really is serious if the man got you to eat soup. When can I meet him?"

"Don't you have to get back to work?"

"I do, but we'll continue this. Get some rest, and I'll check on you later."

"Okay. Promise me you'll consider the fundraiser?"

"Promise. Send me the details."

The call ended, and Taylor immediately sent a message to Liz. The request had gone better than Taylor had expected. She only hoped Geena wouldn't change her mind over the next few hours or days.

AUSTIN PICKED at the skin on the side of his thumb while he sat in a small metal and plastic chair. Cops in and out of uniform bustled around the front of the station. It smelled like ammonia and coffee and last night's drunks in the waiting area.

He'd been there for twenty minutes already, and the person at the desk told him Zeke should be out any minute.

Thankfully, Austin had heard from Taylor shortly after he got there, so that was one less thing for him to worry about. Her roommate, Ellie, assured him she'd be there all day, but he'd still wanted to know if Taylor was better or worse today. He'd check in with her again, but hearing that her fever had broken was a weight off his mind for now.

A few minutes later, Zeke walked out from the back. A police officer followed behind him, stopping to hand papers to the guy at the desk. Zeke looked like he hadn't slept in a week, and his hair was as rumpled as his black T-shirt and jeans.

If he relaxed his eyes and dropped his burning hatred for a second, he could see the same Zeke that he used to walk to the field with after seventh period. The same guy who annoyed the hell out of him, even back then, but who he could tolerate for brief spells. Long enough to grab pizza with after a game, at least.

But despite the clothes and hungover expression, this wasn't that same teenager. This Zeke had bags and crow's feet around his eyes. And he didn't look like he would crack "your mom" jokes any time soon.

Without a word, Zeke followed Austin outside into the bitterly cold air. He felt bad for not realizing the guy wouldn't have a jacket, but it was a short walk to his car, and the inside warmed up quick enough.

They drove in silence through downtown, and it wasn't until the next red light after that before Zeke spoke. "It was just weed, man."

"I didn't ask. Don't need to know."

"I know you know what the charge was," Zeke continued. "I want you to know it wasn't for anything worse than that. I just bought from the wrong guy. Undercover cop was after my guy. I didn't give him up, though."

"How noble of you."

"Don't be like that."

"I'm the one picking you up from jail as a favor for my *mother*," Austin said. "I get to be like however I want."

Zeke raised his hands in defense. "All right, all right. Fair."

"Don't worry. Mom will get the charges dropped, anyway."

Not that Austin knew personally how that worked, but he figured his mother knew enough people and had amassed enough favors over the years to get that done. If it was indeed just pot charges, like Zeke said.

"If she doesn't, my dad will." Zeke scoffed. "Can't have me tarnishing the family's *reputation*."

He said the word with such venom that Austin couldn't help remembering Zeke's dad at some of their games. Not many, but enough to leave an impression. And not a good one. The guy never had a nice thing to say. About his son or the team or the coach or anyone.

"I know you don't approve of me and Melinda," he continued. "I get it."

Oh, jeez. Not this conversation. They'd been avoiding this conversation for the past year. Why did they have to end that streak now?

"We don't have to talk about this," Austin said.

"Like you said, you picked me up from the police station. I kind of owe you."

"Talking about you and my mom isn't how I want any favor repaid. Ever."

"Well, maybe I need to say this."

Zeke slumped in the passenger seat, utterly defeated. Austin almost felt sorry for him.

Almost.

"Melinda's always been nice to me."

Austin cringed at the use of his mother's first name. Plenty of people used it around him, but it sounded wrong coming out of Zeke's mouth.

"I know you think I'm a joke," Zeke continued. "Hell, everyone thinks I'm a joke. My own family always did. That's why I figure I might as well beat people to the punchline. Give 'em what they expect. It's easier that way."

Jeez. He did not need sob story Zeke stinking up his car with pity vibes. He just wanted to pick this guy up, drop him off, and pretend none of this ever happened.

"That's how we met, you know. At some gala thing my folks insisted I attend for them while they were off at some other bullshit. I was cracking jokes like always, and I made her laugh. This totally in-control ice queen lost it over some ridiculous joke I made. I don't even remember what I said, just the sound of that laugh. It was like a drug, man. I was hooked."

Austin tried imagining his mother letting out anything other than a well-controlled chuckle in public. He couldn't.

He couldn't even remember if his dad had ever made her laugh. He'd died when Austin was a kid. It sucked, but he tried not to think about how losing him must have sucked even more for his mom. Thinking about that hurt too much.

So if she got a little enjoyment from being around this clown, who was Austin to judge?

He was going to have to cut them some slack, wasn't he?

"It's not just the jokes, I swear," Zeke said. "I'm not some court jester."

"I never said you were."

He'd sure as hell thought it, but Austin had been careful not to say it out loud. Not to either of them, at least.

"It's the whole control thing, man. She doesn't have to be like that around me. She's honest and lets her guard down, and I listen. I like feeling important to somebody that way, you know?"

Yeah, Austin knew.

He just didn't guess *that* was what was going on behind the scenes.

Honesty. Huh. He never would have guessed that would be the glue holding those two together. But it was important, and so many relationships lacked it. Even his own.

For all he valued honesty, he wasn't being upfront with Taylor about their relationship at all. Sure, he hadn't promised anything, but they also hadn't discussed where their relationship was heading. They hadn't talked about the fact that he'd be leaving soon and what that would mean for them.

They definitely needed to sit down and have that talk. Once Taylor felt better, of course. And he couldn't believe he might have Zeke, of all people, to thank for pushing him to do that.

"I'm the only person on this planet, besides you maybe, who isn't looking to get something from her. I don't want or need her money."

"Zeke, I'm gonna call bullshit on that right there." Austin turned into his mom's neighborhood. Her orders had been to bring him there, not Zeke's apartment. Probably to discuss how she would make this all go away if he could figure out how to lie low. "Didn't she front the start-up cash for your little scam?"

"Stop calling it a scam," Zeke said. "And yes, but I didn't ask her to. It was a gift. Because she believes in me. Whether or not *you* believe that."

He didn't.

But maybe he should.

Zeke had no reason to lie right now, and he sure as hell didn't look like he was. Maybe this is what his mom saw. A broken guy who was just looking for honesty and respect, who made her laugh and didn't ask for anything in return.

Crap.

He did not want to end up liking Zeke.

"Since we're being honest and all," Austin said, "I want to ask you something, and I need a straight answer."

"Okay, shoot."

Austin pulled into the driveway and put the car in park. "Did my uncle give you money? Or loan you any?"

Zeke turned to look at Austin with a shocked expression on his face and confusion in his eyes. He wasn't that good of an actor, so Austin figured that was his answer before Zeke even spoke.

"No, man. Never. I told you, I didn't want their money."

"I know what you said, but I had to ask."

Zeke narrowed his eyes. "Why are you asking that?"

"Don't worry about it," Austin said. "And we never had this conversation."

Zeke looked confused still, but nodded. "All right, man. But if I can help—"

"You'd better get in there."

Zeke looked at the house for a second, then got out of the car. "Thanks for the ride."

Austin watched him use his own key in the door. A weird sight, but one that made a lot more sense after that conversation.

He wasn't sure if he could trust the guy, and he couldn't completely rule him out on his uncle's death. Not just yet. At least, not until he looked over the accounts and got a copy of the will.

He never thought he'd think this, but now he really hoped nothing pointed to Zeke as the killer.

owntown Breaux Bridge hummed with walking traffic Sunday morning when Taylor found a parking spot and crossed Main Street. The tiny corner restaurant she was looking for sat at the end of a strip of antique shops, galleries, and a coffee shop. It was a quaint, touristy little restaurant, and Cajun music slammed into her the moment she pulled open the dark wooden door.

Taylor warmed her hands together as she scanned the tables. In a back corner, she spotted Sierra and Liz conspiring over an array of papers scattered over a red checkered tablecloth.

"Hey there!" Liz gestured across the table. "Have a seat."

"Hope y'all haven't been waiting long for me." Taylor thought she'd left early enough, but she hadn't accounted for the few extra minutes it would take to park and walk to the restaurant.

"You're right on time," Liz assured her.

"We got here early." Sierra aimed a thumb at her friend and business partner. "This one wanted to get a head start."

Taylor hung her coat on the back of the tall wooden chair and sat. "I'm really excited to see what y'all have planned."

They'd called her the night before to ask if she wanted to go over the fundraiser plans with them, and they thought having the meeting here instead of at the shelter would be fun. Taylor couldn't argue with that. She'd take a lunch business meeting any day.

"Glad you could make it," said Liz. "Looking forward to your input."

"You sure look better than when we saw you Wednesday," Sierra said.

"Dang it, Sierra."

"What? She does!"

"You don't have to say it like that though."

"It's fine," Taylor said. "And I feel much better. Thanks."

She hadn't run fever since that night, and after spending all of Thursday resting on the couch, she felt well enough to go to work Friday. By Saturday, she was tired but okay, and today she felt back to normal. Austin was right. That really was magic soup.

"Great!" Liz placed her palms on the papers on the table. "Because we've got a lot to throw at you."

"First up, photographer," Sierra said. "Any luck?"

Taylor had almost forgotten about the conversation with her sister after the last few hazy days. "I think she might do it if the date works with her schedule. But she doesn't have kids, so her weekends are usually flexible."

"Then let's start with nailing down that date, so you can get a commitment from her," Liz said. "That'll be the biggest piece to all of this."

"We're thinking next month," Sierra said.

"Is that enough time?" Taylor didn't know how long setup for an event like this would take, or how much setup was involved. But a month sounded like not enough. Especially with all the other work they were doing to get the shelter up and running.

Liz laughed. "A month is practically a year in animal rescue time. For this though, we mostly need time to promote and get people to sign up."

"How do you like Valentine's Day?" Sierra asked.

"In theory or for this?" Taylor asked. "Either way, I love it."

"It falls on a Sunday this year, so we're thinking about the Saturday afternoon right before the holiday," Liz said. "We could decorate with the whole theme. Use props."

Sierra put a finger in the air. "*No* costumes."

"Costumes at the owner's insistence only," Liz said as a compromise.

Sierra grumbled, "Fine," and broke off a hunk of French bread from the napkin-covered basket in the center of the table. She held up her chunk and butter knife. "Want some?"

"Not yet, thanks." Taylor was starving, but she wanted to focus on all the information in front of her first. She pulled up her calendar app and gasped. "Wait, that's only three weeks away."

"Well then, we'd better get this rolling," Liz said, completely unflustered by the timeline. "Text that sister of yours to see if she's free to help that day."

Taylor did as commanded and sent a quick text to her sister with the proposed date. A moment later, she got a response. "She wants to know what time that day."

"Still working on that," Liz said. "I'm guessing most of the afternoon and whatever time she needs to set up."

Through a mouthful of bread, Sierra chimed in. "Tell her we'll feed her."

"She's not worried about food, I promise." Geena would bring a smoothie or something healthy to keep her going, no doubt. Taylor sent the information, then she panicked as she waited for the response. What if Geena and Ricky had Valentine's weekend plans? They'd probably want to go out on Saturday instead of Sunday, knowing them.

But her worries were appeased a few moments later with Geena's reply.

Fine. I'll do it. For YOU. Let me know when I can see the location to plan for lighting.

"She's in!"

Liz clapped her hands. "Hot damn!"

The elderly couple at the next table was not amused. But when the old woman turned up her nose and opened her mouth to say something, Sierra shot them a glare, and they went back to sipping their gumbo or bisque or whatever they had in their small white cups.

"Sweet," said Sierra. "*Now* can we order?"

They examined the gigantic plastic-covered menus, while Liz insisted multiple times that Taylor should order anything she wanted. This was their treat. The problem was that everything sounded delicious, and Taylor's stomach growled in agreement. She hadn't eaten much the last few days while she recovered from her illness. But she didn't want to go wild on ordering, no matter what Liz said.

The seafood gumbo sounded yummy, but Taylor had enough of soup-like foods for the next several months. She ordered the fried shrimp and hoped the potato salad tasted as good as it looked on the tray a waiter passed with for another table.

Once everyone ordered, she pointed at one paper near Liz. "Are these the promotional materials?"

Liz slid it towards her. "My friend sent these screenshots so we could all see what the posts and event page will look like once we finalize the time and details."

The graphics were adorable. They used stock photos of the cutest dogs in fancy poses, and the text and fonts looked great to Taylor. Not that she knew anything about that stuff. All she knew was that it was all very professional-looking, but also fun and inviting.

"Love it. I think lots of people will sign up for this." Taylor's eyes landed on the location details. "I thought you said you had a place in Lafayette you were using?"

"If we can get it ship-shape, the shelter will be a much better option," Sierra said. "Parking, setup, atmosphere."

"I wasn't sure we could pull off the construction work in time, but we're making good progress out there, so it'd be nice to show off the place," Liz said. "We can introduce ourselves and give tours. It'll be great."

"Assuming the skunks don't make an appearance," Sierra added.

That did sound great. Three weeks wasn't long, but if anyone could pull this together, it was these two women.

"Wait, did you say skunks? As in more than one?"

Liz nodded. "A whole family it looks like."

"Can we... I don't know," Taylor said. "Relocate them?"

Sierra scoffed. "Skunks gonna skunk. No way around that."

Taylor had learned that Sierra was still working part time as a naturalist, so she figured this was her department. If there was a way to get the skunks out before the event, Sierra would figure it out.

"We can decorate it for Valentine's Day," Taylor added.

Sierra chuckled. "That sounds like a you thing."

"If you want to head that up," Liz said, "knock yourself out. Go hearts wild."

Taylor clapped excitedly. "Okay, I'm loving all of this."

Liz and Sierra exchanged a knowing look. Liz said, "We had a feeling you would. In case we haven't mentioned it recently, we're really glad to have you on the team."

"I'm glad to be on the team."

"How's that foster of yours doing?" Sierra asked.

"Tink's doing great," she said. "He's warmed up to me and my roommate and is pretty relaxed in most of the apartment now. He's going to make a perfect cat for someone."

"Still puking?" Liz asked.

"Just a little, and just early in the morning," Taylor said. "It's weird. But since he's still doing it, I'm going to take him to my other job this week, probably tomorrow, to run a senior panel on him."

Liz nodded. "Sounds good. Give them my number, and I'll handle the payment."

"Thanks," said Taylor.

The waiter arrived and placed their plates in front of each of them. Everything smelled delicious.

Taylor's cell dinged as she grabbed her fork to test out that potato salad. She flipped the phone over, expecting to find another text from her sister, but it was Austin.

"What is *that* face for?" Sierra asked. "Or *who?*"

"Stop being so nosy," Liz said.

"It's the guy that dropped off Tink," Taylor said, still staring at the phone. "Austin."

"You and Austin are texting buddies now, huh?" Sierra had a teasing tone to her voice. Liz didn't chastise her this time, though, since she was equally interested in the answer.

"He came over while I was sick this week."

"This is a real thing?" Sierra asked. "Not just a thing I made up in my head?"

"He took care of you while you were sick, *and* he's cute?" Liz nodded in approval. "That one is a keeper for sure."

Taylor couldn't hide the grin on her face. "I had dinner with him last weekend too."

"Oh, that's right," Liz said. "Wait, wasn't it dinner with his mother or something wild like that?"

"With a bunch of his family, actually. It was… interesting."

She figured she'd leave it at that. Didn't think she should get into the whole murdered uncle thing. They hadn't seemed too happy about her getting involved the last time she mentioned her suspicion, so she kept quiet on the rest of the details.

"What are you waiting for?" Sierra asked. "Text him back."

"He wants to hang out this afternoon."

After the conversation with her sister Thursday, Taylor couldn't shake the thought that maybe she and Austin needed to have a talk about where this relationship was going. She didn't want to, but they had to eventually, she figured. She was falling hard for this guy, and at some point, she had to trust her instincts and be honest with him about her past and their future.

Maybe this afternoon was as good a time as any for that.

Liz pointed a fork at her. "Then you'd better eat fast."

"Yes," Sierra agreed. "And we'll be expecting a full report."

17

The hood of Austin's car was warm beneath his jeans. Coupled with the sunshine and rising temperatures, the late January Sunday afternoon felt almost springlike. Austin could wait as long as necessary out there and be perfectly happy.

Okay, that was a lie.

With every second that passed, he grew more anxious as he waited for Taylor to appear on the steps. She'd told him to wait for her outside, and she refused to take questions on the matter.

Austin had checked on her twice each day since he'd sat with her through that fever. She'd sworn she felt much better after that first day, and the energy returning to her voice, along with her more cheerful emoji selections, confirmed that. He didn't think Taylor would outright lie to him about anything, but she had certainly proven she'd soldier on and try not to bother anyone until she ended up in the hospital.

The second-floor door opened and Taylor exited, locking the door behind her. She was carrying something in her arms, but Austin couldn't see what it was until she reached the stairs.

Tink.

Taylor cradled the big furry bundle against her body as she descended, taking one carefully placed step after another until she stood in front of Austin. She wore navy leggings and a white, oversized long-sleeved T-shirt with a rainbow stripe encircling each arm. Her blonde hair was slicked back neatly in a ponytail, and she had a huge grin on her face.

"Surprised?"

Austin returned the smile. "The best surprise. But do you think he'll actually walk with us?"

While Tink had always been friendly with him, Austin knew he wasn't an acceptable replacement for his uncle.

"Pretty sure." Taylor held up her arms and turned to aim the cat at him. "I found an almost matching harness and leash, so I've been testing it out and taking him for little walks around the complex. He seems to approve."

She was clearly proud of the surprise. As she should be.

Austin felt a surge of gratitude that he'd found her and that rescue. He couldn't imagine a better place for Tink to have landed.

He scratched Tink's head and inspected the leash. It was almost identical to the one he remembered. A slightly different shade of purple and no red trim with rounded rhinestones instead of heart-shaped ones. But Tink didn't mind the difference.

"Do you want to hit up the park where you'd pass the two of them?"

"If you're up for that?" She snuggled Tink and looked up at Austin with big, brown, hope-filled eyes. Eyes he couldn't say no to if he wanted to. And he very much wanted this.

He held an arm in front of him. "Lead the way."

Taylor cut through the apartment complex, Tink in arms,

with Austin sticking close beside them. He couldn't shake the feeling that they were a little family taking their cat kid out for a Sunday stroll through the park.

"He seems to be doing better." Austin took another look at Tink and couldn't help smiling. The big guy looked perfectly content in Taylor's arms. So content there that Austin was slightly jealous. Tink's eyes were alert, though. He took in every building and car with interest, but he didn't seem frightened.

"He's doing great." Taylor lifted the cat and kissed the top of his head. "But since he's still hacking up a bit of nothing in the mornings, I'm going to bring him to work with me tomorrow for a blood draw. Just to be safe and check everything out."

His worry kicked up again. Taylor wasn't overly concerned, but what if something really was wrong with Tink? Austin couldn't handle losing him, too. Not so soon.

"Thanks for taking such good care of him," Austin said. "It helps to know he's in the best possible hands."

They reached the back of the complex and a long, narrow park stretched out before them. The Vermilion River bordered one side of the park with a fence and walking path running alongside it.

"Is this where you'd usually pass them?"

She nodded toward the opposite end. "I'd cross them as they'd walk from that direction."

Austin looked ahead and realized that he was staring at the back of his uncle's neighborhood. Uncle Kenny's house was only a block away from the other end of this park. He hadn't known just how close he'd been to Taylor this whole time. The drive through the neighborhood and around a few blocks had messed up his direction and distance sense. He could easily have walked to meet her here.

The weather was gorgeous. It was almost sixty degrees,

which was warm even for South Louisiana in late January, and the sky was all sunshine and puffy clouds on a crisp blue palette. A few kids ran around the grassy open space, chasing each other and an eager-to-please puppy. There was a small climbing play set with slides and a couple swings at the far end of the park, but this half was mostly filled with families and couples sprawled out on blankets to enjoy the beautiful day.

Taylor continued to grip the leash with one hand as she gently placed Tink on the sidewalk. He sniffed the ground and squinted while he rotated his head, taking in the sights and smells of the park. When he felt satisfied with his recognition of the familiar surroundings and their safety, he began walking down the pathway.

Austin couldn't believe it.

The cat really walked on a leash.

Not that he'd doubted Taylor's story or the idea that his uncle walked his cat regularly. It was just one of those things he had to see to truly understand.

People gave strange looks while others giggled and waved and pointed as they passed the trio. Tink didn't notice the extra attention, though. He continued on his way. A cat on a mission.

"How has your weekend been?"

"Good. Busy, but good." He realized he hadn't told her any of the stuff that had been going on that week. He'd wanted her focused on getting better, not on his problems. "Zeke got arrested."

She stumbled with the surprise of the information, but Tink didn't allow for any dawdling. She recovered quickly, and they continued down the path. "For what?"

"Minor drug stuff. Mom will make it go away if she hasn't already."

"Oh." Taylor almost sounded disappointed. He understood the instinct to assume Zeke would get nailed for something bigger and scammier.

She convinced Tink to pause briefly while a little girl admired him. The big guy even sat politely while the kid pet him. It really was a marvel to witness.

When the girl's parents urged her to return to their blanket in the grass nearby, Tink stood and was ready to continue. But Taylor hesitated, looking at how far they'd come. "Should we go back? I don't want to overdo it on his first walk out with me."

Austin turned around with the two of them as they headed back toward her apartment complex. "Want to hear the best part?"

"There's a best part?"

"I had to pick him up from the police station."

Taylor slapped a hand to her mouth, then pulled it away to gasp, "No."

He nodded. "It was an enlightening car ride."

"As in villain confession monologue interesting?"

"Nope." Austin laughed. "That would be convenient, but mostly he talked about his relationship with my mom."

He had to force the word "relationship" out like a hairball.

"That sounds more uncomfortable than interesting."

"It was," Austin said. "But after talking to him, I don't want to think he had anything to do with Uncle Kenny's death."

In fact, he hadn't stopped thinking about that since Thursday. He'd twisted everything fifty different ways to shove Zeke back in the suspect mix, but he just couldn't. The guy didn't seem motivated enough to do anything but make Austin's mom laugh, much less execute a whole murder.

"Well, I still don't like the guy."

"Don't blame you," Austin said.

"You think it was one of the other relatives? Someone I met last Friday?"

"Maybe." Austin had decided not to tell her about the attempted break-in or the new security system he installed. No point worrying her about that. But if that and his uncle's death were connected, then that ruled out someone at the dinner party. "I'm meeting with the attorney tomorrow to go over the will, so that might help clear things up too. And I saw Uncle Kenny's best friend the other day. She mentioned a guy I'd never heard of named Brandon. I don't know if he's got anything to do with this, but I'm not ruling him out yet either."

Tink paused to stare at a family of ducks floating by on the river. When Taylor tried to coax him to continue, he refused to budge. Austin offered to carry him back, but Taylor scooped him up and insisted she was fine with the job.

"What about you?" he asked. "You said you had a rescue meeting earlier, right? How'd that go?"

"Great. We're working on a fundraiser. It'll be a portrait studio thing at the shelter where people can take photos of their pets. We'll get to show off the new place and raise some money for more supplies and operations and vet care once we're up and running soon."

"That sounds amazing."

"Yeah, except my sister is going to be the photographer."

"And that's a bad thing?"

"Remember our bet about who had the worse family?" She shifted Tink's weight to a more comfortable position as they entered the back of the apartment complex. "You haven't met my sister yet."

He laughed. "She can't be worse than my mother. Or Zeke."

"Technically Zeke isn't family, so you don't get to stack

the deck with him." She gave him a sly smile. "And she might not rival your mother, but I'd bet money the two of them would get along swimmingly."

"I'm not taking that bet. When is the event?"

"The day before Valentine's Day."

They continued up the stairs, but there was a noticeable, bloated pause in the conversation. The awkwardness of that holiday was always a weight on any new relationship, but in this case, Austin felt especially pressured to address it. And not in a way he normally might. The promise of flowers and chocolates and a fancy dinner couldn't erase his leaving soon. Hell, he didn't even know if he'd still be in town three weeks from now. He hoped not.

Or had that changed?

They reached the top of the stairs, and Taylor turned toward him as she struggled to dig her keys from her pocket while balancing Tink on one arm. "Do you want to come inside for a bit?"

An unsettling buzzing sensation ripped through his nervous system. He knew what he had to do. He just didn't want to do it.

But this was as good a time as any to have the conversation he'd been putting off for too long.

"We should probably talk."

Taylor blinked at him several times. Then she looked at the door handle and back at Austin. "Ellie's home. Let me put Tink inside, and we can sit out here to talk on the steps."

He waited while she disappeared inside the apartment and returned a few moments later without Tink. He sat on the top step and wiped his sweaty palms on his jean thighs.

"Is everything okay?" Her voice had a slight shakiness to it.

"Yeah, sorry. Don't mean to scare you." He took a deep

breath to settle his buzzing nerves. "I think we need to talk about… this."

"This," she said. "Okay."

"I like you," he blurted out, not wanting her to think for one second that anything else might be the case. "I *really* like you."

She smiled shyly at that. "I really like you too."

Why was this so hard?

Because he didn't want to say these words. Didn't want them to be true.

"The thing is, though… I'll be going back to the Northshore as soon as I wrap things up here."

"Right." She drew out the word, and he could see the wheels behind her eyes spinning, processing what he was saying. "So… you want to end this now?"

"No," he blurted. "I mean… I don't know."

He absolutely did not want to end this now. Or maybe ever. But what choice did he have?

"I've never done a long-distance anything." Sadness weighed down each word as the meaning sank in.

"Me neither." He reached over and grabbed her hand resting on her knee, lacing his fingers with hers. "My spring schedule is packed with baseball. I'm afraid I'd be a crappy companion at any distance for the next few months."

"That's okay. I have a feeling I'm going to have my hands full with the new shelter anyway once it opens up. I don't even know when that will be yet."

He squeezed her hand. "The last thing I want to do is make promises that I can't keep. Or let you down."

"So you don't want to see each other anymore?"

He could see his own pain and inner turmoil mirrored back in her eyes.

"Okay, correction. The *last* thing I want is to not see you again." He lifted her hand and kissed the back of it. "But I don't know how to do that and also not disappoint you."

"You wouldn't disappoint me by caring about your job or those kids. Especially if I know what I'm getting into and we're both honest with each other about our other commitments." She took a big breath and stared down at his hand holding hers. "And I guess I need to be honest with you, too. None of this might matter, anyway."

"Honest about what?" His stomach sank, wondering what dark secret she might be about to reveal. He couldn't think of anything that would make him turn away from her, but his mind was also clouded with wanting things to work out.

She swallowed and exhaled, then looked up at him with those big brown eyes filled with sadness. "There was a reason I was so upset about going back to the vet clinic last week. The same reason I quit." Another deep breath, and she averted her eyes again. "I slept with my boss."

Austin waited patiently for the rest of the story. Not a why or how or the details around what she'd just said, but the rest of what she thought was so horrible that he'd turn his back on her. "Wait... is that all?"

She shook her head and wiped at her face. "He's married. He said and did all the things he could to manipulate me, but that doesn't erase the fact that I knew."

Whoever her boss was, Austin wanted a *word* with the asshole.

Clearly, whatever happened with that situation had upset her. And it wasn't like he would blame her for something like that or hold it against her. She realized she'd made a mistake, but the power dynamic of her married boss crossing a line like that made Austin want to hunt the guy down for a *talk*.

The thing that bothered him the most right now, though, was that she thought it would make a difference in how Austin felt about her.

He released her hand and wrapped his arm around her shoulders, pulling her close against him and kissing her forehead. "I don't know this guy, but you were an employee, and *he* crossed a line he shouldn't. *He* was also the married person. You don't need to take on the guilt for his actions. And none of that makes a difference to me."

"Really?" She looked up at him with red-rimmed eyes and genuine confusion on her face. "You really don't care?"

"No." He kissed her forehead again. "I only care that you're upset. And that you have to work at that place another week."

She shrugged. "I'll live. It's like my penance, I guess."

"You don't deserve punishment for that. I'm glad you're quitting, and I'm glad you found some great new bosses. Those two women seem fun."

Taylor laughed. "They are."

He released his grip on her shoulder and rubbed her back. "So if that's the worst you've got for me—and I stand by my assessment that your relationship past is a non-factor here—then we're back to the question of what to do with us going forward, knowing that I'm leaving and we'll both be mostly unavailable for the next few months."

"It's only two hours away. It isn't like you live across the country."

"True," he said. "Which might work out if we're both busy during the week, anyway."

"Right. But you'll have baseball on the weekends, I guess?"

"I'll have baseball all the time in the spring."

"Maybe I could come see a game or two?"

"Don't you hate sports?"

She shrugged. "Maybe I could be convinced. Besides, I like that you care about those kids so much. It makes me want to care."

Austin had never heard sweeter words in his life. "And we

can text and video chat. I just don't want you disappointed because I'm unavailable until the summer."

"Like I said, it looks like I might be pretty unavailable with the rescue stuff for a while, anyway."

"So this might work out perfectly?" he asked.

Taylor cracked a tiny half-smile that lit up the universe brighter than that sunshine beaming down beside them. "Looks like it might."

He leaned in to kiss her, waking every nerve in his body. She returned the kiss with the same passion he felt, then pulled away abruptly but held his gaze. Her big brown eyes were filled with want and hope.

He felt that too. Want for her. Hope for their future. Everything within his reach. For now.

"Want to come inside?"

Austin continued to look into those eyes of hers and squeezed her hand. "Yeah. I really do."

18

*T*aylor placed the large carrier on the metal exam table, then opened the crate door and waited for Tink to poke his little pink nose out of the opening.

"Come on, buddy."

"You weren't kidding," her coworker said. "He's a beast." Wendy peeled the plastic wrapper open to free a syringe and prep the rest of the supplies.

Taylor coaxed Tink out then placed the carrier on the floor while continuing to pet the big guy and reassure him he was safe here with her. She wasn't sure how he would react to the next step, but whatever he had in store for them, Taylor and Wendy had seen worse and could handle it.

Hopefully.

Howl!

Wendy shook her head in disbelief. "Does he sound like a foghorn all the time?"

"Pretty much."

"You want to hold him while I do the draw?"

"Sounds good. He's fairly chill, so we can try the front first."

Taylor scooted Tink close to her edge of the table with his back pressed against her body while Wendy rubbed one of his forelegs with alcohol. Then Taylor wrapped her left arm around the front of him and held his head upward. Once Wendy was ready, Taylor took hold of his leg near the alcohol and placed her thumb in just the right spot to make the vein stand up.

"That's a good boy," Taylor whispered to Tink, as Wendy inserted the needle and extracted a sample.

"There we go," Wendy said in her soft voice, reserved only for the animals, never any humans she interacted with. She removed the syringe and pressed a cotton ball to the site. "All done."

Taylor continued to hold him still, but released her hold enough to scratch the sides of his neck. "Not so bad, huh?"

They traded off holding the cotton against him while Wendy secured the blood sample and wrapped bright pink tape around his leg. "This is your last week, huh?"

"Yup."

Wendy gave a half-grin and a side-eye. "Feels good?"

Taylor and Wendy had come to a sort of truce since Taylor had put in her two-weeks' notice. They never talked about it, mostly because they didn't talk much about anything. Not since Taylor realized Wendy knew their boss was a creep and couldn't be trusted to have Taylor's back. Once someone was out of Taylor's circle of trust, they were *out.* For good.

But that didn't mean Taylor needed to hold a grudge. Quite the opposite. Once she booted someone from her circle, she no longer had to care what they thought of her, or vice versa. Her relationship with Wendy had never been better since Taylor had booted her coworker from her sphere of caring.

"Yeah, it feels good."

"I'm kind of jealous." Wendy's half-grin stretched into a full-blown one. "But not of working for a rescue. You really like suffering, don't you?"

"Why would you say that?" Taylor scratched the sides of Tink's face. "Look at this guy. I get to help animals like him find new homes. What could be better than that?"

"Uh, not seeing the ugly side of humanity on a daily basis?"

Sure. But Taylor preferred not to think about that. At least not while she didn't have to.

"Lucky for me it's just an empty building for now."

Wendy shook her head and chuckled. "This place is going to miss your Pollyanna bullshit, that's for certain."

Taylor ignored the remark. "All right, buddy. Sorry about this, but it's time to get you in a kennel until I'm done here for the day."

"Hey, wait," Wendy said. "Do you want to do an x-ray while he's here? Just to make sure there's not an obstruction or mass?"

Taylor didn't think he had an obstruction, since he was using the litter box normally and his stool was normal. But she hadn't considered a mass. The blood work would give a hint if they should look for something, but the results would take a couple of days. At least. And while she hadn't thought of a mass before, now that Wendy mentioned it, Taylor wouldn't be able to stop thinking about that possibility.

But there was one problem.

"I guess I should ask Jason." The words brought the taste of bile to her mouth.

"Screw that guy." Wendy cringed. "I mean, not literally."

Taylor wished she and Wendy had gotten off to a better start here. She liked this Wendy. The one who wasn't scowling at her all the time.

She shook off her initial urge to second guess her decision. This was the right choice. She would love working in animal rescue and *not* working here. Even if she ended up missing a coworker or two. Just a little.

"Don't we need him to approve that?"

"I can do it. We do most of the stuff around here, anyway." Wendy grinned. "What's he going to do? Fire us?"

"I don't care if he does, but you still work here."

Wendy shrugged. "Not for long."

Taylor decided not to push for more details, and Wendy didn't seem inclined to offer more. What Wendy did with her career wasn't any of Taylor's business, but she relished the idea of everyone quitting and leaving Jason high and dry to do all the work around here himself. Or any work at all, for once.

After Wendy made a quick check down the hall to note that Jason was still taking lunch in his office with the door shut, the trio moved to the x-ray table. Tink was perfectly agreeable, snuggling in Taylor's arms during the brief transport, and stretching out once they reached the table.

"At least it doesn't look like he needs any sedation," Wendy said over his loud purrs. "Just keep him happy, and I'll handle the rest."

Both women slipped on radiation aprons. Then Taylor gave Tink full-body pets while Wendy targeted the machine over his belly. They rolled him over, and Wendy took an image of his other side as well. Taylor laughed as the cat then stretched and relaxed flat on his back for her to pet his stomach.

"I think he wants you to take one more angle." She laughed as she pet his tummy, then she moved her hand so Wendy could quickly get another image.

"I guess it's nothing major if he's letting you pet him like that," Wendy said. "I wish they were all this easy."

"Right?" Taylor carried Tink across the room to the

empty recovery kennel she'd set up. She hated having to leave him in there, but she had little choice.

Howl.

"I know, dude," she said. "I promise we'll be home again before you know it."

She hoped the rest of the day went by quickly for her own sake, too. She couldn't wait to get out of here and maybe have good news to tell Austin. Hopefully, it was just like Wendy said, and there was nothing seriously wrong with Tink. Austin could use some good news.

Wendy clicked at the computer, and she had the first image up when Taylor walked over to look over her shoulder.

"Is Jason going to notice extra x-rays saved on here?"

Wendy scoffed. "What do you think?"

An image popped up, and after a few seconds, Taylor pointed at a particular spot on the screen. "What's that"?

"It looks like someone had a little extra something with their breakfast one day." Wendy zoomed in and adjusted the image until it came in clear. "The good news is it doesn't look attached, so foreign object not mass."

Taylor squinted. "What do you think it is?"

"I don't know. Something round-ish. No sharp edges or pointy ends is a good thing." Wendy clicked some more. "Let's try a different angle." A few seconds later, she let out a curious, "Huh."

Taylor leaned in a little more. "Is that... a ring?"

"Looks like it." Wendy rotated the image and adjusted the darkness so they could clearly see an empty center. "Yeah. Maybe."

"Where the heck did he get a ring from? And why would he eat it?" Taylor hadn't noticed him being mouthy. Some cats chewed on everything they could get their mouths on, like a teething puppy. But she hadn't noticed Tink chewing things. Then again, it wasn't as if she had random small objects lying around her bedroom. The poor guy must have had that in there since before he got to her place.

"It doesn't look big enough to block anything. It's just... there," Wendy said. "But that's also not exactly great news either."

Taylor nodded. If he hadn't passed this by now after two weeks, the odds weren't good that he'd pass it on his own. At his age, surgery was the last option they wanted.

"What do you think I should do?" Taylor hoped the answer wouldn't be to ask Jason. "Whatever it is, I'll have to run it by Liz and Sierra."

"Who?"

"The owners of the rescue," Taylor said. "He's technically their cat. I'm just his foster and can't sign off on anything."

"Right," Wendy said. "The way he is with you, I forgot he isn't actually your cat."

Taylor pressed her lips together, fighting the urge to comment on how she was forgetting that, too. Because that wasn't a thought she could have.

"I'll call them this afternoon on a break."

"We can try giving him an emetic while he's here today," Wendy said. "Then if it doesn't work they can decide what to do after that."

Taylor sighed. Any next step would require getting Jason involved. Not her preferred route, but she would face Jason or anyone else to get Tink whatever he needed.

"I'll call them now and see if they want to start that."

"HEY, Austin. Good to see you again."

He met the attorney's firm grip for a handshake. "You too, Danny."

Danny Stutes stood several inches shorter than Austin, but his confidence overshadowed his stature. A direct product of both his net worth and his ability to square across any board room table and emerge victorious.

He'd been their family's attorney for almost as long as Austin had been alive, overseeing his father's estate and his mother's business affairs. Uncle Kenny had often spoken fondly of him. Even Austin's mother had never said a dismissive word about him that Austin could ever remember.

"Come in." Danny gestured inside. "Have a seat. Can I get you anything? Water? Soda? Coffee? I think we've got donuts left."

"No, I'm good. Thank you." Austin sat at the long, narrow table across from Danny's piles of papers. He placed his own stack of folders in front of him. "I think I have everything. The accountant was very helpful. He even made a checklist so I can see what's mentioned in the will and what's not accounted for."

Danny sat and adjusted the jacket of his expensive gray suit. Austin had put on a blue dress shirt and charcoal slacks for this meeting, realizing that it was the first time he'd worn anything other than jeans and T-shirts and the occasional polo shirt since Uncle Kenny's funeral.

"Great," Danny said. "This is pretty straightforward, but you'll need that for your records, anyway."

Austin eyed the man while he tapped a pen on the stack in front of him. He didn't like the troubled look on the man's face. Danny Stutes was *always* in control. Troubled never appeared in his emotional vocabulary. "Is there a problem?"

"Not exactly." Danny drew out the last word as he stared at the paper. "More of an interesting detail."

"An interesting detail?"

Danny looked up suddenly and flashed a wide, toothy grin. "Let's start with the straightforward matters." He pointed at Austin's folders. "I said you'll need that because most of his accounts are yours now."

All the sounds vanished from the room. The humming from the central heating. The faint buzzing from the fluorescent lighting. Danny's pen tapping. All gone. Austin could only hear the blood rushing through his head.

"I'm sorry, what did you say?"

"I said you are a very rich man." He laughed. "Well, richer than you already were, thanks to your father's trust. Although I know you like to pretend otherwise."

Danny wasn't wrong. Pretend wasn't exactly the word Austin liked to use. Ignore sounded better. He *ignored* the pile of money his father had left to him. The pile of money his mother liked to remind him of every time she looked at his car or remembered he was paying rent instead of buying up investment properties.

He appreciated that the money was safe and available should he ever need it or whenever he came across a worthy cause in need. He just didn't personally need it right now.

The sound in the room returned, along with the reason he was here.

He might not need money, but he needed answers.

"Wait, you said most," Austin said. "Who else did he leave money to?"

"He left a small investment account for your mother. I believe he said it was stocks she would be interested in. And he was still a silent partner in a restaurant."

"He was?" Austin thought he'd sold off all his restaurant ownership. But he could see Uncle Kenny keeping a toe in somewhere if it didn't require any work from him. Austin must have missed that in the accountant's notes. Although, in his defense, there had been a lot of accounts and numbers and information. His eyes had glazed over real quick, no matter how hard he'd tried to keep it all organized and make sense of it.

"Yes. He left his part ownership in that to…" Danny consulted a paper a little way down in his stack. "Nadine. His sister, yes?"

"That's right."

Austin chuckled. Of course, Uncle Kenny left that to Nadine. He'd given her a job that she didn't have to do. Exactly the kind she loved. But Uncle Kenny had also known his sister. There was no way Austin's aunt would be able to keep her nose out of that business. The not-silent partner in that venture must have had some payback due. Leave it to Uncle Kenny to play the long game.

Still, this wasn't exactly the smoking gun he'd been looking for. He couldn't imagine Nadine killing her brother over a restaurant she didn't know about and likely didn't even want.

"There's just a couple more items to deal with. Let's see. He left the car to Patricia."

"Good." If he'd ended up with it, Austin would have given it to Patricia, anyway. Hopefully, she could take that trip to the Grand Canyon in it. "Okay, I can't take the suspense. What's the interesting bit?"

Danny cleared his throat. "Well, he also left you the cat."

Austin flinched.

He hadn't thought about Tink being in the will. But of course he was. He was family, just like if Uncle Kenny'd had a kid who needed custody.

But now Austin felt guilty about dropping Tink off at the shelter. Sure, he was in excellent hands there, especially with Taylor, but it felt like he was going specifically against his uncle's last wishes by not keeping him. Even though that couldn't be helped. Austin had tried to convince his landlord, but with no luck. Taylor and a new home were Tink's best choice.

"That's not all." Danny made a weird face, like he didn't want to say what came next. "He also left a savings account for his care. It's... a lot of money. And it's specifically marked for Tink's guardian."

"That will be an interesting wrinkle since I surrendered him to an animal rescue organization a couple weeks ago."

Danny raised a brow at that. "Interesting indeed. I need to do some research on how to handle the details of a feline trust fund. You can connect me with them in a few days, and we'll figure everything out. There are other instructions here that I'll have to go over with them."

Austin chuckled, imagining the looks on those two women's faces. And Taylor's. She'd be thrilled to hear that Tink would live out his days as a spoiled cat with whoever adopted him. Hopefully, they'd keep that part quiet, so as not to attract any greedy potential adopters.

"I can do that," Austin said. "Anything else interesting in there?"

He couldn't imagine anything more interesting than a Tink trust fund, but this was Uncle Kenny. Nothing would truly surprise Austin at this point.

"Actually, I have one more thing."

"What is it?" Austin didn't know what other assets his uncle might have squirreled away.

"Well, I'd assumed the house would go to you or your mother, but this is a name I don't recognize."

Austin didn't care about the house. Not for his own purposes, at least. If it went to someone who appreciated it and Austin got out of having to sell it, all the better. He could get back to work and his life.

His stomach dropped at the thought of leaving. His chat

with Taylor had ended well, with plenty of hope for their future.

But he felt closer to her than ever now, and he didn't relish the idea of not seeing her regularly.

Austin couldn't think of anyone who might want that house, much less anyone his uncle might have left it to. Patricia, maybe, but Danny knew who she was.

"What's the name?"

Danny slid his finger down the page until he landed on the paragraph and name he was looking for. "Ah, there. Brandon Wiltz."

19

The pen fell from Austin's fingers and clattered against the table. He stared at the open folder in front of him, his eyes glazing over as the rows and columns of account numbers and balances blurred.

"Do you know who that is?"

Austin blinked the world back into focus and looked up at the attorney sitting across from him. "I think so. Although I've never met him."

"It seems your uncle knew him well enough to leave him a whole house." Danny raised his brow at the paper. "And everything in it."

Brandon Wiltz.

Austin tried to remember what Patricia had said about him. He couldn't remember the exact words she'd used, but "possessive" had been the impression he remembered. Could he have bullied his way into Uncle Kenny's life? It didn't make sense. Uncle Kenny didn't respond well to that kind of behavior.

But what if that's exactly what happened and exactly how Uncle Kenny died?

If he'd grown tired of this Brandon guy's possessiveness, maybe the guy pushed him during an argument. Maybe Uncle Kenny was breaking things off and hadn't changed his will yet? Maybe this wasn't about money, but some crime of passion instead.

Crime of passion?

How had all of this gotten to where Austin was using words like *crime of passion*?

"How long can you hold on to this before you have to notify him?"

Danny gave a sympathetic smile. Probably thinking Austin just wanted to live in the house a little longer, to be closer to his uncle or something. Danny had no idea what was really going on in Austin's head.

"How long do you need?"

"Can you give me a week? Maybe two?" Austin rubbed his face with both hands, scrambling for some kind of plan. "I'd like a little time to process this. And talk to the guy myself. Maybe tell him in person."

"Sure," Danny said. "I can give you a copy of the will to give to him yourself if you'd like. I was going to give a copy for your mother. And your aunt and Patricia, if you'd like as well."

"That would be great," Austin said. "Thanks."

"Still no luck?"

Wendy leaned against the surgery table with her arms crossed. A look of concern blanketed her face. A look that mimicked Taylor's internal thoughts.

"Not yet," Taylor said.

"You know, it's way past—"

"I know, I know." Taylor stuck a hand through the bars of

the recovery kennel and scratched Tink's face. She'd come in every half hour to check on him, but no luck. No vomit. No foreign object. "I already called Liz. We're going to see what the blood work says, make sure it's not affecting his health, then decide on the next step."

"Sorry," Wendy said. "I was rooting for puke."

"Me too." Taylor looked at the clock on the wall. It was after five. Their final patient for the day had just left. "Is Jason still here?"

She hadn't been outright avoiding him for the last week, but... yeah. She'd been avoiding him. Only saw him for five to ten minutes at a time to hold animals during appointments. And she was never in a room alone with him. The plan was working out well so far. Only four days more, then she would be completely free of him and this job.

"Left early. Again. Had an 'appointment,' he said." Wendy used air quotes around the word appointment.

They all knew that was code for him meeting someone who wasn't his wife. The only new thing was, it wasn't the tech who started training that morning to replace Taylor. Maybe because of Taylor giving her a heads up about Jason.

"Do you mind if I head out early?"

Wendy nodded at the doorway. "Get that guy home. He's been through enough today. I'll finish here and lock up."

Taylor gave an appreciative smile. "Thanks."

"No problem. Take care of that big floof." Wendy winked at Taylor. "We all know he's going to end up yours."

"I'm just fostering," she insisted as Wendy left the room.

"Sure you are!" Wendy's voice rang out from down the hall.

Taylor grabbed Tink's carrier and placed it on the floor in front of the kennels. "Ready big guy?"

Her phone buzzed with a text.

Want to come over? I miss you. :)

Taylor smiled and texted back, *I just saw you yesterday... but I miss you too. ;)*

A moment later, he replied with, *I could also use a second brain to help process this will.*

Right, that was this morning. She'd been so busy worrying about Tink she'd forgotten about his meeting with the attorney.

Just finishing my shift and taking Tink home. Can drop him off on my way. Send me the address.

She grabbed Tink from the kennel and placed him in the carrier with only a couple of protest howls.

Bring him. He can snuggle on the couch with us while we talk and order food. Or I can cook

Taylor smiled at the screen. *You can cook???*

She didn't know why that surprised her. But now she couldn't stop thinking about big, strong Austin in an apron. With ruffles. It was the sexiest thought that had hit her brain in months. Years, probably.

Well, now I'm definitely cooking, he replied.

Competitive much?

Very. But I just realized I'm low on groceries, so that'll have to wait for another time. A moment later, he added, *looking forward to seeing you both soon.*

Taylor's grin stretched even wider as she grabbed bowls and a sample bag of cat food to take with her. She doubted he still had anything there for Tink's dinner.

She smiled, thinking about his offer to cook. She'd have to take him up on that one day since she couldn't remember the last time she'd had a date cook for her.

Had she *ever* had a date cook for her?

Sheesh. She really needed to pick better people.

But maybe she was doing that already. Maybe Austin was her road to better.

Or maybe he was the final prize?

Just that thought felt self-indulgent and wrong. But also very right.

AUSTIN SQUINTED at the laptop screen sitting on the kitchen counter. He relaxed against the red barstool and backed up the security camera footage to re-watch that section again.

It couldn't be.

He hit play and watched the short figure enter his uncle's house through the side door, the same one that had been damaged a little over a week ago, prompting him to install the camera.

The figure shuffled inside with something in their hand and wandered through the whole first floor. They scanned every surface and corner until they paused beside the couch in the living room and shuffled back out through the side door. He backed up the video again, just a few seconds this time, and paused on a frame showing the individual's face.

It was Patricia. No doubt about it.

Flo Rida's "My House" played through the house. Not the "Funky Town" tune, indicating someone was at the kitchen door. Instead, this was the front door chime.

Austin left the laptop open and hurried to the foyer. Taylor stood in the doorway with a big smile, sea green scrubs, and her long blonde hair in a messy, end-of-the-day ponytail. He liked this look on her just as much as the dressed-up version of her at his mom's dinner party. Maybe more.

She held a plastic bag in one hand and tapped the carrier in her other hand. "Brought a friend for a visit."

Austin moved aside and gestured for them to come in. He was happy to see both of them, but he couldn't find words yet. His mind was still trying to make sense of that video.

Taylor set the carrier on the floor once they reached the living room. She turned to Austin with a look of concern. "Everything okay?" Then she shook her head. "Of course you aren't. The will meeting. Sorry. That must have been hard."

"I'm okay."

Was he? No, that was a lie.

But he was better now that Taylor was there. Her and Tink. Something about having both of them with him made everything feel a little more right in the world.

"Would you like to put him in a particular room? Or maybe close any doors to places you don't want him in before I let him out?"

"He can have the run of the place. And if he hides, he can spend the night," Austin said. "Crap. I forgot I don't have his litter box and stuff anymore. Hang on, I'll see if I can find a container in the kitchen or—"

"I've got it." Taylor held up the plastic bag draped over one arm. "Litter, box, food, and bowls. I figured you weren't set up for him."

He took a step closer and put both hands on the sides of her face. "You are a beautiful, thoughtful human. Do you know that?" He kissed her, then pulled back slightly to stare into her eyes, making sure she knew he meant every word of that.

She put her hands on his, while he still held her face in his palms. "I'm going to want more of that. But let's get him out of there first. He's had a long enough day at the clinic."

"Right." His stomach dropped as the words sank in. He'd been so distracted today with the will and those revelations and now the video, he'd forgotten the reason Taylor had brought Tink with her to work today. "Did you get any insight into what might be wrong with him?"

Taylor opened the carrier door, and Tink poked his pink nose out of the carrier to sniff the air. Then he took one cautious step out onto the living room floor, his eyes wide with recognition.

"I think we found the root of the problem," Taylor said, "but we're still waiting on blood work to be sure."

"What do you think it might be?"

"It looks like he swallowed something small. Maybe a ring."

They watched Tink take a few more tentative steps until he emerged completely.

"A ring?" Austin had never heard of a cat swallowing a ring before, but he didn't have a lot of experience with things cats might eat. Or any animals. His mother had been opposed to the mess of animal ownership, so Austin never had a pet of his own.

"The good news is it doesn't look sharp or big enough to cause an obstruction."

"Is there bad news?"

Taylor shrugged. "Waiting for that blood work to know. And since he still hasn't hacked it up, even with a little of our help today, it doesn't look promising for him getting it out on his own."

"Can't he just poop it out?"

"Maybe," Taylor said. "That's our next hope once we know from the blood panel that everything else is okay. We want to avoid surgery, if we can."

Surgery?

Austin watched Tink sniff and rub his face against the couch. The poor guy had been through enough. Surgery sounded like the worst cherry on this cat's shitty sundae.

Taylor filled a small pan with litter and let Tink sniff before placing it on the floor near a wall. "Is this okay here?"

"Yeah, fine. Anywhere is good," he said. "I can get his water."

She handed him an empty bowl, which he filled with

water from the kitchen. When he returned, she'd already put out a small bowl of food that Tink dug into greedily. Austin placed the water beside it.

"His stomach should be settled by now from what we gave him earlier," she said. "Especially since he didn't vomit."

"If he does, I'll clean it up."

Austin chuckled internally. At least he didn't have to worry about selling the house. Tink could puke wherever he wanted now. It wasn't Austin's concern anymore beyond the initial cleanup. Stains would be Brandon's problem.

"Hungry for something in particular?" he asked. "We can order from anywhere."

"Whatever you would normally get is fine with me."

"Thai? I assume you've eaten at the place around the block."

"Love it," she said. "Their green curry is the best."

"Chicken? Shrimp? Tofu?"

"Ooh, shrimp," she said.

He made a mental note of that choice so he could put that sparkle in her eye again sometime. Austin ordered their selections, then closed the window for the delivery service.

Taylor pointed at the laptop screen. "I can go hang out with Tink if you were working on something."

"Actually, I could use another set of eyes. Take a look at this."

He backed up the video to when Patricia entered the house. Then he pressed play and waited while Taylor watched intently, taking her assignment as seriously as he'd expected from her.

"Is that here?"

"This morning," Austin said. "I had some damage by the side door a couple weeks ago that looked like someone maybe tried to break in, so I set up cameras. I watch the recording from every time I leave the house now. This was recorded while I was at the attorney's office going over the will."

Taylor furrowed her brow at the screen. "She used a key, and it doesn't look like she's taking anything. Maybe she's looking for something in particular. Do you recognize her?"

"Her name's Patricia. She was my uncle's best friend."

"Wait." Taylor pointed at the screen, prompting Austin to pause the recording. "What's that? It looks like she left something on that little table. Did you see what it was?"

She was right. When Patricia paused in the living room, she appeared to place whatever was in her hand on the side table. He'd missed that the first few times through.

He got up from the barstool and headed back into the living room, with Taylor a step behind him. She peered over his shoulder as he picked up an envelope with his name on it.

"Sorry." She took a step back. "I'm just being nosy."

"No, it's fine." He opened the card inside and held it out so she could see it, too. "You can tell me if I'm overreacting."

"It looks like a note to thank you for whatever you gave her previously. Some of your uncle's things?"

"I gave her a box of stuff last week. But why didn't she just call and thank me? Or drop this off when I was home? Why break in?"

"She didn't exactly break in," Taylor corrected. "She used a key. Your uncle obviously trusted her if he gave her a key to his house."

This was Patricia they were talking about. If there was anyone in Uncle Kenny's life that he trusted, it was her. Austin was just being paranoid. The attempted break-in and the possible murder had him freaked out and searching for suspects around every corner.

Still, something was bothering him.

"What do you think she was looking for? And why didn't she ask me about whatever it is?"

"Maybe she wasn't looking for anything," Taylor said. "Maybe she just wanted a minute alone in here. To say goodbye?"

Austin felt sick to his stomach.

Of course, that's what it was. She'd been so upset the last time she'd been over. And she hadn't been in the house since Uncle Kenny died. Taylor was right. She probably did just want one more look around the place before someone else took it. Before *Brandon* took it.

He wasn't looking forward to *that* conversation, but he supposed he needed to be the one to break that news to her. Patricia had her own place, a nice house with a gorgeous garden from what his uncle had told him, plenty big enough for her and her dogs. But the way she'd spoken of Brandon, Austin didn't think she'd take the news of him living here very well.

Taylor pointed at the letter in Austin's hand. "If she was doing anything shady, I doubt she'd leave evidence that she was here."

Austin laughed. "Very true. I guess I'm just a mess from today."

"Want to talk about it? Tink and I are good listeners." She smiled at the couch where Tink was already curled up against the pillows and sleeping peacefully. "Well, I am. At least, I think so."

They walked together to the deep-seated, bright purple couch in the center of the room. Taylor sat beside Tink on one side, so Austin sat in the middle to be next to her.

"Did the will give you any insight into who might have wanted to hurt your uncle?"

Austin shook his head. "Not really. Patricia gets his car. My mom gets an investment account, but it's not much."

Taylor turned slightly greenish. "You don't think your *mom* is a suspect, do you?"

"No, not at all," Austin said. "She's got more money than she needs already."

Taylor bit her lip and hesitated before her next question. "What about Zeke?"

"He said he doesn't want my family's money, and I'm inclined to believe him. On that, at least," Austin said reluctantly. "And I don't think whatever my mom is getting would be enough for Zeke or anyone to commit murder over. It sounds like it's a special interest kind of thing that only she would appreciate."

"What if Zeke *thought* she'd be getting more than that and found out she wasn't? Or maybe your uncle was supposed to help him with his business and decided not to, and Zeke lost his temper?"

"Anything is possible," Austin said.

"But you think someone else did it? What about the other relatives?"

"They didn't get anything," Austin said. "Except my Aunt Nadine, who got his silent share in a restaurant no one knew about."

"Maybe she knew about it?" Taylor suggested. "Or your cousin who would also inherit that from her mom, eventually?"

Her brain was a spectacular machine of possibilities, and he loved watching the questions spark out of her. Especially when he felt so overwhelmed or stuck that he didn't know where to look. He had to admit they made a pretty great team.

"Maybe," he said. "I didn't even know about it, so it's unlikely. But I'll mention it to the detective."

"So wait, if Patricia got the car, and your mom got one account and your aunt got the restaurant, did he split his money between the rest of you? Because that sounds like a lot of money and plenty of suspects."

Austin shook his head. He hated this part. But it had to come out eventually, he supposed. He just didn't like how the knowledge of this kind of money could change people and how they looked at him.

He cleared his throat. "All the other accounts went to me."

Taylor's eyes widened as a hand covered her mouth. She mumbled against her palm, "All of it?"

"All of it." Then he laughed and corrected himself. "No, wait. There's a trust fund for Tink. A fairly large one."

She looked down at the sleeping cat beside her and back up at Austin. "You're kidding."

"Nope. And since I already signed him over, the shelter will inherit a sizable care fund that goes to whoever becomes his permanent adopter. So no worries about whatever this thing in his stomach costs. Not that I wouldn't have paid for it, anyway."

Taylor removed her hand from her mouth, but her eyes were still stretched out wide. "I thought pet trusts were a myth."

"Apparently not."

Taylor collapsed against the back of the sofa, sinking into the huge pillows behind her. Her mouth hung open in disbelief as she looked around, finally taking in the decor of this room. She let out a giggle when her eyes landed on the Jeff Goldblum clock. "Does that mean you've inherited this place too?"

"I forgot to tell you the wildest part."

"Wilder than Tink's trust fund?"

"Yup," he said. "The house is going to some guy I don't know. Never even heard of him until my mom gave me a list of names. Patricia confirmed he was a friend, but that he seemed a bit possessive to her."

Taylor cringed. "And he's getting the house?"

"Looks like it," Austin said.

"If your uncle was fond enough of him to leave this house to him, why didn't he leave Tink along with it?"

"My House" played through the living room to announce that their food delivery had arrived. Austin stood to get the door, but his eyes remained locked on Taylor, processing the logic of her last statement.

"*That* is an excellent question."

20

*A*ustin found a table beside a window and placed the envelope he'd brought, his phone, and his to-go cup of café au lait in front of him. Patricia had mentioned something about needing to meet her niece across town, so he wasn't sure how long they'd be here.

The place was bustling as usual that Saturday morning. He'd been lucky to grab a table just as his order was ready and a man was packing up his laptop. Austin had swooped in with his coffee and a smile to ask if the man was leaving. He'd learned long ago, definitely not from his mother, that a smile got you a lot further than a scowl or demands. He tried to remember that as much as possible with the team.

Mike had sent the final official roster that morning, along with some stats and updates from practice that week. Austin couldn't wait to get back and join them. Now that he didn't have to sell the house himself, it looked like he'd be able to go home sooner than planned. Another week or two and he'd be on his way.

Assuming he could stomach handing over the keys to this Brandon person.

Austin had done a little more googling since Monday, but nothing shady turned up about the guy. Nothing that rang any obvious alarm bells. Still, something didn't sit right with him about this whole thing. Hopefully, Patricia could shed more light on the situation before he officially met Brandon.

His phone buzzed with a message from Taylor. He laughed at the smiling cat face emoji and the heart with the arrow through it and clicked the link she'd sent. A Facebook post for the St. Martin Animal Sanctuary appeared. It had a cute photo of three dogs, different breeds and sizes, with a description of the Valentine event and a sign-up link.

"Good to see you laughing again."

Patricia hovered over him, stuffed into a bulky tan coat that reached down to her knees. She looked genuinely pleased by his amusement.

Austin stood to hug her. "Good to see you always."

She gave him a solid hug and pat on the back, then waved her hand at his phone. "Don't hold out on me. Whatcha laughing at there? I could use a giggle myself. Is it one of those mee-mee things?"

Austin blinked at her for a few seconds while his brain caught up and realized she was talking about a meme. "No, just a promotional post."

Patricia's nose wrinkled as she sat across the table from him with her giant purse in her lap. "A funny ad?"

"Not exactly." He held out his phone screen for her to see the three dogs. The tallest one was properly at attention, while one of his companions had a goofy grin with its tongue hanging out and the other dog lay on the floor with its feet in the air. "It's a photoshoot fundraiser for a rescue group."

Patricia tilted her head back and looked down her nose at the screen. "Well, I'll be damned. That's the cutest thing I've seen in a while. A fundraiser, you say?"

"The shelter that took in Tink."

"Send me a link to that. I'll have to sign my boys up for pictures. Especially feel like I owe them for taking care of that cat. How'd you find out about it?"

"The vet tech who's fostering Tink texted the link a minute ago."

"Texted?" A sly grin stretched slowly across Patricia's face. "You text all the vet folks in town, or is this one special?"

"You don't have a coffee yet." Austin pushed his chair back. "What can I order for you?"

"Oh no, sit down, young man." Patricia narrowed her gaze. "Spill it. You like her?"

It was none of her business, but he figured he owed this woman at least to humor her a bit after being such a good friend to his uncle for all those years. So Austin took a deep breath, put aside all his worries about the future of his relationship with Taylor and said the honest answer. "Yes. Very much."

"Good," she said with a firm nod. "You need someone who makes you smile like that. Laughing's even better. And Kenny would be happy for you, too. If she's taking care of that cat, you know she'd have his seal of approval."

"Thank you. I think so too." He cleared his throat and lifted the envelope. "Speaking of Uncle Kenny. I know you have somewhere to be this afternoon, so I'll get right to the reason I asked you to meet me."

"What's that?" A second later, her eyes widened with realization. A bit of color drained from her face.

Austin nodded. "A copy of his will."

She stared at the envelope as tears welled in her bottom lids. "He was always so generous. I don't need whatever's in there. He's already given me so much. His friendship meant everything."

Austin dug in his pocket and placed the Mercedes keys on

top of the envelope, then he slid it towards her. "He adored you. Which is why he left you something he cherished."

It wasn't the most expensive thing he owned, but he loved that car more than anything in the house. Not counting Tink, who he considered family, not a possession.

"We'll need to take care of the paperwork to put the title in your name, but it's yours whenever you're ready for it."

She leaned forward and placed a hand on Austin's, squeezing gently. "Thank you. There's no rush. I don't know if I could even bring myself to sit in it again."

"I understand," Austin said. "But I'm sure he'd want you to go on that trip. You could take the dogs in that car."

"Trip?" She looked confused, her eyes still on that envelope and her mind off somewhere in the past.

"The one the two of you were planning together. The Grand Canyon? You said you were supposed to rent an RV together, but maybe taking his car might be like the spirit of Uncle Kenny would be there with you."

"Oh, gosh. My mind has been on festival season and how I'm going to get through that without him by my side this year." She smiled. "But I think that sounds wonderful. Not as good without him, of course. Maybe by the summer I'll be up for that."

He put the keys back in his pocket and slid the envelope to her side of the table. "I'll check with you next week, and we can schedule a time to take care of the title before I leave."

She took the envelope, paused, then waved it in the air. "You really think you can get that house ready to sell in a couple of weeks?"

"Actually…" He cleared his throat. "I won't be selling the house."

Patricia clapped. "You're keeping it? Does that mean you'll be moving back here after the school year?"

He only knew this woman through his uncle, but he still

felt guilty for disappointing her. "It's more that I'm not the one inheriting the house."

He waited while the words sank in.

"Then who? Your mom, right? Because what the heck would I do with that big ol' thing?"

He'd been dreading this part of their conversation all week. But it was better that she heard it from him. "Brandon Wiltz."

Her lips puckered into a scowl as her face reddened. She tapped her fingers on the table and composed herself. "What else did he weasel away with?"

"The house and contents."

Austin couldn't imagine anyone would want all the decor in that place, but he supposed some of it could be valuable as collector's items. And the furniture itself wasn't invaluable. Just a tacky, hodgepodge collection.

"That snake got what he wanted then."

"Any particular reason you think that?" Austin asked.

He had to tread lightly here. Austin didn't want to alarm Patricia, but he needed more information before he contacted Brandon. He wanted to know exactly what he was walking into and what questions to ask.

"He didn't need your uncle's money. Although I suppose everyone gets tempted by the greed monster now and then." Patricia's scowl deepened. "But his eyes were always scanning that house. Mentally appraising its value or redecorating it in his head for his own purposes if I had to guess."

"Do you think Brandon was manipulating Uncle Kenny?" He paused, then asked the thing he needed to know. "Was Uncle Kenny maybe planning to cut things off with Brandon before he died?"

Patricia flinched at that, confusion setting into her eyes. "Why would you ask that?" She made a tiny gasp and whispered, "Did he do something to Kenny?"

"No, no, no," Austin stammered. "Nothing like that. I'm just trying to get a feel for the guy and his relationship with Uncle Kenny before I meet with him."

Patricia seemed to buy that explanation and relaxed a bit. "I'm sorry you have to be the one to meet the snake. But I don't know what to tell you. Kenny knew my feelings about him, and we agreed to disagree about Brandon and stopped discussing him between us."

That made sense. Austin's uncle wasn't fond of conflict, especially not with the people he held dear. So he could imagine him tabling any talk of Brandon around Patricia if it caused stress between them.

"One more thing," he asked. "Do you know any reason he didn't leave Tink to Brandon? Like why he didn't specifically leave Tink with the person getting the house so Tink wouldn't have to be displaced?"

Patricia looked confused by that bit of news as well. "I don't know. That is curious. Although I imagine he would have wanted Tink with the person he trusted most in this world, which was clearly you since he left you to handle all of his affairs."

"You're probably right. It just struck me as odd."

"The whole thing is odd," she said. "How the universe can just take someone away so suddenly with no rhyme or reason. It makes no sense. Of course, you're trying to make sense wherever you can."

She was right. He was trying to make sense of too many things. Maybe it was just the randomness of the universe.

He needed to call the detective again to see if he'd found anything useful. That might stop Austin's mind from spinning out of control.

"How is that cat doing?"

"He's great," Austin said. "Apparently he swallowed something though."

Patricia looked horrified. Probably afraid she would lose Uncle Kenny and his cat all in one big swoop. "What was it? Is he going to be all right?"

"He's fine, really. I promise," Austin assured her. "It isn't causing him much trouble at the moment, but they're trying to avoid surgery."

"So puke or poop, huh?"

"Pretty much. And they already tried the puke route, so it's nature's turn, I guess."

"Let me know how it goes. That old boy's been through enough. I want the best for him. Just wish my boys would tolerate him, but alas, they're jerks." Patricia stood and slipped her coat back on. "Well, I'd better head out. My niece is waiting for me. I'm watching the kids for her while she goes to the doctor."

"Everything all right, I hope?"

"Oh, yes. Just an annual checkup, but she doesn't want to drag littles along. They get to stay with Tante Pat instead."

Austin stood and walked around the table to give her a parting hug. "Oh, and I got your card. You didn't have to go to that trouble. You're very welcome."

"I did have to. I'm so forgetful these days, it would have sat on my counter forgetting to put a stamp or mail it. Sorry about barging in like that, but you weren't home, and I didn't want to forget it in my purse. Gave me one last look at the place, anyway."

"I didn't even realize you had a key." Although, the more he thought about it, the more sense it made. His uncle would have left her in charge of the place if he ever went somewhere. Patricia was his person, essentially.

"Speaking of which." She dug in her purse for her keys and slipped one off the ring. "Give this to the snake. I hope he chokes on it."

"THIS IS IT. TURN THERE." Taylor pointed at the long gravel driveway leading to the Acadian-style home. "Isn't it gorgeous out here?"

Geena steered the car down the driveway between the rows of pecan trees and stared off at the bare crepe myrtles dotting the property. "It is… something out here."

"Oh, come on. It's beautiful. And peaceful," Taylor said. "No traffic. No digital billboards."

"You say that like those are bad things."

"Geena, this is nature. I know it's not something you're used to, but it's wonderful. Give it a chance."

"Lucky for me, I'm not the one taking a job out here, so I don't have to give it a chance."

Taylor sighed as they parked in the grass beside Sierra's Forerunner. "Just promise me you'll be nice today."

"I'm always nice."

"No, you're not," Taylor said. "You dress nice, and you're *polite*. That's not the same thing."

"Isn't it?" Geena got out of the car and smoothed the front of her crisp white shirt dress over a hunter green turtleneck and leggings with dark brown riding boots. After brushing aside the bangs of her sharp blonde pixie cut with one finger, she pulled her camera case from the floor of the back seat, slipping the strap over a shoulder. "Fine then. I'm promising polite. Take it or leave it."

"Fine," Taylor grumbled, leading the way up the porch steps.

Geena pointed at the yard along the side of the house. "What are *those*?"

Taylor turned to look at whatever had Geena in a tizzy. "That's a skunk, genius."

"It looks like a badger." She hurried up the steps and

stayed far away from the side with the offending creatures. "Why are they so big?"

Sierra joined them on the porch and caught the end of Geena's shrieking. "Those are pretty small. The bigger one is the female. Probably about to have those babies soon. It's been a mild winter."

"*Babies?*" Geena shrieked. "You're breeding skunks out here?"

"Not on purpose." Sierra shrugged. "Skunks gonna skunk."

Geena looked at her sister with horror in her eyes. Taylor decided it was time to change the subject and get them all inside as soon as possible before Geena bolted.

"This is my sister, Geena," Taylor said. "She's going to be taking the event photos."

"I'm Sierra. Thanks so much for helping us out."

Regret blanketed Geena's face as she shook Sierra's hand. Taylor swooped in and tucked her arm around her sister's.

"Let's get you inside so you can check out the lighting situation."

Taylor guided Geena through the front door, exchanging a quick glance with Sierra, who immediately shrugged off the whole introduction.

"This is the main welcome room," Sierra said. "It's the biggest room with the most windows. But if you want to isolate in one of the smaller empty rooms, feel free to explore those too."

"Do I hear company?" Liz's voice boomed from down the hall, and a second later she appeared in an oversized, black, Witchy Kitty Rescue sweatshirt hanging off one shoulder and black leggings over comfy-looking, furry slipper boots.

"Liz, this is my sister, Geena. She's here to check out the lighting for the portrait fundraiser."

Geena, who had composed herself since the skunk sighting, extended a hand politely. "Pleasure to meet you."

Liz shook her hand. "Same. I'm Liz. Sierra and I run the place. Or, at least, we will once it's up and running. Shouldn't be too long now. We're awfully grateful for your help."

"I'm glad I can help." Geena glanced over her shoulder at Taylor. "Anything for my little sister."

Liz narrowed her eyes and smirked at Taylor, obviously catching on to the unspoken tension. "We're really happy to have Taylor on board with us too."

After an awkward pause, Geena said, "Sierra mentioned something about rooms we could potentially use? I could check those out first before testing the lighting out here."

"Yes, of course," Liz said, gesturing down the hall. "Follow me."

"Have fun doing lighting stuff," Taylor called out after them. "I'll be planning decorations and the heartstravaganza!"

Sierra placed a hand on her shoulder. "Never use that word again."

"What? I think it's cute." She giggled and looked around the welcome area. There was a lot of wall space to fill and plenty of space to hang things from the ceiling. She was going to have a blast shopping at the party store later today on her way home. They might need to bring in more tables, though. "I was thinking we could put out some treats and refreshments for the animals and the humans."

"Not a bad idea," Sierra said. "I'm not baking them, but maybe you can twist Liz's arm to help."

"I can get my roommate to help with that. She's a fabulous baker. And she's a vet tech also, so she knows what does and doesn't belong in a dog treat."

"Perfect," Sierra said. "Any luck with that cat you've got?"

Taylor shook her head. "Not yet."

Tink's blood work had come back clear, so whatever he'd swallowed wasn't toxic. And since it wasn't blocking his output or causing any other problems, for the time being, they decided to wait it out and give him a little lubrication help and wait.

Sierra nodded down the hallway and raised her brow. "That one gonna be able to handle a bunch of smelly animals?"

"Geena? She'll be fine," Taylor said. "Geena's a snobby complainer, but once she's committed to something she'll follow through."

"Good. Just make sure she doesn't wear white that weekend. We don't have a dry cleaning budget."

Taylor laughed as her phone rang in her back pocket. She didn't recognize the number, so she let it go to voicemail.

"I get a ton of those lately," Sierra said. "Pain in the butt. They drive Marc bananas."

"Your boyfriend?" Taylor asked. "Will I meet him at the event?"

A mischievous grin stretched across Sierra's face. "That is a *fabulous* idea."

"Why do I feel bad for Marc?"

"Don't," Sierra said with a chuckle. "He knew what he was getting into with me. Oh, forgot to tell you, our slots are already halfway filled. Almost met our goal on the first day of sign-ups."

"That's fantastic!" Taylor's phone dinged with a voicemail message. "Probably just a bot recording." She hit play and listened to the message.

It wasn't a bot.

"What's that face for?" Sierra asked.

When the message ended, Taylor held the phone out, staring at the screen in shock. "It's Austin's mom."

"The hot guy with the cat? His *mom?*" Sierra asked. "Ew. What does she want?"

Taylor stared at the screen a second more, then she looked up at Sierra, unable to hide the horror from her face. "She wants me to have lunch with her next week."

---

21

*T*aylor slipped on her most comfortable pair of sweatpants, the ones reserved only for midweek days off work. Although it was only Tuesday, she'd had off Saturday, which meant a two-day weekend, work on Monday, followed by today off again. Her payment for that was being scheduled for the next four days in a row through next Saturday.

But soon she would be *free* of that place and free of hiding from Jason and her guilt and everything that went with that job. She couldn't wait.

There was a long road ahead, but she planned to make the most of today with her comfiest pants. At least until she needed to get ready for her scheduled lunch date.

You up?

She smiled at the phone and replied: *barely.*

Then her smile grew wider as Austin texted that he was in the parking lot and on his way up. He'd been making random stops at her apartment for the past week. Quick visits to drop off coffee or grab a brief kiss or snuggle at the end of one of her long workdays. He didn't mind that her skin smelled like disinfectant—worse some days—or that her hair reeked of sweaty dog if she didn't shower before he came over.

Austin would wrap her in his arms anyway, and they'd usually watch tv on the couch until she passed out against him. He'd either place a blanket over her and slip out or wake her to go to bed before he left, depending on how tired she was.

Taylor had never been so smitten with anyone in her entire life. This man had proven himself to be reliable and caring, and he made her question if she'd ever actually felt love before.

Because this was it. Love. Nothing else she'd experienced before came close.

She hadn't said the word to him, though. They hadn't known each other a month. A voice in her mind told her she couldn't *really* be in love, could she?

But she was. She just wasn't ready to expose her inner belly and say it out loud yet.

Even though she'd fallen hard and fast, that didn't mean he felt the same way. She had to give him time to figure out his own feelings before she vomited up her confession of undying devotion.

Great. Love had made her incredibly dramatic on top of everything else. But she certainly wasn't complaining if that was the worst side effect.

She grabbed the roll of paper towels and cleaning spray that now lived on the night table beside her bed and attacked the spot where Tink had been sitting. To her surprise, there was no spit-up.

Come to think of it, she hadn't heard him retching either. She turned to find him licking his paw contentedly, his post-breakfast routine.

She thought back over the last hour to consider if

anything was different. He'd hopped on the bed as usual, then climbed onto her stomach to sit there and howl. Same as always.

But…

This morning she'd gotten up instead of rolling over to hit snooze and ignore him for a few more minutes. It was her day off, but Taylor had drank a bunch of water before bed and had to pee. That was the only thing she could think of that had changed.

She walked across the room to check the litter box. Nope. Nothing yet. But he usually waited until after breakfast to do his business.

Maybe the ring was on its way out?

Or maybe her change in routine had something to do with him not puking this morning?

That couldn't be it. Could it?

She scratched Tink's head and pet his back, deciding to run some experiments over the week to see if her getting up early was the variable making the difference. It sounded unlikely, but animals did weird stuff for unknown reasons sometimes.

A soft knock rapped against the apartment door. Austin's morning knock, quiet in case Ellie was still sleeping. Taylor never thought she could find consideration so sexy.

She opened the door to Austin in his soft brown jacket with two cups of coffee and a smile surrounded by short, freshly trimmed facial hair. "Good morning."

He met her mouth with a kiss, sweet but passionate, like he hadn't seen her in weeks instead of a couple of days. Taylor loved being in this man's beam of attention. She'd never felt so understood or accepted or appreciated as when she was around Austin. His charm came with genuine goodness, and Taylor was grateful every day that she'd chosen to trust her instincts on this man. He was proof that her ability to assess people wasn't completely broken.

"Good morning to you." He handed her a coffee as he entered the apartment and followed her to the couch. A few seconds later, Tink joined them, jumping up to squeeze between them on the cushion, then placing his front paws on Austin's leg in anticipation of pets. Austin didn't make him wait long. "There's my guy. Good morning to you too."

"To what do I owe thanks for coffee and a kiss this morning?"

"Your beautiful face." He leaned in for another kiss. This time, it was interrupted by Tink's slightly squished howl from between them. Austin laughed against her mouth, tickling her with his beard. "Sorry, dude."

Tink resumed kneading his paws on Austin's leg.

"I think he forgives us." Taylor laughed and looked back up at Austin. "But really, where are you off to so early?"

"The detective returned my call last night and said he can meet with me this morning. So I'm heading to the station and wanted to see you first for a quick second."

"He has news?"

"I couldn't tell. Either he was busy at that moment or didn't want to discuss details over the phone." Austin took a sip of coffee, but the caffeine and sugar boost didn't hide the worry from his face. "I'll find out in a little while, I guess."

"You're going to ask him about Brandon, I assume?"

Austin had become increasingly concerned about the guy during their last several conversations. He'd been putting off contacting the man as long as possible, but he couldn't avoid the matter forever. Taylor still wasn't letting Zeke off the hook in her own mind just yet, but Austin seemed lasered in on Brandon and why he inherited the house, but not Tink.

"I want to see if the detective knows anything about the guy before I meet with him." Austin scratched at his beard nervously. "I left a message with Brandon last night. Told him who I was and that I'd like to meet later this week. So, that's happening, I guess. He hasn't returned my call yet though."

Taylor placed a hand on the side of his face. "I'm sorry, this is all such a mess. It's got to be hard enough losing your uncle without worrying about if someone killed him and why."

Austin nodded and smiled gently at her. "It is. Having you to listen while I talk through it helps."

"Good." Taylor gave him a quick kiss, and Tink let out another howl. This time, he hopped off the couch and stormed back to the bedroom.

"I guess that's his opinion on the matter," Austin said.

A few seconds later, Taylor heard the telltale sound of him shuffling litter around in the box.

"I think he's going to poop in protest." With a grin, she asked, "Want to help me check for that ring or whatever it is?"

"I'll have to pass on that invitation." He gave her another quick kiss as she stood with him. "I need to head to the station."

"Good luck with that."

Austin nodded toward the bedroom. "Good luck with yours, too. I'm not sure which of us has the less pleasant task this morning."

Taylor smiled and kissed him goodbye, trying to force out any anxiety from her expression. She didn't mind those regular poop checks, so Austin had the edge on unpleasant tasks for now, but she hadn't revealed her lunch plans to him. Taylor had debated all weekend, but in the end, she'd respected Melinda's wishes and didn't tell Austin about their meeting today.

She wasn't sure what made her more anxious. Meeting his mother alone for lunch, or hiding the fact from Austin.

"THANKS FOR COMING IN."

Detective Langlinais shook Austin's hand and gestured at the small chair across from his desk. He was a roundish balding man with a dark mustache and a rumpled gray dress shirt. It was as if he'd woken up that morning, pulled up an instruction manual for how to look like a middle-aged detective, and ran with it.

Not that Austin should talk. In his red polo shirt with his school's cougar mascot embroidered on it and his khaki slacks, Austin probably looked like he'd gone shopping for his own "high school baseball coach" look.

"Thanks for meeting with me." Austin sat in the chair and tried to ignore the overwhelming scent mix of coffee and cheap tropical air freshener.

The detective knocked his knuckles on the desk softly while he glanced around at his mess until he found the file folder he was looking for. "I wish I had more to tell you. To be honest, we still don't have a lot to go on in your uncle's case."

Your uncle's case.

"Does that mean it's…"

"We're keeping it as quiet as possible, but yes, we've classified it as a homicide investigation."

Austin felt the blood drain from his head and the room faded for a moment. He shut his eyes and drew a few calming breaths before opening them again. Detective Langlinais sat patiently, waiting for Austin to absorb that bit of news.

"What does that mean now?"

"It means I can do more digging than I could without the official classification." He cleared his throat and laced his fingers in front of him, placing both hands on the file. "But I'm going to be honest with you. There isn't much to tell you about so far."

Austin was overcome with white-hot frustration. They were supposed to have access to information he couldn't get. Documents. Records. *Something*. Anything that would clue them in to whoever killed his uncle. If they couldn't find the answer...

"What do you mean, there isn't much? I have a whole greedy family who've been waiting in line for him to die for years. You're telling me not one of them even smells guilty to you?"

He felt an instant pinch of guilt. It wasn't this guy's fault. Probably. But Austin needed answers, and he'd been hoping to get some this morning.

"I'm aware, and they've all checked out," Detective Langlinais explained. "They've got alibis. Or, as you've discovered, they didn't stand to gain anything by his death."

"Maybe they didn't know that? Or what if they did and were angry about it?"

The detective gave a patient, sympathetic smile. "We're still looking into this, I assure you. But so far none of them look good for it." He cleared his throat. "We also have to consider the possibility that this was... more random."

"What does that mean?"

"There had been some break-ins reported in the area in the weeks surrounding your uncle's death."

"But nothing was taken."

"That you know of," the detective said. "We don't have a record of cash or prescriptions that were in the house, so we have to consider that perhaps your uncle walked in on someone."

Austin thought about the damage to the door frame.

Technically, that could have happened then. Maybe Austin didn't notice in those first couple of weeks. But that felt too coincidental. Especially when there were other suspects.

"Did you clear Zeke?"

He held his breath, waiting for the answer. As much as he still didn't like Zeke, Austin hoped—at least for his mother's sake—that he wasn't a murderer.

The detective nodded. "He was fishing on a charter boat miles away. We checked it out."

Relief washed over Austin, followed by the reality that they had narrowed down the suspects. "Have you looked into a Brandon Wiltz?"

Maybe Austin was imagining things. Maybe he was looking for signs that weren't there. Maybe the coffee he'd picked up was extra strong that morning. But he could have sworn Detective Langlinais stiffened slightly at the mention of that name.

"We are aware of that individual, yes."

"And?"

"I'm sorry, Mr. Champagne. I can't give you any more details on the case than that at this time." He sighed. "I wish I had more for you, but I don't. Not yet. But I promise we're working hard to find whoever did this."

Maybe it was the sincerity in the man's eyes. Or the mustache. Or his own desperation. Whatever the reason, Austin believed this guy.

"I'm meeting with him later this week," Austin said. "To give him a copy of the will and discuss the transfer. Did you know he inherited my uncle's house?"

Detective Langlinais nodded silently.

"Is there anything I should know about him before then?"

"All I can tell you is that this is an active investigation, and I can't reveal any details of the case." He stood. "I'm sorry.

We're working on it, and I'd appreciate it if you wouldn't discuss the case with Mr. Wiltz."

Austin stood, and a chill ran up his back beneath his jacket. "Why not?"

"Just let us do our jobs, okay?" Detective Langlinais extended his hand. "Hopefully, I'll have more information for you soon."

22

Taylor had a feeling Melinda was one of those "on time is late" or "early is on time" people, so she arrived at the restaurant fifteen minutes before their lunch date. Melinda was already waiting for her.

Austin's mother wore a crisp white blouse open low enough to reveal a gorgeous blue statement necklace and earrings to match. Her short blonde bob was styled perfectly, not a strand out of place as she made an elegant gesture at the chair across from her.

"Have a seat. Lovely to see you again."

"You too." Taylor placed her purse and jacket on the back of the chair and sat as commanded, flashing a big smile at Melinda. "Thank you for inviting me."

"Thank you for coming." She said it as if this were some kind of business meeting instead of a casual lunch.

Wait…

Was this a business meeting?

Taylor's brain attempted to sift through what she remembered of their text exchange. It was so hard to interpret meaning and unspoken intentions from texts. She loved the short form communication and the ability to send emojis and have quick exchanges, but she struggled with interpreting messages from people she didn't know well.

Although Austin had been different. Taylor could read him well right from the start. She'd doubted her skill at that, but looking back, her instincts with him had been spot on from the beginning. And while she'd second-guessed every text, her first impressions of his messages had been on the mark each time.

If only she could read his mother half as well.

"The weather's lovely today, isn't it?" Taylor said. "It's so good to see the sun again."

It had been gloomy the last couple of days. The clouds had been so thick that past Sunday that Taylor had skipped Tink's walk for fear it might rain on them. Carrying the cat back to the apartment was one thing. Carrying a wet, cranky cat through an unexpected rain shower might have been more than she could handle.

Melinda made a noise that sounded like it could be agreement, but it wasn't an actual word. She picked up her menu and flipped it over to examine the lunch side. "The candied pecan chicken salad is excellent. Their balsamic dressing is the best I've had in this city."

Taylor barely glanced at the menu, much less considered the options, before the server arrived with her water and asked what they'd like to drink. Before she could say that water was fine, Melinda chimed in.

"Do you like white wine?"

Taylor struggled for words. It wasn't quite noon yet. On a Wednesday. She didn't normally drink with lunch. That seemed like a thing much fancier people did.

But fancy Melinda was waiting for an answer. The mother of the man she was dating.

If she had a drink, would Melinda tack that up in some

pro/con list about her? And if she *didn't*, would Melinda think Taylor was judging her for doing so?

No. Melinda didn't seem the type to give a crap about what anyone thought of her. And the question at hand wasn't actually if she wanted a drink, Taylor reminded herself. Melinda had only asked if she liked white wine.

"Yes." The word came out more like a question than an answer, but Taylor was just glad she could force it out at all.

"We'll have two glasses of the Fletcher Valley Sauvignon Blanc." She lowered her menu. "Are you ready to order?"

Taylor opened and closed her mouth. She didn't know if she wanted salad or a sandwich or maybe one of the lunch pastas, much less *which* of those she should order. But she didn't want to say that in front of Melinda. Taylor got the distinct impression that she shouldn't show her indecisive underbelly to this woman.

"It looks like we'll need a minute," Melinda told the server. "Check back with us when you bring the wine."

"Sorry to hold you up. I could have picked something quickly."

"No, you couldn't." Melinda gave her a knowing smile. "My late husband was the same way with a menu. And no, you aren't holding me up at all. I take it you haven't been here before?"

Taylor shook her head and studied the menu some more. "It all sounds delicious."

"It is. But don't get the panini. Trust me."

Taylor bit her lip. Curiosity tugged at her to ask why, but she kept her mouth shut and mentally settled on a salad. The one Melinda mentioned earlier. She didn't think her stomach could handle anything heavier than that.

The server returned with their wine and disappeared after they gave their selections. Taylor placed her napkin in her lap, smoothing it and fidgeting with the edges, giving her hands something to do so she didn't dive head-first into the glass of wine to swim in it.

Taylor lifted her glass for a sip once Melinda had tasted her own first. The wine was light and dry, a perfect lunch selection. "I hear we'll be getting rain and a cold front tomorrow. I hope it doesn't freeze."

Melinda frowned in reply. Taylor didn't get the impression the frown was for the rain.

"I abhor small talk. Don't you?"

Taylor withdrew slightly, wishing she were a turtle that could retreat entirely into her shell. She *did* enjoy small talk. She found it an excellent way to ease into a conversation and settle in with a person, keeping things light and positive to set the tone before they dug in to meatier discussions.

But she certainly wasn't about to admit that now.

Melinda continued, not waiting for an answer. "So let's get to why we're both here."

"For lunch?"

One corner of Melinda's mouth lifted with amusement. "You truly are a delight. I can see why my son adores you."

She felt her cheeks flush. "I really like Austin."

"I believe you." Melinda's face turned serious. "But your feelings are not the only matter at stake. And my son has just become a more tempting prize."

Taylor blinked at the woman. *Prize?* "I'm sorry, I don't understand."

"Whatever feelings the two of you have, this is a new relationship," Melinda said. "And as I'm sure you know, Austin inherited quite a large sum from his uncle. If you intend to stay with my son because the monetary reward has increased, I'm here to remedy that."

"It's not that, I—"

Melinda stopped her with a raised hand. "I want to believe your intentions are respectable, but one never knows what's truly in another's heart until they reveal it. And I will not take chances with my family. Especially my son. I never have before, and I'm not about to start now, no matter how delightfully suited you seem for Austin."

Taylor's brain slowly processed the strangest, most sideways compliment she'd ever received, but she got hung up on another part of the speech.

I never have before...

How many of these lunches had she had with Austin's past partners?

"Whatever you're after," Melinda continued, "let me head you off right now. My son need not be involved in this if you're set on acquiring anything more than his heart."

After a few moments more of processing things and putting bits and pieces of this conversation together, Taylor came to a terrifying conclusion.

"Are you trying to pay me off? To break up with Austin?"

Melinda laughed. A villainous laugh that made Taylor wonder if she was the one about to be served up and sliced on salads for lunch.

"Don't be ridiculous. Of course, not." Melinda held Taylor in her intense gaze as she took a slow, deliberate sip of her wine. She set down the glass, that gaze never wavering, and the hint of a smile played at her lips. "I wouldn't dream of it. First off, Austin would never speak to me again. Second, that tactic never works."

Taylor got the distinct expression that Melinda's last statement was spoken from experience.

"Then I don't understand." Taylor was actually afraid she clearly understood the unspoken threat being delivered: mess with this woman's family and pay the price.

"My son likes you. I like you. I think you could be very good for him."

"Thank you?"

Taylor wasn't even sure why she answered at all, much less with that. But she didn't know what else to say, and not saying anything didn't feel like an option.

"But let me be very clear," Melinda continued. "If you hurt him, I will no longer like you. And if I have misjudged you and you intend to manipulate him for monetary reasons, know that I have a team of well-paid lawyers and a protective drive that you do not want to trigger into action. Do we understand each other?"

Taylor nodded.

"Good." Melinda switched gears and flashed a great big smile and raised her glass. "Then a toast... to you and Austin."

Taylor raised her glass, then set it back down. "Wait. First, I'd like to say something."

No, no, no. Her brain screamed. *We don't want to say anything. Just drink the wine, smile, shove some lettuce in your face, and let's get the heck out of here!*

But Taylor's mouth wasn't listening to her brain anymore. She ignored her reactive, protective anxieties and trusted her deeper instincts.

"I like your son," she said. "A lot. I might even love him."

Melinda raised an amused eyebrow at that. "Go on."

No time for regret now.

"I liked him before I knew he had any money. When he walked in with nothing but Tink and his grief. When all I knew about him was that he cared about that cat, his family, and those kids he coaches. So no, I'm not here to manipulate him out of his money or anything else. I don't care if you believe me or not, it's the truth."

Melinda crossed her arms and leaned against her chair, eyeing Taylor appraisingly. Taylor's stomach flipped and flopped and her lizard brain screamed out with regret, but she refused to take back a word of that speech. It was long past time she started listening to that deeper intuitive voice in her gut.

Melinda gave an approving nod. "I think you two will be very good for each other. Maybe you can even convince him to move home."

"I have no intention of trying to convince Austin of doing anything he doesn't want to do," Taylor said. "We've discussed the location logistics and our busy lives and how we'll make this work for now."

Melinda chuckled. "You remind me of Austin's father. I loved that man, but he never saw the long game either."

"I told you, I'm not playing any games." Taylor wondered how long she could keep this up. Honesty was fine, but she wasn't conditioned for going head to head with someone like Melinda. Being this direct all the time was exhausting.

"Everything is a game. Just not the way you think." Melinda raised her glass again. "But that's a discussion for another lunch."

Taylor sagged with the weight of that promise.

Threat?

Why did everything with this woman feel like a threat?

"There is one more thing I want to discuss with you today." Melinda set her wine down again and placed her hands in her lap as if she had serious business to explain. Something even more serious than threatening her son's girlfriend if she tried to take advantage of him.

"Oh?"

"I know he's looking into Kenneth's death." Melinda put a hand in the air, palm facing Taylor. "Please don't waste either of our time denying it in some attempt to protect him. I know what he's doing, and I know better than to try stopping him once he has his mind set on something."

This wasn't the direction Taylor expected this conversation to take. Not that she'd expected anything in particular, but she was wholly unprepared for this.

"Then what is it you want to discuss?"

"Assuming that you are sincere in your relationship intentions, I want you to look out for him."

"I don't understand. I mean, certainly, but what exactly are you asking me to do?"

Of course, Taylor would "look out for" Austin. To her, that meant listening to him. Talking things out with him. Being there for him emotionally. But she had a feeling Melinda was asking for something else.

"If he's in over his head, I'd like for you to come to me," Melinda said. "I know you wouldn't want to betray his trust, but I hope you care enough that if you see he's headed for danger of any kind, you'll do what's necessary to protect him. And I have the means to do so."

Taylor wanted to ask what those means were, but that wasn't the point.

Melinda was asking her to snoop. Snitch? Something.

"You don't have to say anything right now. I just want you to think about it, and if you sense danger, I want to be the call you make. Do you understand?"

Taylor nodded. She understood. She wasn't ready to agree to that, but she understood.

"Good," Melinda said. "I'm sure you've noticed his ridiculous white knight streak already. Kenneth is dead. He doesn't need saving. And he wouldn't want justice at the expense of Austin's safety. I'm trusting you to remember that and this conversation."

The server arrived with their salads, saving Taylor from elaborating any further than her simple response.

"I'll remember."

TAYLOR LEANED against her apartment door once she was safely inside and breathed a sigh of relief. She might have been holding that breath since she left the restaurant.

She'd never had a more exhausting lunch in her life. Skipping small talk? Who does that? Never mind the not-so-veiled threats.

Still, she might like Melinda even more, despite all of that. The woman was taxing, but she was also fiercely protective of her son. Taylor couldn't fault her for that. Even if she was appalled that Melinda wanted her to be some kind of spy.

Taylor pushed away from the door, dropped her keys and bag on the couch, and went to the bedroom to hunt for Tink. A few snuggles with that guy would improve her mood.

But the moment she walked in, the smell of fresh poop hit her like she'd run face-first into a wall of it. Tink left his bed and pranced over to greet her and show off his creation.

"Nice, buddy." Taylor grabbed the trash can and scoop and squatted beside the litter box. "Let's see if you left me a present today."

She dug around in the box and began her routine: unearthing the pieces and breaking them up to inspect the insides. Not exactly a glamorous job, but a necessary one if they wanted to find whatever he'd eaten.

When she flipped over the last remaining piece, Taylor spotted something purple sticking out of it.

Huh. She'd been looking for a ring all this time. What the heck was this?

She broke the poop apart to get at the purple thing and discovered that it was, in fact, a ring. After poking at it with the corner of the litter scoop, she confirmed it wasn't metal, maybe some kind of rubber or silicone.

"Where did you get this?"

But it made a lot more sense why this ended up in his stomach. Cats weren't garbage disposals like dogs, but some had chewing preferences, particularly cardboard, plastic, and elastic hair ties. A rubber ring could have been just the texture to tempt this guy, then whoops... into the belly. It made more sense than a metal ring.

The big question was where he got it from.

She'd have to ask Austin later. Send him some pictures or have him come over to look at it.

After she cleaned it up.

She glanced over at Tink. "I should make you do this part."

Tink gave a howl in reply, and Taylor kissed him on the head before walking to the kitchen for gloves and cleaning supplies.

23

*A*ustin slid into the dark wooden booth and looked around. He'd picked this meeting place because it was quiet and didn't gather a crowd until later in the evening, when the Friday night jazz combo began their first set.

So far, the dimly lit bar in the back of the modern Italian restaurant was a ghost town. Reputable but private enough for a serious conversation. Plus, the bar had the best cocktail menu, and they could still order food if this guy wanted a meal. Not that Austin could stomach anything right now.

He glanced at his watch. Twenty minutes early. Good. No one arrived more than fifteen minutes before a meeting, so arriving before that gave Austin the advantage. He got to pick his seat. To relax. To settle in to his position of power and mentally prepare to maintain control of the meeting.

Like it or not, he had picked up a few things from his mother over the years.

He hadn't intended to, but watching her command a room, in both formal and casual settings, he'd absorbed some of her techniques. Although she'd deliberately conveyed this verbal lesson many times over. For once, he was grateful a lesson had stuck.

But now he had twenty minutes to kill. Or at least five, if this guy was the conscientious type.

The problem with showing up this early was that Austin didn't relax with a lot of time on his hands. He was glad to have his choice of seats, so he could see the door from his position, but with every second that ticked by, he grew antsier. Austin didn't like sitting still and doing nothing. Doing nothing gave his brain time to wander.

He'd already let his brain too much time to wonder about what this Brandon guy might be like. What he might have done to Uncle Kenny. What Austin might do if his suspicions were confirmed.

He ordered a whiskey on the rocks and pulled out his phone. Without thinking, he opened his messages and sent a smiling sun face to Taylor with the message, *hey sunshine*. Then he scrolled back through previous few days of conversations, and his eyes locked on the last photo she'd sent him on Wednesday. The purple ring.

Austin had recognized it immediately. It could always be seen on his uncle's finger, though he hadn't realized it was a silicone ring. And he definitely didn't know it was inscribed with, *Never give up*. Austin wasn't sure if those words had any meaning for his uncle, but the man was tenacious, so it could be as simple as a reminder for himself. Or it could be a song quote Austin didn't recognize. Either way, the mystery of the ingested object had been solved.

But, according to Taylor, not the morning vomiting. She'd insisted it wasn't too worrisome, since Tink's blood work was clear and there didn't seem to be any concern now that he'd passed the ring.

Austin didn't know how that ring ended up in Tink's stomach, but since Taylor said it happened all the time with chewy, rubbery things, he decided not to worry about it. It must have fallen off during the fall, or Tink grabbed it when his uncle took it off.

The server placed a rocks glass with light golden liquid over ice in front of Austin just as he caught sight of the man he'd been waiting to meet.

Austin might be returning soon to his Northshore life, but he wasn't leaving without getting a few answers. Even if he couldn't solve his uncle's murder, he was going to follow through with this as far as he could.

The man entered the dark bar, and Austin recognized him immediately from the internet photos, particularly a photo of him and Uncle Kenny smiling together at that Mardi Gras ball. Brandon's face was the same oddly disarming mix of features: squared jaw, full lips, intense eyebrows, and soft cheeks. He wore an impeccably tailored gray suit, and his short dark hair was trimmed and styled to professional perfection.

Austin stood and extended his hand as the man approached. "Brandon?"

When he shook the guy's hand, Austin got an instant picture in his mind of this man shoving his uncle down the steps. He'd tried to stop picturing that all week, but facing Brandon brought the image back.

"You must be Austin. I'd recognize that smile anywhere." For a moment, he appeared joyful. Then his expression fell. "Sorry. I know you're his nephew, but I wasn't prepared for you to look so much like him."

Austin gestured at the booth beside them. "Really?"

No one had ever commented that Austin looked like his uncle. His dad, sure. Lots of times. And since his dad and Uncle Kenny were brothers, it made sense that Austin might resemble both of them. Aside from their matching light brown hair, he'd never picked up any similarities in appearance before.

Maybe it was guilt making this guy see things that weren't there.

"It's the eyes. And the smile, of course." They slid into the booth and Brandon nodded at Austin's drink. "Whiskey?" When Austin confirmed the guess, Brandon smiled. "You know, I would have expected all these similarities might be difficult to handle, but seeing him in you in so many little ways... I don't know. It's comforting, I guess. As comforting as it can be in a world where he isn't anymore."

Dramatic much?

Austin choked down his anger and washed it back with a sip of whiskey while Brandon ordered a clover club.

Interesting choice.

While Austin was busy worrying about his position of power and maintaining control in this conversation, the suspected murderer across from him was ordering a pink drink with egg white foam.

Interesting.

Maybe that was his own power move?

Austin pushed away all speculations about this man's drink. He was channeling his mother too much now. A color was a color and a drink choice was a drink choice. Nothing more.

This murder investigation was making him question everything. Even his own judgment.

"Do you want to order food?"

Brandon shook his head. "I don't think I could stomach it. Seeing you is nice, but this is all still... a lot. You know?"

Austin did know. The only thing Austin doubted was this guy's act right now.

He was good, Austin had to give him that. Anyone else might find him wholly convincing. But Austin owed it to his uncle to remain unmoved by the performance and get to the truth.

"I'm glad you agreed to meet with me."

"Of course," Brandon said, fiddling with his fingers resting on the table. "My regret is not reaching out to you sooner. And that we couldn't meet under better circumstances. Your uncle had been hoping for a dinner party for the next time you came into town, and I'd been looking forward to that. He spoke so fondly of you. Whenever your name came up, his eyes sparkled with admiration. I hope you know how much you meant to him."

Austin blinked and willed his eyes to remain dry. As dry as they could in this dank bar with his uncle's name and memories hovering over them.

"The feeling was mutual."

Austin didn't know why he felt the need to add that. He didn't owe this man his feelings about his uncle. Didn't owe this man anything, whether he had something to do with his uncle's death or not.

"How's Tink?" Brandon laced his fingers together and tapped his clasped hands on the table gently. "That poor cat must be a wreck without Kenny. Gosh, he loved that animal more than anything. How's he adjusting? Lost without his person, I'm guessing."

"He was, but he's doing well now."

Brandon's shoulders dropped with what looked like relief. Austin reminded himself that even a killer could care about a cat.

"I'm so glad to hear that."

Austin felt that familiar stab of guilt, but for some reason, he told the rest of Tink's story. "I found a home for him. Temporarily. I can't take him with me back to Northshore. Believe me, I tried." He couldn't help the searing pain of that guilt ripping through his gut at the disappointed look on

Brandon's face. "But he's with a wonderful woman. A vet tech. Taylor. He's staying with her until they find a permanent home. She'll make sure they're the right people."

The server placed Brandon's bright pink cocktail in front of him, and he adjusted the lemon twist so he could take a sip.

"I can't say I'm not disappointed he isn't with you, but I understand. Kenny trusted you, so I know you'll do right by Tink. And with everything else."

"I guess that leads us right into why I asked you to meet with me this evening." Austin slid the envelope with Brandon's full name on it across the table. "This is a copy of Uncle Kenny's will."

Brandon stared at the envelope, not making a move toward it like it was laced with poison or something. "I don't think I can read that right now."

"It's your copy, so whenever you're ready." Austin paused, not sure why he felt compelled to offer Brandon any kindness. His uncle had never mentioned him to Austin. Patricia didn't have a single good word to say about him. And while he'd left him the house, Uncle Kenny hadn't trusted him with Tink. Nothing added up to imply that Austin owed this man an ounce of compassion.

But as his mother so often reminded him, sometimes you needed to grease things up a bit, if you wanted something from a person. Especially information.

"Would you like me to tell you what he left you?"

"I never wanted anything from him," Brandon said. "Only his companionship. And he can't leave that behind, so it doesn't matter."

Austin didn't know what to say to that. It was exactly the kind of thing someone might rehearse to seem sincere. Or the kind of thing someone overtaken by grief might say.

"He left you the house."

Brandon's head snapped up, and his gaze shifted from the envelope to Austin across the booth. He stared in shock for a bit, then a nervous, delighted chuckle fell out. "Of course, he did." He shook his head. "I'd expected him to give it to you, but this makes sense."

"Why?"

One-word answers and questions. Another lesson from his mother. Let your opponent fill in the blanks as much as possible.

"Like I said, I only wanted his company. And what could he leave behind that is most *him?*"

Austin nodded.

It was the first thing that made sense. The house really was his uncle personified.

"I may have been the only person on this planet who loved that place as much as he did," Brandon said. "Not because I loved the aesthetics or the individual pieces or anything, but because it made him happy. Because it was everything he loved. Except for Tink and you, of course."

"I just have one question." Austin had a lot of questions. But he was going to limit this interrogation to just one for now. "Why didn't he leave Tink to you? With the house, I mean. Tink would be more comfortable staying there."

"Oh, that's easy," Brandon said. "Aside from the fact that Kenny trusted you most, I'm allergic to cats. I had to load up on meds every time I went there. It was worth it, and if he'd asked me to move in with him, I would have happily lived the rest of my life on those pills, snuggled up with him on that purple couch watching his favorite movie every night." His expression turned sad again. "But we never got to that point. We talked about moving in together down the road. We're both older and independent and had separate lives, so we were taking it slow. But things were headed that way."

While Austin couldn't say for sure what happened that

day on his uncle's staircase, he was certain this man believed every word coming out of his mouth right now. Brandon loved Uncle Kenny, that much Austin was sure of. The question remaining was if the feeling was mutual.

"Since you lived independent lives, then you weren't upset that he went so many places with Patricia?"

Brandon narrowed his eyes thoughtfully. "No, it didn't bother me that he spent time with her. I can't say she felt the same way though, as I'm sure she's made clear to you already."

"Why would you say that?"

Another Melinda lesson: ask questions, never give answers.

"Because she told everyone how she felt about me. Although I can't say why she felt that way."

"She seems to think you had a... tight hold on my uncle."

Okay, so he wasn't as good at this as his mother would be. He could live with not being a carbon copy of her, as long as he got the answers he was looking for.

Brandon sat up a little straighter, tightening his grip on the stem of his delicate glass. "I never tried to influence who your uncle spent time with or how he spent his time."

"You weren't at all jealous of their trip? Or being left out of their plans?"

Austin had expected a response, maybe a glint of jealousy in the man's eyes or a twitch of anger playing at his lips. But he hadn't expected the utter confusion he was witnessing.

"What trip?"

"They were planning to rent an RV and drive to the Grand Canyon together with Patricia's dogs."

The confusion settled deeper into the lines on Brandon's face. "Well, I suppose he must have been planning two trips then. I would have loved for all of us to go together, but I doubt Patricia would have agreed to that. And then there's the matter of Tink and the dogs not being able to travel together. Huh…" Brandon paused, lost in thought for a moment. "Do you know what he planned to do with Tink during their trip? Because I'm surprised he hadn't asked me to look after him. When was their trip?"

There was no anger in his voice. No resentment in his tone or expression. Only confusion.

"Later this year," Austin said. "I think she said this summer, maybe. Wait, what do you mean two trips?"

Brandon took a sip of his drink as if to steady himself and process the information coming his way. "Your uncle and I planned the same trip. Minus the dogs, of course. The two of us and Tink."

"Are you sure?" Austin asked. "Maybe he just mentioned it in passing but planned the trip with Patricia instead?"

Maybe you were jealous and angry and shoved him down the stairs when you found out?

This was it. This was the piece of information Austin had been missing. The thing that could have set this murderer over the edge and cost Uncle Kenny his life.

Austin just had to keep this guy talking. Too bad he hadn't thought to record their conversation. He could have brought this to the detective. Especially if that drink loosened Brandon up even more.

"No, we *planned* it. I have a copy of the RV reservation."

"Maybe you jumped the gun and reserved it for a trip he was planning with someone else."

Austin tried to keep his tone light and conversational, but even he could hear the accusatory edge of each of his own words.

"I have the email. Kenny made the reservation himself and forwarded a copy to me. It was a surprise. He reserved it for the week of our one-year dating anniversary."

The two men stared at each other in confusion. Austin

didn't think anyone could be this good an actor, and he could look up the email confirmation on his uncle's account for himself. Lying about this wouldn't make any sense.

So maybe there really were two trips planned. Maybe his uncle had been trying to appease both people he cared about and didn't tell them each about the other trip to avoid more tension between them.

But where did that leave the investigation?

If Brandon and Uncle Kenny were on good terms still, then who murdered him?

24

"*I*s it bad?" Sierra asked the moment Taylor and Geena entered the shelter loaded down with camera lights and cookie trays. "It's bad, isn't it?"

Geena shot them both a disgusted look that spoke volumes. Taylor's sister had chosen a more sensible outfit for working with animals today. Dark wash skinny jeans with a black tank top and a long, mossy green cardigan. The outfit looked expensive and would surely be covered in hair by the end of the day, but at least all the pieces looked washable.

"I'm sure it'll be fine," Taylor said. "Maybe we can put a diffuser out on the porch?"

What else could she say? It wasn't as if they could do anything about it. People would arrive for the first appointments within the hour, and, like Sierra said, skunks gonna skunk.

Sierra raised an amused brow at that. "You want us to diffuse... what? The whole property? The wooded river line? All of Breaux Bridge?"

With a shrug, Taylor said, "Just the porch."

She placed her cookie trays on one of the folding tables

along the wall. Colorful confetti hearts dotted the white plastic tablecloth with small vases filled with paper conversation hearts on sticks designed to look like flower bouquets. There were real flowers too. Small bunches of daisies and carnations. Taylor had set up yesterday and hardly slept a wink in anticipation of this event. She couldn't believe this was her actual job.

While she arranged the snacks, plates, and napkins, two brown paws and a little black nose appeared to check out her work. The bone-shaped peanut butter doggy treats Ellie made last night obviously smelled as enticing as they looked.

"Puck, no." Sierra clapped and called the dog away from the table. "Sorry. I brought him over to be our test appointment this morning, but he's more excited for treats. Marc and Luna are coming to pick him up in a little while, so he'll be gone before anyone else gets here."

Taylor had met Luna one day when Liz stopped by after picking up her daughter from school. Luna looked about ten years old and was a sweet, introspective child with a big heart for animals. Taylor had learned that they all live in two houses on this road, which made for a perfect arrangement to help Liz with single mom child care.

Taylor held out her fist for Puck to sniff before petting him. "Nice to meet you, Puck."

"I'll get set up, and we can take some test shots with him in a minute." Geena headed down the hall toward the first small room on the right that they'd designated for the photo studio.

"Do you and Marc have plans for tonight or tomorrow?"

Sierra froze with a mouth full of cookie that she'd snuck in there while Taylor was setting up the other table. "For what?"

"Valentine's Day?" Taylor made an elaborate gesture at the decorations.

"Oh, that." Sierra scoffed. "Not my jam. Marc's either. Although I'm sure he'll probably have something dorky set up for after this shindig, mostly because he'll think he's supposed to. Not that I haven't told him otherwise. That man's gotta find stuff out on his own though." She squatted beside Puck to let him lick her face. "It's kind of cute. Sometimes. What about you and that hunky teacher of yours?"

"I'm helping him pack tomorrow."

Sierra scrunched her nose at that and stood. "That sounds decidedly unsexy."

"He's going back to the Northshore tomorrow night." The words flew out of her mouth in a fast flurry. It was better to launch them out all at once, she figured. Like ripping off a bandage. Still hurt, though. "He's got most of the business stuff wrapped up, so he'll just need to return for a day or two to finalize the house and car transfer. Everything else is done."

Done.

Like them.

Taylor cleared her throat and reminded herself to get a grip as she placed a stack of cups near an empty ice bucket. This whole long-distance thing was making her uncharacteristically dramatic.

The worst part? Being mopey and dramatic on Valentine's Day weekend.

She would not let this ruin her day or her enjoyment of this event.

"Well, that sucks." Leave it to Sierra to put an honest, no-bullshit cap on a thing. "Sorry about that. Y'all gonna still make it work? Northshore isn't too far."

"We're going to try," Taylor said. "We'll both be busy for the next few months anyway, so we'll see how it goes and reassess this summer."

Sierra laughed. "You and your chipper practicality are adorable."

"Thank you? I think?"

Sierra glanced at the clock on the wall. "We'd better get rolling before people show up. You ready to get your picture taken?"

Puck did a little spin before following Sierra down the hall to where Geena was setting up.

Taylor finished fussing with both of the snack tables—one for the humans and one for the animal friends—and walked into the kitchen area where the schedule sat on a counter. Their first appointment was in less than half an hour. A husky. Followed by a Ragdoll cat named Rupert.

Today was going to be a blast.

AUSTIN PUT money in the meter and headed down the sidewalk. It was a dreary February afternoon. The sun hadn't poked its head out all day. And while his jacket kept his body warm, the icy wind slashed across his cheeks as he crossed a downtown intersection.

"The guys will be glad to have you back with the team." Mike had called while Austin was on his way to the station. He'd been thrilled to hear that Austin would be with them again before the first game of the season on Tuesday. "And I'm glad too. Not sure if you know this, but you handle a lot of stuff around here. It'll feel good to hand some of this back to you."

"I will forever be grateful to you for carrying the load while I was gone this past month and a half."

"No problem, man. Just glad to have you back soon." Mike paused, then added, "If you're sure you're ready. I know I joke that it's a lot, but I can handle things as long as you need me to."

"Appreciate it, but I'm done here. I'll just need a day or two later to finish up some things, but I'm ready to get back to my classes and the team."

His life.

It was time to get back to his life. And he was doing that tomorrow.

Those first weeks all he could think about was getting back to Northshore. Now it was time.

"So why do you sound so *not* ready?" Mike asked.

That was a simple answer. A one-word answer.

Taylor.

"I'm good," Austin insisted. "Listen, I'm picking up some of my uncle's things from the police station, so I have to go. I'll call you tomorrow when I get to the apartment."

"Sounds good, man. Talk to you then."

Austin stuffed his phone into his pocket and entered the station, heading straight for the front desk. He told the officer that he'd gotten a call to pick up his uncle's things that were no longer needed as potential evidence after the autopsy, and she instructed him to have a seat while she got someone to bring those out.

He grabbed an empty chair along the wall, remembering the last time he'd waited here. His car ride with Zeke. How far he'd come from that day just three weeks ago. Austin had been so worried that Zeke had murdered his uncle, but he'd been wrong about that. Just like he'd been wrong about so many things.

All week, ever since his meeting last Friday night, Austin had been wondering if maybe he'd also been wrong about Brandon. The guy seemed sincere. Austin couldn't imagine he was *that* horrible a judge of character.

Maybe, at worst, there had been some terrible accident.

Or maybe, like the detective suggested, there had been a random break-in.

Regardless, Austin had to give up the idea that he would be the one to stumble on it. Because he was at a complete dead end with theories and clues. If the truth came out, the police would have to find it.

"Mr. Champagne?"

Austin hopped to his feet and launched himself at the counter. "Yes?"

The woman held out an enormous plastic bag filled with a few small items. The bag had a white label sticker with a bunch of numbers on it.

"Here you go." Her tone was upbeat, like she was handing him takeout and not the items that had been on his uncle's body at the time of his death. "You have a blessed day."

He took the bag and stared at it for a while, not sure what he was supposed to do now. Take it back to the house, obviously. But then what? Rummage through the contents of his uncle's pockets?

He turned to leave, but something purple at the bottom of the bag caught his eye.

Austin held the bag up and used the fingers of his other hand to manipulate the position of the purple ring. He angled the ring and squinted at the inscription through the clear plastic.

Never surrender.

Was he seeing things? Or had he been so desperate for something from his uncle that he'd hallucinated what he thought was his uncle's ring?

"Is Detective Langlinais around?"

The woman at the desk hollered at a uniformed officer walking past them. "You seen Randy?"

"He left a little while ago," the man answered. "Said he'd be gone most of the afternoon."

Austin thanked them and walked out of the station with the bag and a head full of questions. When he reached his car, he sat behind the wheel and stared at the ring peeking at him.

Then he caught sight of his uncle's phone next to it inside the bag.

He pulled out the phone, but the battery was dead. Thankfully, it worked with his charger, so he turned on the car, plugged it in, and waited. A few moments later, it powered up, and he clicked open the photos app.

Austin scrolled through his uncle's pictures, not entirely sure what he was looking for. Maybe there were a bunch of those rings. Like it was a group thing. There had to be some explanation.

He didn't spot anything initially, but what he did eventually discover was photo after photo of Brandon Wiltz. Brandon smiling in the park. Brandon looking drowsy on the couch with Tink. Selfies with Uncle Kenny and Brandon together.

Austin began to tear up at how happy they looked. The photos were time-stamped up to the day before Uncle Kenny's death. There was nothing to show that he had anything but continued love for the man.

After scrolling back to last fall, Austin stopped on a picture at a local music festival. He zoomed in and found what he was looking for.

Austin's heart raced.

No. There had to be some explanation.

Maybe he was right. Maybe there were a bunch of them floating around, and the one he was looking at in this photo meant nothing.

He pulled out his own phone and made a call. "I have a question I'm hoping you have and answer to."

"Okay." Brandon's voice was a little shaky, stunned by Austin's panicked tone. "What can I help you with?"

"Uncle Kenny's purple ring. What did the inscription on his say?"

Brandon laughed softly. "Is that all? Never surrender. It's a line from Galaxy Quest, his favorite movie. Also, the reason for the purple couch too."

"Were there a bunch of other ones like it? Do you have one too?"

"No," Brandon said. "But there are two rings, and his was a gift. The full quote is, 'Never give up. Never surrender.' "

Austin's blood went cold. Somehow, he forced out the last question. The one that could put all the pieces together. "Brandon, who gave him that ring?"

After a long pause, Brandon revealed the answer Austin didn't want to hear.

"Patricia."

25

"This was wonderful." The woman slid a knit cap over her cropped natural hair. She gathered her Maltese adorned with blue polka dot ribbons into her long arms and held out a business card. "If I can be of any help here, please reach out."

Taylor examined the simple design and the woman's information. She was an attorney here in Breaux Bridge. That could probably be useful.

It also reminded Taylor that she needed to poke Liz and Sierra about getting that newsletter set up. Although, she was afraid if she poked too much, they might suggest she help with that. Tech and marketing were *not* high on Taylor's list of skills.

"Thank you," Taylor said. "We appreciate the support. Especially from the local community."

"I want to see this place succeed, and I know lots of folks who are excited about your potential as well." She lifted the furry bundle in her arms. "I'd better get this spoiled darling back home. Looking forward to getting the photos. Hope you all have a great rest of your day!"

Taylor held the door open for the woman. "Thanks. You too!"

The skunk smell on the porch had faded over the last few hours, but Taylor quickly shut the door before it and the cold air could flood into the building.

Thankfully, no one had complained about the stinky situation all day. At least, not to her. If they'd complained to Sierra, Taylor surely would have heard about it.

"Nice work." Sierra appeared from the kitchen with a bottle of water in hand and Liz by her side. "You're a natural. We should make you Head Schmooze in Charge. That's an official title, right?"

Not only did that sound terrifying, but Taylor also doubted her qualifications for that position. "You do *not* want me schmoozing anyone."

"You're way better at it than this one." Liz aimed a thumb at Sierra. "And me, if we're being honest."

Taylor shook her head. "I am not good at that kind of peopling. I'm the worst salesperson."

"This is different," Liz said. "This is being chipper and friendly to people who have big bucks to donate. Flashing smiles and talking about their pets with heartfelt enthusiasm. No sales pitch required. Just being your genuine, sparkly self."

Sparkly? Was she sparkly?

"I sparkle?"

"Oh, yeah." Sierra laughed. "You definitely sparkle. And rich people eat that up. Especially rich animal people. You're a gem."

Taylor wasn't sure if she wanted to be a gem. Or sparkle. Or schmooze anyone. But she had to admit she did like talking to people. Especially all the pet owners she met today.

She handed the card to Liz.

"Thanks." Liz waved it in the air. "We can talk about all this later. Maybe have our first official staff meeting Monday."

"Ew," Sierra said.

Taylor smiled. "Sounds good."

"What's up next?" Sierra rubbed her hands together eagerly. "I hope not too many more. They wiped out our snacks."

Taylor glanced at the mostly empty trays. All the treats were a hit, especially Ellie's homemade dog biscuits. There had been lots of requests for the recipe. Maybe Ellie would share it. That could be something they could send out in a newsletter or give little recipe cards out with adoptions.

Liz examined the spreadsheet. "Just one appointment left."

They were a few minutes ahead of schedule, so that last appointment hadn't arrived yet. Taylor was eager to finish the day and get home to her bed, but also sad that the event was ending. Talking to people and helping Geena with the photos had been a ton of fun. Taylor could hardly believe this was her actual *job*.

She'd been having so much fun that she realized she hadn't checked her messages since lunch. Geena joined them in the front room just as Taylor was opening her one missed message from Austin.

"How's the afternoon been?" Liz asked Geena. "Sorry I haven't checked in with you much."

"It's been fine." Geena used her polite, professional voice, but her accompanying smile was genuine. It was subtle, but Taylor could tell the difference. Geena had enjoyed herself today. "You all kept things running smoothly, and the photos themselves went well. A little challenging but I expected a few hiccups."

Taylor giggled. "Like that Ragdoll? Rupert."

"Cats are the worst models," Geena said with a sly smile. Then her eyes lit up with an idea. "Maybe next time consider having someplace set up for outdoor shots if anyone wants them. For the dogs, at least. It would take some thinking and logistics because we can't control the weather or lighting, but it might be a nice option."

Sierra and Liz exchanged a look.

"We were actually going to talk to you about future possibilities," Liz said. "Can you stay a minute after the last appointment? If not, we can set something up later."

"Sure," Geena said. "I assume Taylor won't mind sticking around a few minutes longer?"

Taylor put her phone away and returned her attention to the group. "I won't need a ride home. Austin is meeting me here, so I can ride with him. I guess he wanted to check out the place now that it's mostly finished."

"So I get to check *him* out?" Geena raised her brow with intrigue.

"You'll like this one," Sierra said. "Checks all the boxes so far."

"Let's go look at the boring computer stuff before we stick our noses all the way in their business," Liz said. "Holler if you need anything, otherwise we'll be out in a bit to clean up after this last session."

"Sounds good." When Taylor turned back to Geena, she found a sly grin still plastered on her sister's face. "What?"

"Nothing," Geena said. "I'm just looking forward to this."

"Sierra's right. You'll like him."

Taylor hoped so. Not that she expected or even wanted her sister's approval on anything, but she was glad that for once she wasn't in danger of judgment or disappointment.

At least, she didn't think so.

She couldn't guess a single reason Geena might not

approve of Austin. But if there was something to disapprove of, Geena would sniff it out.

"Enough about *my* love life," Taylor said. "What do you and Ricky have planned for this evening? I'm assuming you have plans tonight instead of on a big ol' Sunday."

A huge smile had been plastered across Geena's face all day. It was the happiest Taylor had seen her in years. Not that she'd seen much of her sister recently. Still, it was good to see Geena with a camera in her hand again and joy in her heart.

But all that disappeared in an instant, and Taylor immediately regretted her question.

"No plans." Geena sighed and stared at the ceiling. "I didn't want to say anything and ruin the mood here."

Taylor placed a hand on her sister's arm. They'd never been a touchy family, and Geena had always been the most stoic of them all. But this looked like it called for emergency comfort methods.

"What's going on?"

"Ricky moved out." Her voice was ragged and tired. All the joy of the day had drained away. "He left last weekend."

Taylor wrapped her arms around her sister. "Oh, Geena. I'm so sorry."

She'd never liked her brother-in-law. He had a casually cruel sense of humor and seemed to value material objects and making money to gain those more than he valued the people in his life. Taylor only saw him on major holidays for brief chunks of time, but she never got a good vibe from the guy.

So no, she wasn't sorry to be rid of her brother-in-law. But she was sorry her sister was hurting.

"Don't be," Geena said. "I'm not."

"It's okay to be upset." Taylor released her embrace but kept her hands on her sister at arm's length.

"I know, but I'm mad at myself for being upset." Geena let out a laughing sob. "Everyone was right about him. He's a jerk. I picked a *jerk*."

Taylor didn't know how her sister couldn't realize that before now, but it wasn't the time to say that. "Sometimes you've got to try someone on for a while to see if they fit. It happens."

"I knew it. Deep down, I did. But I thought he'd want to change. That we'd grow together. He made me think that. He did and said all the right things for a while. Until he didn't anymore."

Taylor had never heard that man say one right thing, but he'd worked his charm on Geena. Taylor hated him now even more for that.

It was strangely comforting to know that she had something in common with her sister. They'd both fallen for the charm of jerks at least once.

"Anyway, I don't want to ruin the rest of today." Geena wiped at her eyes, delicately brushing away tears without smudging her mascara or eyeliner.

"You aren't ruining anything," Taylor said. "And I'm coming over tomorrow. We're going to spend the afternoon and evening together. We'll go out for margaritas. Or pick up a gallon of them and watch movies and talk. Whatever you want to do. Austin's leaving tomorrow anyway, so I could use a distraction."

Geena raised her brow and teased, "I'm your convenient distraction?"

"If that makes it easier to swallow me caring for you, then yes. Let's go with that."

After a moment, Geena smiled again. "Deal."

The front door opened and a cheerful voice sang out, "Hellooo."

A short, round woman in a bulky tan coat entered, led by

two plump rat terriers on retractable leashes. She had sun-toasted, leathery skin, like she spent a lot of time in a garden or at all the many outdoor music events they had in the region throughout the fall and spring.

"Hi, come on in." Taylor closed the door and extended her hand. "I'm Taylor."

The woman stared at her for a moment with a curious smile. Taylor wasn't sure what it was about this woman's expression that made her uneasy. Maybe it was just exhaustion from a long day. Or maybe it was her sister's unsettling news that had her on edge. Whatever it was, Taylor was ready to herd this woman and her dogs in and out of the studio so she could finish this day and enjoy the last of her time here with Austin.

"Patricia." The woman shook her hand. "Glad to meet you, Taylor."

"Hi, I'm Geena." Taylor's sister shook the woman's hand and aimed a thumb down the hall. "I misread the schedule and pet sizes, so I need to adjust some light heights in there. Give me just a second, and I'll be ready for you guys."

Geena disappeared into the studio room. Patricia's dogs yipped and tugged at the ends of their leashes, eager to do anything but stand still.

"I don't know if Austin has mentioned me, but I was friends with his uncle."

That's why the name sounded familiar. Taylor couldn't remember on the spot what else Austin had said about her. "Austin did mention your name."

"How's Tink doing? I hear he's staying with you for the time being, right?"

"Yes, he is." Maybe she was just tired, but something about the way the woman looked at Taylor made her want to keep her answers simple. "He's doing great."

"No health issues?" Patricia leaned forward as she waited

for a response. "I know he's an older cat, and this whole ordeal must be so stressful for him."

Taylor wasn't great at lying. Okay, she was awful at it. But she also didn't feel like getting into Tink's medical history with this stranger, even if she hadn't been sensing weird vibes.

"He was a little stressed, but he's fine now."

That, at least, wasn't a lie, so Taylor could deliver the line with confidence.

Patricia, however, seemed to doubt it. She eyed Taylor suspiciously. "Well, that's good. I don't know if I could bear anything happening to that cat. Especially after everything."

"Of course." Taylor gestured down the hall. "Let's see if Geena is ready for you all."

"I was so excited about this when Austin told me about it. This is such a wonderful idea. Bo and Rocky have been looking forward to getting their pictures done all week. Haven't you boys?"

Patricia leaned down to let her dogs give her face kisses. Then, as she held up the leashes to aim her pups toward the room, Taylor caught sight of something. Something that grabbed her attention and set off immediate alarm bells in her head: a ring-shaped tan line.

26

---

*A*ustin parked in front of the shelter beside an expensive sedan. It was the only vehicle, but Taylor had said she'd ridden with her sister, so he assumed that was hers. She'd mentioned something about Sierra and Liz both living down this road, so they must have walked here.

He ran up the steps and rushed inside, where it was empty and quiet. The event was finished or they were between appointments. Judging from the bare trays with only crumbs left on them, the fundraiser had been a success. Or at least people and their pets had been hungry.

The shelter owners and a woman Austin didn't know walked out of a back room and headed toward him. Liz gave a big, genuine-looking smile, while Sierra flashed a smirk.

"Well, look who's here," Sierra said.

"Good to see you, Austin," Liz said.

"Hi. Is Taylor in the back?" The words fell out in a frenzied flurry.

The woman Austin didn't recognize asked in a worried tone, "She isn't with you?"

Now it was Austin's turn to worry. Well, to worry more.

Because all he could do on the way there was worry. Especially since he'd missed Taylor's call when he'd had to stop for gas, and she didn't respond to his text after that.

"I told her to wait for me here and that I could pick her up. I thought she'd gotten a ride here with someone."

"That's me. I'm Geena."

"You're Taylor's sister, right?"

They had the same face, the same small features, but everything on this woman seemed more pronounced and commanding, from her sharp clothes to her angular pixie cut.

"Yes, and she rode with me. I went into a meeting after I tore down the lighting, and she wasn't out front. I assumed she'd left with you and forgot to tell me or didn't want to interrupt us."

"No, I just got here." Austin's phone rang in his hand. He raised it quickly with the hope that he'd see Taylor's name on the screen, but it was his mother. "I can't—"

"Austin, is Taylor with you?"

The concern in his mother's voice cast an icy blanket over his heart. He rarely heard her sound anything but poised and confident.

"No," he said. "I'm at the shelter to pick her up, but they don't know where she is."

"She must be outside somewhere," Liz offered. "I'll check around the property."

"Maybe she got curious about the skunks." Sierra followed Liz.

Taylor's sister took a step closer. He wished he had a word or two to ease her concern, but he was struggling to contain his own panic at the moment.

His brain caught up to the situation and his mother's words. "Why are you looking for Taylor?"

"She texted a while ago to ask me something," his mother

said. "When she stopped responding, I tried to call her, but she didn't answer."

Austin put a pin in why Taylor had his mother's phone number and asked a more pressing question. "What did she want to know?"

There was a heavy pause before Melinda answered. "She asked me if I knew whether Patricia wore a ring."

Austin's blood pounded in his ears.

No, no, no.

He kept the phone up and asked Geena, "Do you know the name of the last appointment?"

"Sorry, I don't remember." She was stammering, and Austin could see her mind racing.

"Do you remember what she looked like?"

"She was kind of short. Older. She had two little dogs."

The blood in his veins felt like it had frozen solid. "Mom, I'll have to call you back."

"Austin, you call me the moment you find her," his mother said. "And if I don't hear from you within the hour, I'm calling the police."

Geena held up a finger and hurried over to a counter in the adjoining kitchen area.

"Hang on, let me check the list." She scanned a piece of paper. "The sign-up sheet says her name is Patricia. Do you know her? Could Taylor be with her?"

Austin already knew it was her, but hearing the name out loud for confirmation felt like someone hit a line drive right into his gut.

"Yeah." He stared at his phone, feeling utterly helpless. After trying her cell one more time, he said, "I don't have her roommate's number. Do you?"

Geena nodded. "I'll call Ellie, but Taylor said she's working at the emergency clinic today. Do you have Patricia's number? Taylor must be with her. Maybe they went out for coffee and Taylor's phone died. It must be something simple like that, right?"

Austin wished it was that simple.

"I'll try her on the way." He headed out the door with Geena on his heels.

With the phone to her ear, she said, "Ellie isn't answering. On the way where?"

"I think they might be going to the apartment." He hoped that was answer enough because he didn't know how to connect the dots for her about his uncle and the ring and Tink. And he didn't know where to start or how much Taylor had already told her.

"Why would they go there?"

Austin stopped on the porch. A cold, biting wind sliced across his face as he turned toward Geena. Fierce determination had replaced her fear. He handed her his phone with a new message open. "Give me your number, and I'll let you know if I find them."

"Like hell." But she took the phone anyway and typed her number. When she handed it back, Geena said, "In case we get separated. But you can bet your ass I'm coming with you."

27

Taylor placed the small pet carrier on the ground beside her. While she fumbled with her key in the lock, the hard end of a revolver barrel poked into her back.

"Hurry up."

The dog in the crate Patricia was holding yapped in agreement. Because, of course, Patricia brought her dogs to an abduction. Or whatever this was. And since she couldn't hold both carriers and aim a gun at Taylor, Patricia had made Taylor carry one of her dogs into the apartment.

Tink was going to *love* that.

"I'm hurrying," Taylor said. "I'd be a lot less nervous and open the door faster if you weren't jamming that thing in my back."

"Just a friendly reminder not to try anything funny, that's all."

Taylor turned the key and entered. "I guess you don't want to see the hilarious meme I found this morning?"

Taylor had realized during the ride to her apartment—with Patricia managing to drive and still aim her gun at Taylor in the passenger seat—that her only useful superpower in this situation might be small talk and her sparkling personality. She had no leverage. She didn't even know what this woman wanted from her, except maybe to keep her as a hostage.

Melinda might have been immune to small talk, but maybe Taylor could win Patricia over with it. At least for Taylor to keep herself alive as long as possible.

But Patricia ignored Taylor's meme joke and seemed laser-focused the moment they entered the apartment. She placed the carrier she was holding on the carpet near the front door. "Put Bo here next to Rocky."

Taylor did as ordered. "How long do we plan on being here? Should I get them some water or—"

"Do you ever hush up?" Patricia's tone and demeanor had become noticeably more agitated since they'd entered the apartment.

"Sometimes," Taylor said. "But guns make me a little nervous, and when I'm nervous, I get extra chatty. I mean, I would probably talk less if you weren't aiming that thing at me."

Patricia narrowed her eyes at Taylor and ignored the suggestion. "Where is it?"

"Where's what?"

Despite Taylor asking multiple times, Patricia had never told her what she wanted or why they were driving to her apartment. Taylor had a suspicion, but she felt more comfortable asking questions and keeping Patricia talking.

Taylor's phone buzzed inside Patricia's coat pocket. She'd demanded that Taylor hand it over once they got in the car. After scanning the message and missed call notifications, she had to know that Taylor had brought suspicions to Melinda.

"Popular girl, aren't you?" Patricia's face distorted into an evil-looking smirk. "No matter. My car's packed, and I have my babies. I'll be long gone before anyone finds you here."

"Finds me?"

The statement didn't indicate what Taylor's state might be when they "found" her.

Once again, Patricia ignored her. "How did you know?"

"How did I know what?" Taylor asked. "I don't know why you're holding that gun, much less what you think I might know. I was just taking photos at the shelter until you showed up."

"Then why is Melinda texting you and asking if I'm there? What did you tell her?"

Taylor's sparkling personality and small talk weren't getting the job done anymore. Time to change tactics.

"I saw your tan line."

Patricia looked down at her right hand holding the gun and frowned. "I didn't even notice it was missing until that night. Shows you what kind of shock I was in. Must have fallen off in that split second when I tried to catch him. My skin's been so dry this winter, and I've lost a few pounds sick over this whole thing with Brandon. That'll teach me not to moisturize, huh?"

Taylor wasn't in any place to judge people over ill-timed, stress-induced humor, so she jumped to the real meat of what Patricia had said. "What thing with Brandon?"

"Kenny was going to ask him to move in." Patricia caught herself before she continued with her explanation. "Not that it's any of your business."

"You're kind of making it my business by kidnapping me and demanding… whatever it is you're demanding here."

Taylor had given up on the idea of sparkling and decided straight talk was the way to go. It's all she had the energy and courage left for. Plus, if she kept talking, maybe Patricia would also keep talking. Maybe they could talk their way out of this together. Or at least without a hole in Taylor.

With a wave of the gun, Patricia gave a one-word answer. "Ring."

"Right." Taylor put her hands up. "It's in the bedroom. I'm going to get it. Don't shoot me in the back or anything."

"You're cute, but exhausting. Do you know that?"

"I do now, I guess."

Taylor turned with her hands raised and walked into her bedroom. She could hear Patricia's footsteps on the carpet behind her, then stopping in the doorway. Taylor grabbed the sealed plastic bag from her nightstand and held it in the air.

"Good." Patricia waved the gun again. "Let's go. Out of here."

Howl.

Patricia's eyes lit up for a second, then she narrowed them at the big tabby who'd come out from under the bed to greet the familiar voice. "Ugh. You. I wouldn't be in this mess if it weren't for you."

Sure, lady. Blame a cat for your murder. That makes perfect sense.

"How did *you* know?" Taylor asked.

"Austin said the cat had eaten something. And since I'd combed that house and couldn't find my ring, I put it together."

Taylor remembered the security footage Austin had shown her of Patricia in the house. And to think Taylor had given her the benefit of the doubt and suggested she was just getting one last goodbye look at the place.

Holding the bag in the air, Taylor looked at the purple ring inside. "What does the inscription mean?"

"It's a quote," Patricia said. "Well, part of it. From *Galaxy Quest*. I gave him his half of the ring pair a couple birthdays back when he'd had a health scare that turned out to be nothing." She scoffed at the bag. "I was the one who stood by him.

I was the one who promised to stand beside him forever. But the moment *Brandon* showed up, he—"

A loud knock at the front door interrupted Patricia's pity party speech.

"Taylor?" Austin's voice boomed from outside.

A rush of relief hit Taylor when she heard his voice, but that relief was followed by a wave of nausea at the realization of what he was walking into.

The dogs barked and howled from inside their carriers.

Patricia held out a hand for the bag and waved the gun at the front door. "Well, go on. Let's not keep that handsome man waiting."

28

*A*ustin had suspected Patricia was inside Taylor's apartment long before her dogs announced his arrival.

He'd parked beside her hatchback, noticing that it was packed for a lengthy trip, probably with no return plans. That meant she knew they were on to her, and she had no way out except to disappear. It also meant she had nothing left to lose here, making it difficult to reason with her.

The door opened to reveal Taylor standing in the entrance while the dogs continued to bark somewhere off to her side. She was pale and her eyes sagged with worry. Austin wanted to wrap an arm around her and drag her outside to safety, but he didn't know if that would place her in even more danger.

He was walking into a trap, but he'd walk into a million deadly traps to protect her. He would see this through to whatever end.

Austin tried to project reassurance as he put a hand on her arm and walked inside. The door closed, and he turned to find Patricia standing behind it next to two pet carriers. In one hand, she held the plastic bag containing the ring Tink had swallowed. In her other hand, she held a small revolver aimed at Taylor's side.

"Hello, Austin," she said. "Wish I could say I was glad you could join us, but it would have been better if you'd gotten stuck in traffic. I was just on my way out."

He didn't recognize the woman standing in front of him now. She didn't match the image of his uncle's sweet friend. "I thought you hated guns."

"I do hate them. Never said I didn't have one, though. A girl can't be too careful. Never know who you'll run into. Right, Taylor?"

"Let her go," Austin said. "I don't know what's going on here, but she's got nothing to do with it, and you can take me if you need to instead."

"I'm not taking anyone," Patricia said. "But I think I'll keep her around a bit longer. She makes good insurance so you don't try anything funny."

He nodded at the bag in her hand. "Looks like you've already found what you came here for. Just take it and leave. That's the only evidence. No one will come after you."

"As if I believe you'd let me walk out of here." She scoffed. "After watching you on your little justice crusade the last few weeks? No, sir. We're all going outside together so I can keep an eye on you until I'm on my way." She pointed at the dog carriers. "Each of you take a baby."

"Patricia, can we—"

"*Now.*"

She waved the gun at him as she said the word, but what stuck out for Austin was the steadiness of her hand. No jerking movements. No subtle trembling. Her finger remained poised on the trigger as she held her aim on Taylor.

This wasn't some impulsive reaction that landed her here. She'd planned this exit, and she was clearly committed to *any* outcome.

"Okay, okay."

He stepped in front of Taylor to grab the farthest carrier and block the path between Taylor and a potential bullet. She silently grabbed the other carrier. He watched her movements out of the corner of his eye, while most of his attention remained on Patricia and her gun.

Taylor seemed equally steadfast. Quieter and more reserved than he'd ever seen her, but in control. She was afraid but holding on. He tried not to let his thoughts spin on how alone and scared she must have been before he'd arrived, or how long she'd had to handle Patricia on her own.

"You first, Austin. And know that I've got my eye on your girlfriend here, so don't try anything. Just walk downstairs like nothing's wrong and stop at my car."

He did as ordered, stepping outside and proceeding down the apartment steps. With a slight shake of his head, he hoped Geena got the message not to interfere, in case she couldn't see the full situation from inside his car where he'd told her to wait. Her expression was pained, and he knew she wanted to rush out and rescue her sister as much as he did.

Thankfully, Geena stayed put.

"Wouldn't you rather take Uncle Kenny's car?" Austin said as he approached Patricia's Subaru that was way past its expiration date. "You never came by to pick it up. It would be more comfortable to take a trip in than this one."

"The car." Patricia scoffed again. "Can you believe, after all these years, he left me nothing but *a car*?"

He'd left her quite a nice car. A car he'd loved and that he'd presumably thought Patricia would appreciate. He'd given the things he loved most to the people he'd loved most.

But Patricia was too far gone in her self-righteous anger to see that.

Taylor shivered beside him, and he wanted to reach an arm around her to hold her close. He didn't dare, though. Not until she was safely away from Patricia.

He tried desperately to squash his guilt over bringing this terror into Taylor's life. If he'd never brought Tink to her, never asked her out, never told her about all of this, she wouldn't be in danger.

"Put them on the backseat. One at a time. Taylor first."

Austin opened the door and held it while Taylor loaded her carrier. He motioned with his eyes for her to step aside, hopefully far out of harm's way.

"Now you." Patricia sounded tired. Maybe everything she was doing and everything she'd done was finally sinking in.

Austin ducked into the back and slid the carrier he'd been holding onto the seat, scanning everything inside the car. She had luggage, pillows, and boxes jammed into every corner. Then his eyes landed on something familiar. Something he had never seen, but that had been described to him: a purple harness with red trim and heart-shaped gemstones.

He stared at it, and rage coursed through him. For a second, he'd thought maybe she'd taken it for sentimental reasons. But logic took over, and he realized it was just the right size to fit on one of her dogs. She'd killed Uncle Kenny, then snatched Tink's harness and leash for her own spoiled beasts.

"Hurry up." Patricia's voice was less steady now as a car drove past and pulled into a nearby spot. "I never wanted to hurt either of you. I just need my ring, and I'll be on my way and out of your hair for good."

Meaning they would be safe.

But also that she would get away with everything.

With a quick check that Taylor was out of harm's way

near the back bumper of the car, Austin stood and closed the backseat door. Then, in the same motion he'd use if he'd had an aluminum bat in his hands, he swung his arms across his body and into Patricia's outstretched arm.

Then he heard the gunshot.

29

A scream erupted from Taylor before her conscious brain caught up. It had been busy spinning around the sound of that gunshot.

She heard other things now also, faint and distant, like she was underwater. Patricia shouting. Dogs barking. Multiple car doors opening from different directions. Someone who wasn't her or Patricia screaming Austin's name.

Blood dripped near his foot, but from her position behind him, she couldn't tell where he'd been shot. All she could see was his back, Patricia's stunned expression, and the blood on the ground.

Taylor had seen her fair share of blood at the vet clinic. Her heart broke into a million pieces with every injured animal that crossed her, but she always remained calm and controlled so she could help.

But none of that blood had ever belonged to the man she'd fallen completely and hopelessly in love with these last few weeks.

"Austin." The word came out as a whimper, and she

lunged toward him, not even sure if the gun was still in Patricia's hand or if he'd knocked it to the ground. It didn't matter. Gun or not, she had to help him.

But she couldn't move. Someone was holding her arms now, stopping her.

It was Geena.

"Taylor, wait."

When did she get there?

Taylor's mind was a boundless sea of confusion swirling even more as she heard Austin's name come from someone else's mouth off in the distance. A second later, an unexpected visitor appeared.

Zeke kicked something and slid it aside. The gun. Then he grabbed Patricia's arms and pulled her backward toward the sidewalk, away from Austin and the car. She mumbled over and over how it was an accident and she'd never meant to hurt anyone.

Once Patricia was secured, Geena released her grip. Taylor rushed forward, meeting Austin in two steps as she heard his name again and realized someone else now stood beside them.

"Is he okay?" Melinda asked.

"I don't know yet." Taylor didn't know where the blood was coming from yet, and she realized he hadn't said a word or moved since the gun went off. "Austin, can you hear me?"

His face was a blank expression, with his eyes still lasered on Patricia, who Zeke had full control of now. It was as if the events of the day and maybe even the last couple of months were just settling in.

He blinked a few times, rejoining reality with the sound of her voice. "Yeah." He shook his head, then quickly scanned Taylor. "Are you okay?"

"I'm fine," she said. "Where did the bullet hit you?"

"I was *shot*?"

Definitely shock.

"I need you to sit. Here."

"I don't think anything hit me." He looked down at himself, patting his torso and arms. He winced and cursed when his right hand landed on his left arm.

"Sit on the ground and lean your back against the car while I take a look."

She helped him down and squatted beside him.

Melinda gasped as she processed the blood on her son's jacket sleeve.

"Can you find me a clean shirt or a small blanket? There should be something in the car."

"Look on the front seat!" shouted a shaky voice from the sidewalk.

Taylor shot Patricia a glare, but kept her mouth shut. It wouldn't do any good to waste breath on her right now, and Patricia sure as heck wasn't getting a thanks out of Taylor.

The dogs barked inside their crates on the backseat, and Melinda hurried around the side of the car while Taylor cradled Austin's arm.

"I'm going to take off your jacket to check things out."

Austin nodded and winced as she slid the jacket off of his body, carefully peeling it away from the injured arm. After inspecting the wound, Taylor let out a massive exhale.

"The bullet went through. The bleeding isn't great, but it doesn't look like it hit anything major."

Melinda returned with a flannel shirt and handed it to Taylor. "That's good, right? He's going to be okay?"

"An ambulance is on the way," Geena said from behind them.

"Yes, he's going to be fine." Taylor began wrapping the shirt around the wound to put pressure and slow the bleeding until the paramedics got there. She kissed his forehead. "As long as he promises to never do anything that reck-less and dangerous again."

He flashed that charming smile of his, the one that made her weak even now, as terrified as she'd been just moments ago.

"If someone's ever aiming a gun at you again, I can't make any promises."

Taylor stacked a couple of throw pillows close to Austin so he could rest his bandaged arm on them. He thanked her and leaned his head against the back of the big purple couch.

"Can I get you anything else right now?"

He gave her a goofy grin. "A kiss?"

The pain meds were working. Good.

She kissed him, then said, "I'll let Geena and Ellie know we're settled in here."

After Geena had given her statement to the police, she'd handled bringing Austin's car to his uncle's house while Taylor had ridden in the ambulance. Melinda insisted on following them to the hospital, so she and Zeke gave Austin and Taylor a ride here as soon as they stitched Austin up.

Taylor sent a quick text to Geena, then another to Ellie, who assured Taylor she'd watch over Tink and maybe smudge some sage to cleanse the apartment of Patricia's presence.

"Are you sure I can't convince the two of you to spend at least tonight and tomorrow at my house?" Melinda asked. "I could take care of everything while you both rest."

"We're fine, Mom," Austin said with a sloppy drawl. "And I've got my nurse to take care of me."

"You can still have her at my house," Melinda insisted.

Taylor had found herself agreeable to that suggestion. She

didn't need any help caring for him, but if he'd been more comfortable there, Taylor wouldn't have objected.

Melinda and Zeke had tracked down the apartment after Melinda had insisted that Austin give her the name of the complex on his ride over there. She'd proven herself to be helpful back in the parking lot and had stayed with Taylor while the nurses and doctors worked on him in the ER.

Maybe it was just exhaustion, but Melinda was growing on Taylor. And not in a fungus kind of way.

"I don't blame them." Zeke gawked at every inch of the house. "This place is *sweet!*"

Taylor laughed. Of course, he would love it here.

Austin extended his uninjured arm. "Thanks for today, man."

"No worries." Zeke shook Austin's hand. "I kind of owe you one, but I'd have been there for you, anyway."

"Thanks, Zeke." Taylor couldn't believe they were living in a world where she was genuinely appreciative of this guy, but he'd earned it.

"Well, you're welcome to come over if you change your minds. Even if it's the middle of the night," Melinda said. "Call me if you need anything."

"We will. Thank you." Taylor closed the door behind them and leaned against it. She'd been glad to have them with her at the hospital, but she was now grateful for some quiet and space to process the day and everything that had happened.

As she walked over to snuggle beside Austin on the couch, her phone dinged twice in rapid succession. The first text was from Liz, saying she was glad to hear they were safe and sound, and she wished Austin a speedy recovery.

Geena had filled them in once she got a ride to the shelter to pick up her own car and bring Patricia's dogs to them. The cops had released the dogs to Geena once Liz talked with one of them on the phone and gave the shelter's info. Liz and

Sierra agreed to keep the dogs until someone in Patricia's family could take them.

The second text was from Sierra, telling Taylor she was glad she was safe and that she'd better not show up to work on Monday.

"More well wishes?" Austin put his uninjured arm around her shoulder as she sat beside him.

"Sierra and Liz send their love."

"Ah." He winced as he shifted. "They're good bosses."

"Yes, they are." Of all the decisions she'd made over the last couple of months, trusting her gut and taking that job had been one of the best. "Speaking of work, I'll remind you to call yours and tell them you won't be back on Monday."

"It's not that bad," Austin said. "I should be fine to drive by tomorrow afternoon."

"That's the meds talking. Even if they help the pain, you can't drive on them."

"Fine," he sighed. "Looks like I won't be making that first game after all."

"There will be plenty more. And bright side! Now you get to spend all of Valentine's Day with me instead of packing and driving."

Austin nodded at his arm. "I'm afraid I won't be the most fun company."

"You're plenty fun no matter what." She kissed him and lingered on his lips, grateful that the day hadn't taken an even worse turn. Even more grateful to have this man in her life, whatever the future held for them. "Besides, we can spend tomorrow snuggling right here, ordering takeout, and watching a movie marathon."

He leaned in to kiss her again, then stared into her eyes. "That sounds perfect."

Two Months Later

"Be right back." Austin patted Mike's shoulder and left the dugout.

Mike hollered, "Take your time!"

Austin knew Mike could handle things, whether he was gone for a few minutes, a few weeks, or next season. Which made Austin's announcement earlier that afternoon a lot easier to deliver.

The last couple of months had been busy as expected, but he'd still felt the sharp ache of missing Taylor. It was like the pain in his arm those first few weeks as his body struggled to repair the bullet hole. While that injury had completely healed, he didn't think his heart could recover if a Taylor-shaped hole remained.

So, he'd decided to move back there at the end of this school year.

When he'd heard that the Breaux Bridge High coach was

retiring, he'd reached out about the possibility of taking over there. After a few meetings with administrators, they offered him the job.

Austin never dreamed he'd be so excited to return to that area. But he wouldn't be working in Lafayette, his hometown, with its traffic and oil money and his mother's friends and associates. The school was in a quiet town nearby, only a few miles from the animal shelter. It was a smaller high school with a solid program he could build on. A perfect situation for him. Especially since it put him closer to Taylor.

He was so excited that he was even considering letting his mother scout real estate on his behalf. Austin was looking for a small house, since he had plenty of money now but didn't want a lot of upkeep. He just needed something big enough for a couple of people and a cat.

Later in the summer, he planned to ask Taylor and Tink to move in with him. He just wanted to get everything lined up first. For tonight, he only planned to tell Taylor the good news that he was moving back to the area and that he'd be able to take Tink permanently.

He liked to think Uncle Kenny would approve of the whole arrangement. Especially the part about how Austin also intended to make a sizable donation in his uncle's name to the St. Martin Animal Sanctuary.

He jogged to the edge of the bleachers where Taylor and Geena stood waiting for him. It had been raining almost non stop all week, but the dark clouds had parted that morning to welcome a spectacular spring day. April in Louisiana was usually pretty nice, but this was particularly gorgeous. Cool and slightly breezy with plenty of sun and some bright, puffy clouds. It was like nature wanted to celebrate Taylor's visit as well.

Not caring that the guys would give him crap for it when

he got back to the team, he wrapped an arm around Taylor's waist and gave her a quick kiss.

"Hey, Geena. Glad you could make it too. Good drive here?"

"Traffic wasn't bad at all," Geena added.

"Good." He held Taylor close, looking forward to having her close every day soon.

He hadn't told her about the job yet, but now that he'd told Mike a heads-up, he planned to tell her that evening at dinner after the game. They could all celebrate together over tacos and margaritas.

Despite the horrible start to the year, there had been a lot of good news lately. The team was most likely headed to the playoffs next month. Brandon had moved into Uncle Kenny's house. Patricia had confessed and taken a plea deal so they could all avoid a long, drawn-out trial. And Taylor had even solved the mystery of Tink's morning pukies.

After he'd hacked up that ring, Tink had still been gagging or spitting up almost every morning. But after some experimentation, Taylor had figured out that if she got up or petted him when Tink first hopped on the bed, he didn't puke. If she tried to ignore him, his traumatized kitty brain thought she might never wake up... like Uncle Kenny.

It hadn't been a problem when Tink was with Austin because he was such an early riser, even when he didn't have to work. But thanks to Taylor's detective skills and masterful experimentation, the mystery was solved and she could continue to set Tink's poor worried mind at ease.

"Well, I'd better get back," he said. "We'll be starting soon. I'll see you guys after."

They wished him and the team good luck, and he gave Taylor another quick kiss before jogging back to the dugout.

He turned to take one more look at her while she and Geena climbed the ramp up to the bleachers.

Austin didn't care if the team could see the goofy grin on his face. He only cared that she was here for the game and dinner, that he had good news to surprise her with, and that there would be endless dinners together, starting a few months from now.

TAYLOR AND GEENA both jumped to their feet to join the crowd in roaring applause and cheers. A senior player had just hit a line drive in the perfect spot between two outfielders, allowing his teammates to run home.

The scoreboard said it all. Not only did those two runs solidify the home team's win, but it also secured a nice position in the playoffs.

Taylor watched as Austin congratulated his players and celebrated the win with them. Then he herded them all to line up for their show of sportsmanship and "good game" hand slaps.

She still wasn't much of a baseball fan, but after coming to a few of these games, she'd grown to love watching the players' excitement and how they supported each other. She also loved seeing Austin's influence on these guys.

"Ready?" Geena asked.

With a nod, Taylor led the way out of the bleachers and toward the team. She congratulated a few of the players and wrapped her arms around Austin to give him a congratulatory kiss.

"Good game, Coach."

"Thanks." His hands rested on her waist as he stared down into her eyes. "Victory is extra sweet when you're here to witness it."

Her heart fluttered. Missing him was wearing on her, and

she couldn't wait for the summer when he'd hopefully be in town more often.

They were making the long-distance thing work, but it was still hard to only see him for a couple of hours a week. Weekends were equally busy, or one or both of them were too exhausted to make the drive.

She wished she could go to all their games, but it just wasn't logistically possible. Especially not these weekday games, since she had to leave early from the shelter for the long trip.

One thing the last couple of months had proven was that animal rescue was completely unpredictable. She could make all the plans she wanted, but if someone showed up with an animal in need, she had to stick around to take care of it.

They'd maxed out on intakes within a few weeks. Taylor was busier than she'd ever been at the vet clinic, but her heart and soul were as full as her schedule.

"Want us to grab a table at the restaurant while you wrap up here?"

Austin gave her another quick kiss. "That would be great. Thanks. Mike and I will see you there. I think his fiancé is coming too."

Taylor had been dying to meet the woman who'd snagged Mike's heart.

Taylor and Geena headed toward the parking lot as Taylor's phone dinged. It was Ellie. Taylor showed Geena the message with a cute photo of Tink on his back with his paws in the air.

"Aww, he's adorable," Geena said. "Have you told Austin the good news yet?"

"No. I was thinking about telling him tonight. Might as well add to the celebration, right?"

She'd wanted to make sure everything would work out before she told Austin that she'd decided to adopt Tink. Liz and Sierra had given her the obligatory, "You can't keep them all," speech, but they were thrilled she wanted to adopt him.

After just a few months, that big, sweet boy had become part of her life and created a permanent place for himself in her heart. With all he'd been through, she couldn't imagine putting him through the stress of handing him off to someone else.

So she'd double-checked with Ellie that it would be okay and made the decision. Along with taking the shelter job and trusting her instincts on Austin, adopting Tink felt like another excellent choice of listening to her gut.

"What about you?" Taylor asked her sister. "Any good news to add to the celebration? We were supposed to talk about that on the way. Sorry, I forgot to ask."

"Unfortunately, no. Ricky found another way to drag his feet on the paperwork."

"Ugh, I'm sorry."

Geena's soon-to-be ex-husband continued to drag out every step the last few weeks, even though leaving their marriage had been his idea. Their separation and eventual divorce should have been simple. They didn't have any kids and rented an apartment under her name, so the split should have been easy. But he was lazy, selfish, and spiteful, keeping Geena stressed and tied to that jerk for longer than necessary.

They reached the car, and Geena clicked the key fob to unlock the doors. "In good news, I'll be at the shelter this weekend to get photos of the new intakes."

"I can meet you whenever to help." Assisting with photos was Taylor's new favorite unofficial volunteer gig. She brought out dogs and cats and either held them on a leash or waved toys over Geena's camera to keep their attention on just the right spot.

She'd been so happy to hear that Geena agreed to volunteer for the task. It gave her sister something to do to keep her mind off the divorce once or twice a month, and she seemed to get joy out of it too. Especially once she remembered to stop wearing her dry clean only clothes to the shelter.

"So we can add that to the celebration list," Geena said. "I'm here to celebrate as many little things as we can these days."

"Absolutely." Things were definitely improving. Heck, the fact that she and her sister were speaking at all, much less headed out for dinner together, was a minor miracle. Taylor had plenty to cheer about lately, and she had all the confidence in the world that things would start looking up for Geena too.

With her heart overflowing with hope, Taylor aimed the car at the restaurant to celebrate today and all the tomorrows with the people she loved.

ABOUT THE AUTHOR

Leigh Landry is a contemporary romance and mystery author who loves stories with happy endings, supportive friendships, and adorable pets. Once a musician, freelance writer, and English teacher, Leigh now spends her days writing and volunteering at an animal rescue center in the Heart of Cajun Country.

You can find more information about Leigh, news about upcoming and currently published books, and a free story collection at: leighlandryauthor.com.

Made in the USA
Coppell, TX
03 December 2021

67070671R00173